HAVING IT ALL

SEATTLE WHALERS · HOCKEY ROMANCE

Having It All

Emily Bunney

4 Horsemen
Publications, Inc.

Published By: 4 Horsemen Publications, Inc.

4 Horsemen Publications, Inc.
PO Box 417
Sylva, NC 28779
4horsemenpublications.com
info@4horsemenpublications.com

Cover by Niki Tantillo
Typesetting by Autumn Skye
Edited by JM Paquette

Library of Congress Control Number: 2021941800

Paperback ISBN-13: 978-1-64450-272-3
Audiobook ISBN-13: 978-1-64450-273-0
Ebook ISBN-13: 978-1-64450-274-7
Hardcover ISBN-13: 979-8-8232-0685-3

Dedication

I'm dedicating this book to my lovely friend Lana,
who has been there from the beginning. You've
waited so patiently for your happily ever after. I hope
it's everything you wished for.

Table of Contents

Acknowledgements

I'd like to thank my wonderful friends and family for supporting me yet again, especially through my writer's block! I know I've been a nightmare.

Thanks to Jen, Val, and Erika for being so understanding with everything. I love you guys.

To Leticia and Jodi, my amazing alphas. You have no idea how much I appreciate you.

My ARC team, yet again, you've embraced my crazy hockey family and your love for them keeps me tapping away at my keyboard and weaving these stories for you. I have so much more in store for them.

And of course everyone who takes the time to follow me on social media. You allow me to indulge my love of Tyler Seguin and all things hockey.

Thank you again for reading my stories. I never thought I'd be doing this, and it still amazes me every day.

If you enjoyed Thor and Lana's story, please consider leaving a review. You have no idea how much it helps.

Lots of love
Emily xxx

PROLOGUE

Lana

Paris, France

I'm trying not to hyperventilate. I need to get my breathing under control before I pass out and miss my window. I've planned this down to the minute, and I can't fuck it up by fainting like a damsel in a black and white movie. I've spent the last six months being that girl, and I'm done.

It's time to get the fuck out of Dodge. Well, not exactly Dodge, more like the plush apartment in the Notre-Dame-de-Lorette district of Paris—a city that had once been my dream, where I attended Le Cordon Bleu and worked in a rustic Parisian Bistro as a sous chef. However, now it's become my nightmare.

A place where I'm trapped in a gilded cage with a monster.

I tiptoe into the walk-in closet and carefully move the ottoman into place so I can reach the bag I stashed away on the top shelf. Being barely five feet tall, I still have to stretch almost beyond my limit to retrieve the duffel, but finally my fingertips brush the shoulder strap. I grab it and pull the bag down into my arms. However, I underestimated the weight of all my essential belongings, and it knocks my tiny frame off balance, causing me to jump down from the ottoman with a loud thump.

I drop to the floor and freeze, my heart in my mouth, my breathing on the cusp of becoming a noisy gasp.

Shit! My eyes frantically scan the bedroom through the closet door, and I see the figure on the bed, but thankfully, it doesn't seem to be moving.

Hopefully, I haven't misjudged how drunk Etienne is; he got pretty loaded after service tonight, and when he came home, he was staggering and thankfully too drunk to start anything. When he finally passed out, face-down on his fancy four poster bed, I was pretty sure he'd be knocked out until morning.

Once my panic is under control again, I stand up, holding my bag to my chest. I've had to pack light; I can't risk Etienne realizing I've gone until I don't come home from my service at the bistro at midnight, by which time I'll be back on American soil.

Thinking about home brings tears to my eyes, and I spend a moment thinking about all the reasons I have to leave. Actually, the snoring bastard in front of me is the only reason I have to go home. If I leave him but remain in Paris, he may find a way to win me over, even if it's against my better judgement, and despite knowing better by now. I need to break away, so going back to America is my only option at this point.

Picking up my boots and coat, I sneak out of the bedroom, avoiding all the creaky floorboards in Etienne's classic Parisian apartment. I quietly choke down a glass of orange juice and the croissant I'd usually have for breakfast, leaving the plate and glass in the dishwasher. I know Etienne will check what I had for breakfast, so I want him to believe I went about my morning routine as normal. I've packed one set of chef's whites and my knife roll, the items I would regularly take to school, so he'll have no cause to be suspicious when he finally crawls out of bed.

I take one more look around the apartment, looking at all the perfection and beauty. But I finally see it for what it is: a prison.

Quietly, I slip out the front door and walk quickly down the three flights of stairs. I can't risk using the noisy, ancient elevator. I don't want any of Etienne's neighbors to see me leave in the middle of the night. His family owns this whole building so many of the residents know him personally.

Ha! That's a joke. I thought I knew him. What the fuck did I know?

I creep through the marble foyer and exit onto the street where I'm immediately drenched by the cold January rain. God, winter in Paris is fucking miserable. The freezing rain soaks through my light jacket as I hustle down the cobbled street toward the Rue des Martyrs, where I catch a taxi.

"*Gare de Lyon, s'il vous plaît,*" I say to the driver as we pull into the light traffic. I'm heading to the train station first as I need to get rid of my phone. One of the first clues I had that Etienne was a bad guy was when my best friend Zac found a tracker app hidden on my cell. I was furious and mortified; I'm not used to being controlled. But it made sense because I'd leave the bistro late at night sometimes, and anything can happen after midnight. Like a fucking sucker, I bought his bullshit and believed he was looking out for me.

It was Zac's suggestion that I go to the train station to dump my cell and use a burner until I'm back in the States. He's obsessed with shows like *CSI*, so he's picked up plenty of tricks like this one.

So, when I arrive, I pay the driver and hop out, walking quickly into the terminal. My heart is thundering in my chest, and my palms are sweaty as I look around for what I need. At this time, the terminal isn't very crowded, and I feel like I've made a huge error in judgement, but then I see what I need, and I stride toward the ticket booth.

There are two people in front of me in the line and one of them has a large rolling suitcase with an open pocket on the front. I carefully reach into my jeans and pull out my cell, palming it to keep it hidden. I've already put it on silent, so as I step closer to the woman in front of me, I put my own bag on the floor and bend over, close to her case.

Shit, if she catches me tampering with her case, I'm likely to get in a lot of trouble, so I have to be quick and careful. I swallow the dryness in my throat and try not to pant as I rummage around in my bag and covertly slide my cell phone into the open pocket of her suitcase.

I nervously stand up and expect to see the woman looking accusingly at me, but instead she's talking animatedly to the man in the ticket booth.

Thank god, I've done it. Now I just need to get another taxi to the airport, and I'm on my way home. And my cell phone? I've got no idea where that's going, but I'm sure Etienne will be hot on its trail when he finds out I've left.

As I get farther and farther away from the life I've built in Paris, the more nervous I get. Etienne's been my entire life for the last year. I allowed it to happen. He made me rely on him, love him, trust him. He controlled every facet of my life, and while I wonder what my life will be without him, I'm eager to find out.

I'll finally be free to be me.

I guess going back to the US is the only way I'm going to figure that out.

I just hope my brother doesn't mind me showing up unannounced on his doorstep. I've now got a fifteen-hour flight to Seattle to figure out what I'm going to say to him about why I've suddenly walked out on my life in France. There's absolutely no way I'm going to tell him the truth. He'd literally fly to Paris and kill Etienne if he knew what's been going on.

And when your big brother is Matt Landon, massive, badass center for the Seattle Whalers ice hockey team, believe me when I say he could rip Etienne to pieces with his bare hands. And while I know he would totally deserve it, I don't want to upend Matt's life too.

Yes, I need a believable story, and I need one fast.

1

Thor

I huff out a frustrated breath and my floppy blonde hair lifts off my forehead, which is damp with sweat. I always break out into a sweat when I talk to my mom about my dating situation. She's been going on at me for ten minutes about how blessed she is to have three sons married, two already with children. I silently curse my brothers for being such suck ups and emotional overachievers. I mean, I'm the starting goaltender for the Seattle Whalers NHL team with the best shutout record in the league. It definitely isn't too shabby, but it seems that means shit to my family unless I'm married with a baby or three.

"Are you going to answer me, Alex?" My mom's annoyed tone brings me back to the conversation.

Shit, what the fuck did she ask me?

"Listen mama, I have to go," I reply quickly. "I have a team thing to go to, and I can't be late." I drag my hand through my long hair and grimace when I hear her suck her teeth in disapproval.

"I don't like being ignored, Alex. You're a successful man, and you'll be thirty this year. You need to find a wife and settle down. I don't want your brothers to have to hide any more news stories about you and these … these women you seem to attract."

"C'mon, mama. I don't go looking for women like that," I grumble, pacing around the island in my kitchen. "They seem nice enough to start with."

"And where do you meet these women?" she asks in a tight voice.

I huff out another breath. "In bars, I guess."

"Exactly!" my mom crows triumphantly. "You're not going to meet a nice girl to marry in a damn bar."

"I know that. But I don't have time to date like a normal person," I explain for what feels like the millionth time. "Magnus and the others don't have the same sort of schedule I have. I know Ansol and Hugo have their own challenges being a doctor and a vet, but they don't travel like I have to…"

"Excuses, Alex, excuses. You have teammates who are married, yes?"

"Yeah." I'm fully sulking now, like a petulant child being scolded for having his hand in the cookie jar.

"Well, if they can do it, so can you. You're choosing to live your life like a teenager. It's time to grow up." And it seems, as usual, my mom has the last word. "I'll let you go. Please think about what I've said. I don't mean to pressure you, *min skatt*. You're my baby, and I want you to be happy."

She called me *my treasure*. I can hear the thick emotion in my mom's voice; it's the same whenever we talk. I think she still feels guilty for sending me to live in Canada when I was fourteen to help further my hockey career. I was so grateful for the opportunity then, and I've never had any issues with the move, but I know my mom really struggled with the separation.

"I know you do, mama. I promise to keep looking, and I'll try better places. Perhaps a church?" I smirk and chuckle, and I finally hear her laugh as well.

"You're still a smart ass," she replies fondly. "*Jag älskar dig.*"

"I love you, too. Give my love to papa."

"I will. Call your brothers when you get a chance."

I laugh. "You know I will. Now go to bed," I say firmly.

I end the call and lean my large frame against the kitchen counter, gripping the granite work surface with my huge hands. It's crazy that from thousands of miles away, my mom can reduce me to a child—a very large, sweaty child, but a child nonetheless.

I notice that I've sweated through the button-down shirt I'm wearing for the party, so I quickly move through my condo to my bedroom, unbuttoning it as I go. A man of my size finds it hard to get nice shirts, so I'm not going to ruin this one by wearing it all day with pit stains. Entering my walk-in closet, I choose a blue flannel button down that goes with my dark jeans and Timberlands. I give myself a quick, refreshing spray with deodorant and pull the shirt up my thick biceps, buttoning it up on the way back to the kitchen.

Just as I'm searching for the gift bag I left in the living room, my phone pings with a message.

[NATE: We're downstairs already. Hurry up or you can drive yourself.]

3

I snort and shake my head. Fucking kid's getting too big for his boots now he's not the rookie anymore.

[THOR: Calm your tits, kid. I'm coming.]
[NATE: Not a fucking kid. (middle finger emoji)]

Finally locating the gift bag, I grab it along with my phone, wallet, and keys and head down to the parking garage of my building. Several Whalers players live here, including Nate, our young defenseman, so it has a nice team atmosphere. It's also useful for carpooling.

"Jesus, I thought I'd have to send a geriatric nurse up there to help you, old man." Nate laughs when I eventually reach his truck and stuff myself into the back seat.

"Fuck you, kid," I growl, tossing the bag onto the pile of gifts on the back seat. "Don't you think the little one should be in the back seat? It's cramped as hell back here."

At my comment, Nate's girlfriend Beth whips her head round and gives me her famous death stare: her eyes as icy blue as mine, her red lips pulled into a cocky grin. She's the tiniest woman I've ever met, but she's full of piss and bluster. I like her a lot, but she kind of scares me.

"The little one called shotgun, so you're shit out of luck, big one!" Beth sasses, cocking her arrogant eyebrow and sticking her tongue out at me.

"That doesn't count," I argue. "You're fucking the driver!"

I hear Nate snort out a laugh as he pulls out of

the underground garage and sets the Sat Nav for our destination.

"Sucks to be you," she laughs, reaching over to give Nate's crotch a rub. "Certainly doesn't suck to me."

"Fuck's sake, Princess. Now I have a boner," Nate grumbles, batting her hand away and hitting the turn signal. "I can't go to a kids party with a chub on."

Jesus, these two are the worst. Why did I agree to carpool with them again?

"I thought you always have wood when I'm around, cowboy," Beth husks in a sultry voice, her fingers grazing down his neck.

"You two need to knock that shit off," I grumble, kicking the back of Nate's seat, which is pressing uncomfortably against my knees. "I'm not spending the next hour here while you verbally jerk each other off."

Both Nate and Beth burst out laughing at my grumpiness, Beth turning in her seat to look at me with sad puppy dog eyes. "Sorry, big one. We'll rein it in."

I reach out and pinch her cheek like she's a little kid. "Thank you, little one." I chuckle, knowing she hates it when I do that, something she quickly confirms when she slaps my hands away and scowls.

As the Sunday traffic eases, we make our way out of the city, heading toward the Sound. Nate and I talk about our upcoming game against the Edmonton Kodiaks and how they're really a team to watch for a cup run this season.

"I just hope Bugs has his head in the game this year," Nate comments. "It's gonna be hard juggling being the Cap and having a new baby."

"He seems on top of things so far," I reply, thinking

that Bugs and Cam have been amazing, considering their baby daughter wasn't planned and was a result of a friends with benefits one night stand. However, they decided to raise the baby together and in the process of navigating that, they fell in love. Now they have a two-month-old baby girl, Cam has moved into Bugs' massive mansion, and they couldn't be happier. Cam is still on maternity leave from her job as the assistant to our team's General Manager, but last time I saw her, she was still dipping into emails and Zoom calls to help out the woman who's covering for her.

Today, we're heading out to the sprawling waterfront house that belongs to our starting center, Matt Landon, and his girlfriend Mila. We all wanted to throw a party to welcome baby Sawyer to the Whalers family and since no one wanted to bring that sort of stress to Bugs and Cam's doorstep, Mila offered up their house as party central. The whole team and all the coaching staff will be there, along with Don, our GM, and several of the office staff who work closely with Cam. Thankfully, it's a sunny February day with no forecast for rain which seems like a miracle in Seattle, but I guess the gods must be shining on us today.

"At last!" Mila bursts out of the front door and stomps toward the truck as we pull up outside her house. Her red hair is blowing around her head like flames and her cheeks are just as red. She looks a little stressed.

"The party has arrived, lovely Mila," I bellow, flinging my door open, scooping her up into a hug that she tries to resist.

"Damn it, Thor. There's no time for that," she grumbles, wriggling in my arms, but I hold her tight. "You'd better have picked up the cake, or I'll have your balls for earrings."

Her feisty comment makes me howl with laughter and give her one last squeeze before releasing her. She gives me a shitty look and straightens her dress with a huff.

"Of course." I give her a shallow bow. "We have everything from your extensive list."

"I should think so," she replies, a little smirk tilting up the corner of her mouth. I can always make Mila giggle. "Now get your butt in the house and help Matt hang the banner."

With another bow, I leap up the steps onto the porch and enter through the front door, my eyes immediately assaulted by so much pink it looks like the main room has been hosed down with Pepto.

"Wow!" I chuckle, looking around to find Matt trying to hang one side of a huge "It's a girl" banner.

"Dude, a little help here," he calls, looking at me for assistance. His muscular, tattooed arms are stretched to their limit, and he's still inches from getting the banner straight. I trot over to him and join him on the table he's pulled up to reach the high stone chimney that reaches all the way to the pitched roof. We awkwardly switch places without dropping the banner, and I easily reach the place he's trying to hang it; my six feet six inches and huge arm span giving me the advantage over our Assistant Captain.

"Why the fuck did I agree to this?" Matt chuckles

as we clamber down from the table and move it back into position where it'll act as a place to leave gifts.

"Because it's a nice thing to do," I offer, following him to the kitchen where we both grab a beer from the large tub full of ice. "It's been a big adjustment for Bugs. I think it's nice the team is showing him support."

"Absolutely." Matt takes a large swallow of his beer while looking around the room. "Mila went a bit over the top with the pink." Despite his grumpy attitude, I can see the affection and love in his eyes as he talks about his woman, and yet again, I feel a pang of regret that I don't have someone like that in my life.

Apart from a high school romance that quickly faded once I got called up to the NHL, I've never had a long-term relationship—just a succession of short affairs with women who seem amazing to start with but usually end up doing something to reveal their true colors. I've had ex-lovers sell stories about me to the tabloids, post intimate pictures of me online, and I even had to get a court order to stop one of them releasing a sex tape we'd made together. That was not my finest moment, and another indiscretion my older brothers had to hide from my mama. Trust me when I say I won't be doing anything like that again.

Let's face it: my mom has every reason in the world to worry about my dating life. I'm almost thirty years old, and I have no idea what it means to commit to anything other than my career. And an ice hockey career can end in the blink of an eye, especially for a goalie. Of all the positions on the team, we take a lot of the hits, usually playing the full sixty minutes, contorting our large bodies up like a pretzel and being pummeled time after time by a speeding rubber disk. I took a nasty hit to the throat in the last game of our Stanley Cup run last season, and it took me most of the summer to recover from it. My throat hurts almost every day, and the doctor had serious concerns about permanent damage to my larynx. However, I got the all clear to train and play, and even though it takes a while for my voice to get going in the morning, I'm good to go.

"Okay, the guest of honor will be here in an hour, so we need to finish setting up the bar, hang some bunting on the porch, and make sure the caterers know where to set up the food," Mila states as she marches into the kitchen with her clipboard, looking all business. No wonder Coach Casey values her so highly as his assistant. "Do you think we have enough pink?"

Matt barks out a throaty laugh and pulls his woman against his body, smoothing her chaotic red hair out of her face.

"Red, the place looks perfect. Bugs and Cam'll love it." He takes her lips in a searing kiss that makes me feel like I should turn away to give them privacy. "Now stop stressing, get your butt upstairs, and finish getting ready. I got this." He gives her butt a cheeky slap, making her squeal.

"Thank you." Mila giggles, wriggling free from his embrace and handing over her clipboard. "Don't let the caterers leave without putting the mini quiches in the oven to warm through." She points finger guns at him as she heads toward the stairs.

"Sure thing." He smirks, pretending to look at her list, but once she disappears up the stairs, he tosses the clipboard on the counter and gets us both another beer.

"You'd better do what she says, man." I chuckle, accepting the chilled glass bottle. "I don't think today is the day to piss her off."

Matt tips his bottle at me and takes a long drink. "It's all under control. Fancy a game of pool?"

I shrug and nod, following him into the game room. It's not my woman that'll cut my balls off if the mini quiches are ruined, so I see no harm in enjoying a few games of pool while we wait for this party to start. I'm just here for the free food and booze.

2

Lana

I'm dirty, tired, and I'm about to lose my shit if this dick at Customs doesn't hurry up and wave me through. Obviously, travelling with my knife roll raises all sorts of questions, and it takes every ounce of my restraint to smile and explain, again, that I'm a chef, it's an essential part of my job, and they can't confiscate it. Do they do this to Gordon Ramsay? I bet he flies on his own private plane, so he probably doesn't have to go through this shit.

"Let me just try my supervisor again," the weedy looking guy says in his nasally voice, pulling his walkie-talkie off his belt, twiddling the button until it screeches to life.

"Danny, Danny, I need you at the Customs desk. Over."

I huff out an exasperated breath and fold my arms across my chest. I've been travelling for almost twenty hours, and I have zero patience left. I catch a whiff of my own body odor and scrunch my nose up—I need a shower and a warm bed, now.

After what feels like a millennium, a bald man I

11

assume to be Danny appears through a door marked Private and begins talking to the guy who's currently ruining my life. They have a whispered, heated discussion, and Danny looks over at me and rolls his eyes, shoving the other man out of the way so he can approach me.

"May I see your passport?" he asks, smiling kindly and I feel slightly more hopeful that he's at least competent at his job.

"Sure," I sigh, pulling it out of my carryon bag and handing it over. Danny opens it and looks from it to me several times.

"Miss Landon, you're a chef by profession?" he asks, now looking down at my knife roll which is spread out, showing the tools of my trade.

"Yes, I've just finished working in Paris and attending Le Cordon Bleu culinary school. My knife roll is essential for me to work, and it costs several thousand dollars so I'm not in a position to replace it if you…" I can hear my voice getting high pitched and teary, but Danny holds his hand up to stop me.

"That won't be necessary, Miss Landon." He flicks his eyes toward the other man, and he looks less than pleased. "I'm so sorry you've been waiting, but Joel is new and was just being over cautious. You're free to go. Please accept our apologies."

Relief floods over me. I was running on adrenaline, but now that this is done, all I feel is weak and lightheaded. I still don't feel safe, and I won't until I'm out of the airport.

"Thank you. I appreciate the speed at which *you* dealt with this." I shoot Joel a shitty look. "I suggest you train your staff a little better in the future."

I quickly grab my knife roll and hotfoot it away before he can change his mind.

With no other luggage to collect, I find the car rental office and collect a mid-size coupe. I'll have to buy a car at some point, but for now, this will do. My first stop is the hotel I've booked in the city so I can at least recover from my jet lag before I have to face my brother. Tomorrow, I plan to drive out to Matt's new house on the Sound, but I need a shower, a meal that isn't served in a plastic tray, and a good night's sleep before I have to deal with the Spanish Inquisition.

When I finally make it to the hotel, I'm thankful that check in is simple and quick. As I step into the elevator, I feel a more acute sense of panic than I've felt during the whole journey. I'm on the final stage, but part of me is still convinced the doors will slide open on my floor and Etienne will be standing there, ready to take me back to Paris. As the elevator pings through the floors, my breathing picks up until I'm virtually panting with anxiety. When the doors finally open, I'm immensely relieved to find the floor is deserted.

"Get a grip, you idiot," I admonish myself, taking a huge cleansing breath and heading toward my room, fumbling slightly with the keycard. When I'm finally inside, I flick the lock and the security bar and press my back against the door, sliding down it until my knees are drawn up under my chin.

I can't believe I've finally made it. It feels like I've been travelling for weeks, which I have, in a way. I realized it wasn't working with Etienne about six months ago when I agreed to move in with him, and he couldn't hide his drinking or controlling behavior any-more. The first time he left his mark on me, I slapped him back, called him an asshole, and stormed out of the apartment.

Because fuck him!

However, that night he arrived at the Bistro with a huge bouquet of red roses, lots of regret and tears in his eyes, along with promises it'd never happen again, and that he'd quit drinking so much.

Like a fool in love, I believed everything he said.

For a while, it was perfect between us again. He took me on trips down the Seine where we'd drink champagne and he'd tell me all about the history of the amazing architecture; we'd eat at the most expensive restaurants, and we'd visit vineyards and his family's chateau. He'd make love to me like no one had before, and I thought we could make a life together.

At the same time, he couldn't stop drinking too much red wine during service at the restaurant, and I couldn't live up to what he expected me to be. I was either too loud, too sulky, too busy, or too American. Sometimes all of the above. Nothing I did was ever good enough and he seemed to take sick delight in reminding me how his girlfriend should act. He'd humiliate me in public and physically punish me in private. I was embarrassed to admit to all of it; saying it out loud would make it real.

Eventually, I'd had enough and confided in Zac. He went crazy and I had to talk him out of going to Etienne's restaurant and beating the shit out of him. But once he'd calmed down and I finally admitted I needed his help to leave, we began to put the plan into action.

And now, here I am. Back in the States. Too ashamed to go to my folks' place in Florida, my only other option was Seattle. I know my brother can be an overprotective meathead, but at least he'll ask fewer questions than our parents.

Hunger and the need for a shower finally urges me from my place by the door, and I set about unpacking my jammies and toiletries. The hotel is basic but clean and comfortable, and thankfully has a twenty-four-hour room service menu. My body has no clue what time it is, but it's dark outside, so I figure I should eat something and go to bed. I quickly shoot a text off to Zac to let him know I'm safely at the hotel, and I strip off my jeans and sweater as I walk into the bathroom. The hot water feels like a rebirth, and I stand under it until my skin tingles and the pads of my fingers turn wrinkly. At that moment, despite the fact I've freed myself from Etienne, I allow the tears to flow down my cheeks, mixing with the shower water. It's a combination of happiness, sadness, and relief. I may be at the lowest point in my life; I have no home, no job, no friends who aren't thousands of miles away. My life may be fucking pathetic. But it's once again my own.

Hopefully, things will look better in the morning.

The Sat Nav voice tells me to take the next turn down what looks like a dirt track, and as I bump along, I worry I've put too much trust in modern technology. Any minute I'll plummet into the Sound because the stupid device has taken me on a wild goose chase.

I feel much better than I did yesterday; the shower, the food, and the rest have done me a world of good, and I finally feel prepared to grovel at my brother's feet and ask him for a place to stay while I figure out what to do next. I don't think it'll come to that, though.

As I continue along the track, still hoping I won't end up in the water, I begin to notice expensive-looking cars parked on the verges; huge SUVs, Lamborghinis, Audis, and a Tesla line the track and fill the space in front of my brother's large house. Luckily, there's a small space in front of the garage that I manage to squeeze my car into, next to a massive orange Hummer.

From the looks of things, Matt and Mila are having a party, and I don't know if this will be a curse or a blessing. At least he won't be able to tear me a new one with a house full of guests. However, I don't really want to explain my sudden appearance in front of what I assume will be a room full of hockey players. My stomach fills with nerves as I climb out of the car, being careful not to ding the expensive Hummer with my door.

I suddenly notice the pink bunting hanging from the front porch and the pink and white "It's a Girl" balloons swaying lazily in the breeze. *Are they having a baby shower? Is Mila pregnant? How the hell did I miss this piece of news?*

A little pissed at apparently being left out of the loop, I stomp toward the porch. I've been in France, not outer space. That brother of mine sure has a lot of explaining to do.

Just as I'm about to throw the front door open, it

pulls away from me and the doorframe is filled by the biggest man I've ever seen. He literally becomes the door, taking up all the height and much of the width with his huge body. As I drag my eyes up his torso, I take in the way his muscles bulge underneath the soft looking flannel shirt. The sleeves are stretched tightly over his biceps, and it looks like one hard flex could cause them to split open like the Incredible Hulk. When I finally reach his face I'm greeted by a short blonde beard with hints of red around his chin, full soft lips, shaggy blonde hair, and eyes so icy blue they could be chipped from a glacier. His heavy brows are drawn together, but as his eyes drink me in, his lips kick up into a breathtaking smile.

We hold each other's gaze for an embarrassingly long time, and eventually I drag my eyes away so I can try to peer around this behemoth of a man.

"Is Matt home?" I ask in a voice that's tight with anxiety. This huge gatekeeper doesn't seem to be letting me past.

"Who wants to know?" the giant asks, cocking an inquisitive eyebrow and folding his thick arms across his chest. He has a slight accent that I can't quite place.

Jesus, what is with everybody? Am I destined to only encounter idiots now I'm back in America?

"I don't think that's any of your damn business," I snap, stepping forward and pushing against his chest. "Can you move out of the way, please?" However, it's like trying to move a mountain, and even when I put all my weight behind it, he doesn't budge.

A deep chuckle that seems to vibrate through his chest and travel through my fingers makes me look up at the man blocking my way, and I find myself dazzled by his smile. It's open and kind, but also the most infuriating thing I've ever seen right about now.

3

Thor

The little firecracker standing in front of me is the most intriguing woman I've come across in a really long time. I just came out to collect the gift bag I left in the back of Nate's truck, and suddenly I'm confronted with five feet of pissed off brunette. Her chestnut hair falls over her shoulders in a sleek sheet and her denim blue eyes burn with indignation at being stopped at the door. As those same eyes drink in my imposing physique, I size up her luscious curves. She's an absolute knockout, if not my usual type. I tend to go for arrogant, leggy blondes, and look where that's got me.

Her annoyance is cute, and I can't help but laugh at her attempts to shove me out of the way.

"Now, now, little one. What's the rush? Are you here for the baby party?" I ask as she finally gives up trying to move me and stands back with her hands on her sexy hips.

Fuck, I need to stop checking her out like this.

"I'm here to see Matt Landon," she states firmly. "And you're standing in my way." The firecracker digs around in the pocket of her tight jeans and produces

19

the cheapest looking cell phone I've ever seen, holding it up so I can see the contact with Matt's number programmed in. "Now, do I really need to call my brother?"

The last piece of information hits me like a sledgehammer. Shit, this is Matt's sister. I've heard him talk about her plenty, but I thought she lived in Paris.

"Hello? Anybody home?" she asks, knocking the door frame to my left. "Are my words getting through your thick hockey skull?"

I dumbly nod my head and step aside, noticing the smug smirk that tips up her pouty lips, and her sassy attitude makes my dick twitch to life.

"Finally," she mutters as she breezes past me, and her vanilla scent fills my nostrils. I can't help but follow her into the main room like a lovesick puppy; this feisty firecracker has me by the balls, and I think I'm okay with that.

"Jesus, Thor, where've you been?" Beth asks, stalking up to me. "And where's the gift bag? You had one fucking job, you big goon."

My head snaps down to look at the feisty blonde, her red lips pressed together in annoyance.

"Sorry, I got distracted," I reply, my eyes never leaving said distraction as she makes her way through the party toward her brother.

Beth's gaze follows mine. "Who's that?" she asks.

"Matt's sister, apparently," I say, absently watching as Matt finally clocks his sister and pulls her into a massive hug.

"Oh, that's so awesome. Mila says Lana's a blast," Beth enthuses, clapping her hands. "Go get the gift bag." She shoves me in an attempt to get me moving and heads toward the commotion caused by the unexpected guest.

Not wanting to miss a moment of what's about to unfold, I jog out to the truck and retrieve the gift bag, depositing it on the gift table. I find Matt and the rest of my line hanging out in the kitchen, surrounding his sister, who looks a little bit freaked out at all the attention she's getting.

"What the hell are you doing here, Squirt?" Matt asks, his thick tattooed arm draped over her shoulders.

"Don't call me that, dick face," she growls, shoving him in the ribs, making me smirk into my hand. She really is a firecracker.

"C'mon Lana. I thought you had four months of school left," Matt persists. "In fact, I didn't think you'd ever come back. You seemed so settled in Paris." He ruffles her hair, and she swats his hand away.

I notice the uncomfortable look that crosses Lana's pretty face, but it's there one moment and gone the next, and she's back to sassing her big brother.

"Paris is so over," she says, rolling her eyes. "I have enough credits to graduate so I figured I'd come back and get a job here. The Seattle food scene is really happening right now."

"Do Ma and Pop know you're back?" Matt asks, scowling a little.

"Not exactly." Lana laughs nervously, a cute dimple popping out in her cheek, matching her brother's. "Anyway, enough about me. Are you and Mila having a baby? What's this party all about?"

Suddenly, it's Matt's turn to look freaked out, and as his head snaps toward Mila, she bursts out into hysterical laughter.

"Easy, big guy!" Mila soothes once she's stopped laughing. "It's Cam and Bugs with the baby, remember? You are *so* not ready for that yet."

With a smirk, Matt wipes his brow in fake relief and pulls Mila into a deep kiss which elicits gagging noises from his kid sister.

"Is there any booze at this party?" Lana asks no one in particular as her brother sucks face with his woman.

This is my moment.

"I'll show you," I volunteer, which causes Nate and Ford to smirk at me as I push forward and take Lana's arm, leading her toward the bar. She allows me to hold her arm for all of two seconds, and that's all it takes for me to notice how silky her skin is and how good she smells. I'm just beginning to enjoy having her next to me when she steps away and throws me a cautious look.

"I can walk myself, thank you," she sasses, moving her arm away from me and marching off to the bar. Yet again, I can't seem to stop myself from following her, my dick leading the way and doing all my thinking for me.

"What can I get you?" I ask, joining her at the counter where Matt set up the bar.

"I can get it," Lana says, turning to face me. Well, she faces my chest because she's so tiny, but her chin is tilted up, so her deep blue eyes are locked with mine. "Where's your accent from? Are you Austrian, like Arnie?"

What the fuck? She thinks I'm Austrian? But as I look at her in shocked indignation, I notice the cheeky smile that plays on her lips, and I realize she's messing with me.

Before I can correct her and while thinking about spanking her peachy, round ass for being so cheeky, Matt appears again and grabs a beer from the bucket of ice.

"I see you've met our goalie," he says to his sister, obviously not sensing the tension that crackles between us. "Lana, this is Thor."

At the mention of my team nickname, she smirks into her hand and rolls her eyes. "Thor? You hockey players and your nicknames." She laughs, shaking her head.

Damn, this feisty little minx is really turning me on, even when she's laughing at me. "You can talk—Squirt." I chuckle, enjoying the little growl my comment elicits. "Alex," I say, thrusting my hand out for her to shake. "You can call me Alex."

For some reason, my correction seems to take the wind out of her sails, and she stops scowling and looks at my outstretched hand.

"I'm Lana," she replies in a husky little voice that does nothing to ease the tightness in my jeans.

I notice her take a sharp intake of breath as I wrap her hand in mine; it's tiny, but she has a strong grip, and I can feel small rough calluses on her fingers. At that moment, I wonder what it would feel like to have it wrapped around my hard cock. However, as I drag my gaze away from her and notice the angry scowl on her brother's face, I realize that thinking about Matt's little sister and my dick together can end very, very badly for me.

Suddenly, I feel Matt's hand on the back of my neck. "Thor, a word," he mutters, steering me away from eye fucking his sister to a quiet corner where he releases me and fixes me with a death stare. "What the fuck, man?"

"What?" I ask, raising my hands and laughing at how serious Matt looks all of a sudden.

"She is absolutely off limits." Matt pokes me in the chest and the nerve in his jaw twitches. "That's my fucking sister, and if she's hanging around, I'll be telling all the guys the same thing. No one touches her. Spread the word."

"Hey! We were just talking," I protest, still chuckling at what an overprotective asshole he's being. As the youngest of four brothers, I have no idea what it's like to have a little sister, but Matt looks ready to chop my balls off if I don't agree to stay away from his.

"You forget that I know you well enough to know when you're zeroing in on your target," Matt continues. "She is not gonna be one of your conquests, man. Stay the fuck away."

I shake my head and slap him on the back. "Of course, man. You're my brother, which essentially makes her my sister. I'll have nothing but brotherly thoughts toward her."

By the way Matt relaxes, I think my words have calmed him. I just need to give my dick the memo because he still seems extremely interested in the firecracker who's talking to Cam across the room, cooing over baby SJ. As I continue to stare, her sapphire blue eyes catch my gaze and I feel the room fall away.

This is going to be a problem.

4

Lana

"So what's the deal, Squirt?" Matt asks as we settle down on the couch with a cold beer. The party ended an hour ago, so once everything was cleared away and Mila was sent off for a long soak in the tub, I knew I'd have to face my brother's questions.

I take a long pull on my beer and avoid his piercing stare. Jesus, when his career as a hockey player ends, he could totally work for the CIA! His loud huff and the playful shove on my shoulder alert me to the fact that my grace period is over, and it's time to talk.

Swallowing the liquid in my mouth, I prepare to share the half-truth as to why I've shown up on his doorstep.

"Like I said, I'm done with Paris. I'll still graduate, but I'm tired of working for tyrannical chefs who take all the credit for my blood, sweat, and tears," I explain. This much is true. I loved my job as a sous chef, but I constantly felt like my hard work wasn't acknowledged or appreciated. I often developed new dishes for the menu just to see the head chef take all the credit once they became top sellers.

"Okay, I get why you'd want to get out of that situation," my brother concedes. "But why leave Paris altogether? Couldn't you just work at a different restaurant? You've always told us how much you love France."

"I did. I do," I reply, my eyes prickling with tears, feeling the loss of my dream deep in my heart. "I just feel like it's time to come home, see what options are open to me here." I shrug and take another swig of cold beer, thankful for the satisfied look in my brother's eyes. He's buying my story, and I feel a weight slowly lifting from my shoulders.

"Well, it's good to have you home, kid." Matt gives my shoulder a reassuring squeeze and drains his beer. "Take it you wanna crash here until you get yourself settled?"

"Of course." I smirk. "There have to be some advantages to having a rich douchebag for a brother. How many rooms does this place have anyway?"

Matt pulls me into a headlock and scrubs his knuckles through my sleek hair, ruffling it up, which he knows I hate. "Don't be a brat, or I'll make you sleep on a cot in the garage." He laughs as I struggle to release myself from his grip.

Thankfully, Mila chooses that moment to return from her bath, giggling at our sibling wrestling match. "See, this is why I'm grateful that I'm an only child."

At the sound of her voice, Matt releases his grip, shoves me away, and pulls Mila down onto his lap, planting a sloppy kiss on her lips.

"Feeling better after your bath, Red?" he asks, grabbing a handful of Mila's robe-covered butt. Ugh, these two are nauseating! One disadvantage of staying here will be all the PDA I'll have to deal with.

"Yes," Mila sighs, snuggling into Matt's chest. "I feel very relaxed." As she begins to kiss and nibble at my brother's ear, I take that as my signal to leave them to it.

"Okay, I'm gonna head back to my hotel as I paid for tonight already," I say awkwardly, standing up in order to get away from the make out session that seems to be unfolding in front of me. "What time can I come back tomorrow?"

My question seems to get my brother's attention away from his girlfriend, and he gently lifts her off his lap. "I'll walk you out and give you the door and alarm code. Just come back whenever you're ready."

Mila straightens her robe and stands as well. "I'm really excited to have you come and stay, Lana. I'll make up the guest room at the top of the stairs for you." With that, she pulls me into a hug, and I let her warm, lavender scent envelop me. It's comforting and I feel safe for the first time in months. "You're welcome for as long as you need." The way she whispers this in my ear makes me think she knows there's more to my story than I've revealed so far.

"Thanks, you guys. I promise that once I get my job situation sorted out, I'll start looking for a place," I reply, pulling out of the hug and accepting the piece of paper Matt has scribbled the codes on. "I know you two have only just moved in together, and I don't wanna cramp your style."

"No sweat, Squirt. You're welcome as long as you need. You'll just have to put up with Mila screaming my name at all hours of the day and night." He smirks at the crimson blush that stains Mila's cheeks and pulls her into a hug while I open the front door and make gagging noises.

"Dude, that's way too much information," I grumble, stepping over the threshold. "Looks like I'll be investing in a set of ear plugs."

"Can't help it if your brother's a sex god." He chuckles again, despite Mila trying to cover his mouth with her hand.

"Oh my GOD, shut up," she cries as he picks her up, making her squeal. "Come back as soon as you're ready, Lana. I'll make sure this idiot behaves himself."

"Thanks again." I retreat down the steps as they wave goodbye, and my brother slams the door, no doubt getting ready to ravage his girlfriend. Ugh, I'm definitely heading for the drugstore to buy some ear plugs and possibly a blindfold.

It's late by the time I get back into the city, so I order some soup and crackers from room service and try to read. However, my mind finally feels still enough to process everything that's happened over the last seventy-two hours. I begin to wonder what Etienne is doing, whether he freaked out when I didn't come home from work. Did he check his tracker app during the day and see my phone moving steadily away from the city? Has he been to the bistro to look for me or tried to track Zac down?

My phone lights up on the comforter, and I see Zac's name appear. I throw my Kindle down and grab the phone, swiping to accept the call.

"Hey Zac, you're up early," I say, sliding down into bed. It's a little before dawn in Paris.

"Bonjour, babe." His deep voice travels across the ocean to immediately comfort me. "Not up early—I've not been to bed yet." I can hear the mischievous smirk in his voice, and I smile.

"Naughty." I giggle. "Who was the lucky boy?"

"Didn't catch his name, but he was Spanish and didn't speak a word of English or French, so we communicated in the best way I know." He chuckles.

"You're a whore." I sigh good naturedly, knowing my best friend and his reputation for hot, anonymous hookups. "So, what's new?"

The pregnant pause that follows makes my stomach clench, and my palms become sweaty. I subconsciously twirl a lock of hair around my fingers, tugging it until my scalp stings.

"Etienne came to the restaurant."

His words cause a spike of ice to stab through my heart. "Oh god, what did he say? Did he hurt you?"

Zac's deep baritone laugh vibrates through the phone. "Oh baby, don't worry about me. I can take care of myself."

"I know you can handle yourself, but just tell me what happened!" I cry out, feeling all the relaxation leave my body in a sickening wave.

"Okay, Lana, relax," Zac soothes. "It took him twenty hours to track me down, and when he came to the bistro, he was surprisingly calm and sober."

I suck in a breath. "What did he say?"

"He asked if I knew why you'd gone to the Côte d'Azur and why you're not answering your phone. I guess my plan to send your phone on a mystery tour is working."

"Yes, you're very clever." I sigh. "What did you say after that?"

"I told him you were tired of his shit and needed a break and that's when he punched me," Zac replies in a tight voice.

I gasp and tug harder on my hair. "Oh Zac, are you okay?"

He laughs again. "I told you I can handle myself. He got one punch in and split my lip before the guys in the kitchen dragged him off and kicked his ass out."

I feel the tears sting my eyes as I think about my best friend taking a punch to protect me. I know all too well how Etienne's angry hands feel, and I shudder at the thought.

"I'm so sorry I dragged you into this drama," I say in a strangled sob. "If he approaches you again, you need to call the police."

"Don't worry about that, babe. The kitchen porters gave his ass a pretty good kicking in the alley behind the bistro when they threw him out. I don't think he'll be back anytime soon." Zac chuckles. "Plus, I might get a sexy scar out of it."

I sigh and let my body relax again. I know that Zac can handle himself; at over six feet tall, he towers over Etienne's slight, aristocratic frame, outweighing him with lean muscle that's hard earned from time in the gym and hours playing soccer at the weekend. But it still hurts my heart to know he's also suffered at the fists of that asshole.

"So, how did things go with your brother?" Zac asks, bringing me back to the moment. "Did he buy your story? Is he gonna let you stay with him?"

"Yes and yes," I reply. "It's all good. I'm gonna move in tomorrow and then think about what to do for work."

"What about your contacts in Seattle? Have you tried them yet?" he asks, reminding me of the talk we had one night after too many glasses of Côtes du Rhône.

"Not yet, but who knows if anyone's hiring?" I reply. "It's a long shot that any of these leads will come to anything. I have no work history in the States, so who'd hire me?"

"Oh Jesus, would you listen to yourself?" Zac growls. "Where's my badass bestie who can do anything she puts her mind to?"

"She's tired," I sigh, suddenly feeling like my bones are made of lead, a deep aching fatigue that I've been fighting for too long settling over me like a weighted blanket. "I'm so tired." Even as I say the words, I feel my eyelids droop.

"I know, baby. It will get better, I promise. Take some time for yourself. You need to heal."

"I know," I mumble. "Zac, can I ask you something?"

"Anything, you know that."

"Can you stay on the line while I fall asleep?" I feel ridiculous for asking this, but I always feel so safe around Zac, and after his revelations about Etienne's visit, I need that security right now.

"You bet," he replies in a quiet voice. "Snuggle down and I'll regale you with all the gossip while you fall asleep. I love you, babe."

"Love you too," I whisper, and I don't even hear the beginning of his first story as I slip into a dreamless sleep.

Thor

The smell of sweat stings my nostrils as I push through the door into the team gym. Most of my line are already exercising hard on various machines and apparatus, working with the different athletic trainers around the room. I'm only late because I've had a session with the team doctor who is still assessing my throat injury. He confirms it's mostly healed, but he wants to keep an eye on it until the tenderness and periodic voice loss has settled down. Of all the injuries I could sustain as a goaltender, I never imagined this would be a problem. I always thought my knees or hips would give out first. But thankfully, those parts of my huge body seem to be holding up well, especially as I'm about to turn thirty.

As I throw my towel and water bottle down on the mat, I see Coach Casey approach.

"How was your session with the doc?" he asks, running his hand through his silver hair. Coach used to be a kick ass player back in the day, and I respect him immensely as our coach. He's never steered us wrong, and even though he's tough and takes no shit, he's a great leader. It's one of the reasons our premature exit from last season's cup run stung so much. And my part in that exit feels even more raw. I took a puck to the throat in the deciding game of the series against Dallas and had to leave the game. I don't for a second believe that was the sole cause for the loss, because I'm not a completely self-centered asshole, but the goalie is the constant presence in the team, usually playing the entire sixty minutes, so when the reserve goalie had to take my place, it unsettled the team dynamic, and shit just fell apart.

"He's happy with my progress," I reply. "He just wants to keep up the weekly monitoring while I'm still having some pain and voice loss."

"Okay, good," Coach Casey says. "Make sure the equipment team packs your neck defender with your gear. I know you hate wearing it, but I'm not gonna risk another injury." He slaps my bicep and goes back to talking to the lead athletic trainer who's putting Bugs through his paces on the rowing machine.

I decide to warm up with some stretches, so I drop to the mat and begin stretching out my legs, contorting myself into various different poses that mimic what I do on the ice. As my muscles become more elastic, I move into a box split, rolling my hips back and forth, finally pushing forward into my hands and knees, continuing to roll my hips.

"No wonder you're such a hit with the ladies." Knox smirks, dropping down next to me while he chugs water from his bottle.

I just grunt at him and continue my stretching. Knox doesn't seem to get the hint that I don't want to chat, and he continues rambling on about his latest conquest. His light brown skin is slick with sweat, and I'm happy to see him working hard instead of slacking off and dicking around. We all hoped that when Brett got traded to the Washington Sentinels and Knox was called up to the first line that he'd stop his partying and get serious. And even though he's focused and having a great season on the ice, he's still making waves when it comes to his personal life. If I thought I was tabloid fodder, he's their front-page bad boy, constantly being photographed with different women, partying all over Seattle.

"Dude, I don't wanna hear it," I grumble, falling out of my stretch and fixing him with my icy stare. His ramblings about hot chicks just serve as a reminder that it's been a few months since I hooked up with anyone and about the last conversation I had with my mom. Her disappointed words still ring in my ears just to be quickly replaced by sapphire blue eyes, cute freckles, and a peachy ass.

Lana Landon.

The sexy firecracker who happens to be my team-mate's little sister and therefore completely off limits. I've not been able to get her sassy attitude and bright smile out of my head since the party a few days ago, and I'm ashamed to say she's been at the forefront in my mind when I've fisted my cock in the shower.

As if he can sense I'm having dirty thoughts about his sister, Matt strides over and stands over me, scowling. Guilt immediately envelops me, and I swallow the dry lump that's suddenly formed in my throat.

"What's up, man?" I ask, trying to sound as casual as possible.

His scowl doesn't leave his face, and I'm convinced he's going to call me out for perving over his sister. However, he surprises the shit out of me by asking, "How's the throat? Coach said you've been seeing the doc."

Relief washes over me, and I stand, towering over Matt by several inches. "Yeah, he just wants to keep monitoring it. There's no problem. Thanks for asking."

"Of course, man." He slaps my back. "We're a team. Gotta look out for my brothers."

Shit, now I feel twice as guilty about lusting after his kid sister. I need to get this crush under control and put her out of my head.

5

Lana

I've been sitting on Matt's couch for two weeks, and I can literally feel my ass spreading a little more every hour. When I moved my meager possessions into my brother's house, I had every intention of getting straight into my new life. I have a few contacts in Seattle, so I set about reaching out to them. However, after several phone calls and a few lunches, I came up empty. It seems the Seattle food scene is so happening, it's happening without me. No one is hiring and the only jobs I can find online are at fast food joints or a '50s themed diner where I'll have to dress up as a pin-up girl.

No fucking way.

Once my job search became too depressing to continue, I set up camp on Matt's couch and haven't moved since. I've eaten my weight in junk food, watched *Sex and the City* on a loop, and wallowed in self-pity. What the hell was I thinking uprooting my entire life because of a shitty guy? I should have told Etienne to kiss my ass and moved on without such drastic measures. But I've been through it before, and maybe Etienne would have wormed his way back into my life like he's done every single time I broke up with him.

Thankfully, Matt and Mila have had a hectic schedule of games and travel, so other than a few fleeting conversations on their way in or out of the house, I've had the place to myself. This has been a blessing and a curse; if my brother knew that I was putting down roots on his couch and not actively looking for work and a place to live, he'd kick my ass. It's been bad enough putting on a brave face when mom and dad call.

"I can't believe you came back and didn't come to us first," mom scolded during our first conversation. "The weather in Florida is perfect. I thought you'd want some time in the sun after the gloom of Paris in January."

"I'm sorry, mom. I got such a good deal on my ticket I couldn't pass on it," I lied. "I promise to come down with Matt next time the Whalers play Tampa."

"You'd better, young lady. We miss you." I can hear the emotion in my mom's voice, and I feel like absolute shit yet again.

My heart squeezed uncomfortably at her words, and I felt terrible for not confiding in her. But just like my brother, my mom would swim the Atlantic to put her foot up Etienne's ass if she knew what was really going on.

So, other than occasional chats with my parents and Matt and Mila, I've been alone with my thoughts and my hot Cheetos.

"Squirt, don't take this the wrong way, but that couch is new, and I really don't want your ass print on it."

I look up from my Kindle and stare at my brother, sweaty from his run, that cocky smirk on his lips. He and Mila returned from a four-day road trip late last night when I was already tucked up in bed. However, I forgot they were coming home, so I didn't clean up the little nest I'd made for myself on the couch before I went to bed. When I got up this morning, the blanket I've been hibernating under was already in the washing machine, the Cheetos crumbs had been vacuumed from the rug, the trashy magazines neatly stacked on the coffee table, and all my cups and plates were in the dishwasher. My cheeks flared with embarrassment when I realized my secret solitary behavior had been discovered, so I threw myself into the shower and cleaned up, so I at least didn't look like a crazy hermit.

"Give me a break," I grumble, closing my Kindle and tossing it on the couch just as Matt takes a seat next to me.

"You know what? I *have* given you a break," he replies seriously. "I've watched you fester on my couch for two weeks, and before you deny it, I can tell by your B.O. and permanent Cheetos breath that you don't even bother getting up when we're not here."

I feel my cheeks burn with shame and I shift uncomfortably, avoiding Matt's stare but not denying what he's saying.

"I have a feeling there's more to your move home than you're letting on, but I'm not gonna push you into telling me until you're ready." He puts his hand on my shoulder and squeezes it in the reassuring way he's done since we were kids. "However, I will not allow you to wallow on my couch any longer. Tell me your plan, and I'll do whatever I can to help you out—you know that."

My eyes fill with tears at his kindness and understanding, and before I can stop myself, I burst into ugly sobs, covering my face with my hands. While I cry, I'm pulled into my brother's arms, and he hugs me until I'm done crying and the smell of his sweaty T-shirt becomes too much to bear.

"Ugh, you stink." I sniff, pulling out of his arms, but I give him a look that he knows is full of appreciation for comforting me.

He smirks at me and pulls his shirt over his nose, taking a deep breath. "Smells like hard work and awesomeness to me, Squirt." He chuckles, the dimple we share popping in his cheek. "C'mon then, let's hear it. If the restaurants are a dead end, what are you gonna do for work?"

I let out a shaky breath and wipe my eyes. "I don't know. I guess I could take the diner job until I find something more suitable." I shrug, knowing that a demeaning job where I have to cook in booty shorts and a crop top is better than no job at all. Plus, it's a step toward independence, and I know how much I need that.

"The pin-up diner job?" Matt growls, narrowing his eyes at me. "Hard pass. No sister of mine is gonna have guys ogling her butt while she cooks greasy diner food."

I giggle at his alpha overprotective brother act. If I want to take the job, he won't be able to stop me, but I appreciate the fact that he doesn't want me to do something he knows I'll hate.

"So, if that's not an option, I guess I could do

something outside of cooking. I have my business degree, so I could do something in an office." I shrug and feel the dread settle in my stomach at the prospect of sitting behind a desk like a corporate zombie all day long.

Matt laughs. "Yeah, you look thrilled at the prospect of that."

I slump down into the couch cushions and sigh. "Perhaps I should go and stay with Mom and Pop in Florida."

"Hey now, it's only been a few weeks. Something will come up. I can ask at the Whalers. We have chefs for the players' lounge and some who prepare our meal plans," he suggests.

"Maybe," I mutter, feeling less than enthusiastic about working alongside my brother and his girlfriend. It seems too much like a handout.

"For fuck's sake, Squirt, you're killing me." He sighs. "Let me ask you this: what's the dream?"

"The dream?" I ask.

"Yeah, you know, what's the ultimate Lana Landon dream? If you could do anything in the whole world, what would it be?"

"Well, it used to be to live and work in Paris in a Michelin-starred restaurant, work my way up to head chef, and develop my own menus," I say in a tight voice. I still dream about working at an award-winning restaurant, about doing what I love and proving to myself and everyone that I can do it. But it doesn't have to be in Paris anymore. Let's just say the city has lost its luster.

"So why isn't that the dream anymore?" Matt pushes.

I huff out a breath and cross my arms over my chest. "It just isn't, okay? Drop it, would you?"

"Fine." He huffs as well. "What's the backup dream? When I was working toward playing in the NHL, one of my junior coaches told me to have a backup, just in case I didn't make it to the show."

"I guess I've always wanted to run my own kitchen. You know, develop my own menus and cook the way I want. Be my own woman." But even as I say the words, I know this is not an easy feat. "It's a stupid idea. Did you know that up to sixty percent of new restaurants fail in the first year?"

"So that means forty percent have to succeed, right? I know math was never my strong point but even I can work that out." He laughs. "Why can't you be one of the forty percent?"

"It's not just that; for starters, it's the cost of setting it all up. I could try and find some investors, but that takes time and contacts I just don't have …"

"You know that money isn't an issue. I'd happily invest in you," Matt offers without even a second thought. God, my brother may be an overprotective asshole sometimes, but he's so generous. I have already taken advantage of the Big Brother Scholarship Fund when he paid for me to move to Paris and attend Le Cordon Bleu.

"No way!" I hold my hands up. "I can't ask you to do that. You've given me enough, and it would take hundreds of thousands of dollars to set up. You've just bought this house and you have your future with Mila to think about. Absolutely not!"

"Okay, fine. But there must be something I can do

to help?" he asks.

"Once I have that magic idea, I'll let you know." I laugh. "In the meantime, how about I make us lunch? I don't think I can continue with the Cheetos and Snickers diet for much longer."

"Sounds good, Squirt." Matt pats my knee and rises from the couch. "I'm gonna hit the shower. You know where everything is. Help yourself to whatever you want."

I stand as well and put my arms around my brother's waist, resting my cheek against his chest, his arms coming around my shoulders.

"Thank you," I whisper, giving him a squeeze. "I will tell you why I came back. Just not yet, okay?"

"Sure thing, kid." Matt pats my back. "As long as you're alright, I'm happy."

I feel the sting of tears in my eyes and pull out of the hug before I dissolve into another snotty crying fit. "Are you happy with grilled cheese?" I ask, wiping my eyes with the back of my sleeve,

"You know it's my favorite," he replies, wiping his own eyes and quickly disappearing upstairs to shower while I move into his amazing kitchen. Apparently, he had the original one ripped out and replaced with top of the range appliances, marble countertops, and clean modern cabinet fronts. It's literally my dream kitchen, and I'm excited to cook something other than frozen pizza in it for the first time.

After digging around in the fridge, I find some ingredients to make grilled cheese sandwiches. I slice the sourdough bread into chunky slices and smear one side with butter. Then I load up a slice with pepperjack cheese, white cheddar, sliced jalapenos, and some salsa I found at the back of the fridge.

Adding more butter and a touch of oil to the skillet, I heat it up and then add the loaded sandwich, loving the satisfying sizzle when the buttered bread hits the hot skillet. I keep a close eye on it, checking that the bread is crisping up and the cheese is melting, and at the perfect moment, I flip it over and cook the other side. The satisfaction I get from cooking is comparable to nothing else; turning a pile of random ingredients into something that feeds and nourishes people's body and soul is something I've always loved to do.

"Oh my god, what is that smell?" Mila asks, drifting into the kitchen with her nose in the air as I deposit the first sandwich onto a paper towel to drain, adding the next one to the skillet.

"I'm making grilled cheese, want one?" I reply, pressing the slotted turner to the top of the sandwich so it sizzles loudly.

"Yes please," Mila sighs, taking a seat at the kitchen island. "After a week of hotel food, I'm dying for something fresh and home cooked."

"Here." I slide the finished sandwich onto a plate and dress it with some fresh watercress and a pickle. "It's not exactly gourmet, but hopefully it'll fill a hole."

"Well, this is the fanciest grilled cheese I've ever eaten." Mila laughs, picking up the sandwich and taking a large bite. I watch as her eyes roll back in her head, and she moans. "Oh wow!"

"Hey Red, are you eating my sandwich?" Matt laughs, stalking into the kitchen wearing his Whalers sweatpants and hoodie, his hair still damp from the shower.

"Oh babe, you need to try this," she says after swallowing the food in her mouth, holding her half-eaten sandwich out to him.

"I love you, but I'll take my own, thanks." He plants a kiss on her greasy lips and grabs the freshly cooked sandwich from the paper towel and begins to devour it.

"Hey, at least let me put it on a plate for you," I protest, disgusted by his caveman behavior.

"No need, Squirt. This isn't touching the sides," he mumbles, shoveling more crispy bread and melted cheese into his mouth. I finish cooking my sandwich and turn off the burner, sliding it onto a plate with the little salad and pickle.

"Honestly, Lana, that's the best thing I've eaten in ages," Mila says, wiping her mouth with a napkin. I try to ignore the dirty smirk that crosses my brother's face at her comment.

"Thanks. I used to make these all the time in Paris. I have lots of different recipes. I call this one Cheesy Gonzales." I chuckle, remembering when I made it for me and Zac after a night out, and we came up with the silly name.

"You could totally sell these," Mila states, taking a bite out of her pickle.

I laugh. "I'm not sure I could open a grilled-cheese-only restaurant." I shake my head and begin to wipe the cooling skillet clean.

"Who said anything about a restaurant? You could have a grilled cheese food truck," she says off-handedly. "I see them all the time down at the pier and at big events like festivals and those pop-up outdoor movie theaters."

It's like a lightning bolt hits me between the eyes. Why the fuck didn't I think of that before? I've been so focused on restaurants that I didn't even consider the booming food truck movement. It's not really a thing in Paris; there it's all about having an established restaurant in the right part of the city. With a food truck, I could go to all the best spots and all the big events in and around Seattle.

I race round the kitchen island and pull Mila into a hug. "You're a genius, you know that?" I laugh, feeling buoyant and excited for the first time in months.

Mila laughs and hugs me back. "What did I do?"

"You just came up with my new dream, that's all!"

6

Thor

The Whalers fans are some of the loudest and most passionate in the NHL, and as the Vegas center powers toward me, the puck at his blade, I take strength from them. We're one goal down against the Gamblers, and I can't let this goal in with four minutes left on the clock. I fill the doorstep of my goal, my long arms outstretched, sliding side to side all whilst keeping the lurking winger in my peripheral vision. Nate is hot on the player's tail and just as he's about to wind up to hit a slapper at me, Nate picks his pocket and flies round the back of the net, passing it to Bugs who skates away back up the ice.

While the battle to equalize rages at the other end of the rink, I take a moment to lift my helmet and squirt water into my mouth and over my face. I'm already a big guy, weighing in at almost two hundred and forty pounds, but when you add another fifty pounds of gear on top of that, it's a Herculean feat to even skate onto the ice, let alone play sixty minutes of high-adrenaline hockey.

As I toss my bottle back onto the top of my net, I

lower my helmet just as Knox scores at the other end, tying the game.

"Fuck yeah, rookie!" I yell, thrusting my oversized goalie stick into the air while Knox skates backward with his fists pumping in his signature celebration.

However, there's no time to rest on our laurels as we go to a TV break and Coach Casey calls us over for a briefing of the next play, calling the first line to power through and play the remaining two minutes to get the win. I can see all the guys are dog tired, but they're just as pumped to get the win against the Gamblers.

"Are you ready to win this?" Coach yells over the deafening noise of the home fans.

"YES COACH!" we yell back, skating into our positions as the TV break ends and Bugs goes to the center for the puck drop.

"You ready to eat rubber, Bergman?" I hear the familiar, hard Slavic voice of Orlov, the Vegas winger. He's one of the best players in the NHL, but he's also an enormous asshat, and we've come to blows more times than I'd care to count.

"As long as you're ready to feel my blade up your ass," I growl, keeping my eyes firmly fixed on the puck drop that's just about to happen. He does this all the time, trying to get inside my head and making me lose focus. But I'm older and wiser now. I'm not the green kid who used to throw my gloves down for the slightest thing.

"Oh wow, I had no idea you were gay." He chuckles. "Congratulations on coming out. I guess all those bunnies you fuck around with are just a smoke screen, huh?"

I can feel my blood boiling. It's just like Orlov to throw around homophobic slurs in hopes it'll wound my masculinity enough that I'll take my eyes off the puck.

"If I was gay, you'd be the last man I'd tell and certainly the last man I'd fuck." I see the puck drop and the Vegas captain wins it, skating like lightning toward me. I hear Orlov as he continues to throw insults my way, but he's now just an annoying gnat and of no consequence. I have a job to do, and as the players begin to battle it out on the blue paint, I fall into a wide split to block the sliding shot, flicking it back out onto the ice with my skate. It thankfully hits the end of Matt's stick, and he flies off toward our goal, the Vegas defensemen, who seem to have fallen asleep on the job, chasing him down. But they're too late. I hear the horn and the red bulb behind our goal lights up to indicate that Matt has scored a goal that should give us the win, seeing as there's mere seconds left on the clock.

By the time the celebrations are finished, and the puck is dropped again, we manage to just run the clock down, and when the buzzer sounds, the place erupts into an explosion of cheers. "Jump Around," the Whalers fight song, blasts over the PA and the players flood the ice, coming over to offer their thanks, hugs, and slaps to my helmet for a great game. I didn't get a shutout and haven't had one since before the new year, but this was a good win for the team, and it gets us one step closer to a conference win and a spot in the cup run.

"O'Connell's tonight?" Bugs yells over the noise of the locker room. It's Saturday and we have a free day tomorrow, so we'd already made tentative plans to go out after the game, depending on the outcome.

"Fuck yeah!" Knox hollers, ripping his jersey over his head and whirling it round his head like a lasso, launching it toward the laundry bin with pin-point accuracy.

"Calm your tits, kid." I laugh. "You know Coach Casey is watching you like a hawk to make sure you're behaving."

Knox fixes me with an irritated stare. "For fuck's sake, I get into one little fight with a pap outside a club, and suddenly I'm on social probation."

"Correction: you smashed a photographer's very expensive equipment and broke his nose because he took a picture of you fingering a bunny in an alley behind a club." I fix him with my own irritated icy stare. "You need to smarten up, kid. You keep getting yourself into scrapes like this, Coach will bench your ass for the rest of the season."

Knox snorts out his disinterest and continues to remove his sweaty gear. "Fine, I'll come to O'Connell's and behave myself. It's like a fucking old man bar in there anyway. None of the chicks are hot, and the beer is always warm."

Jesus, this kid! He may be as close to a natural hockey talent as I've ever seen, but his head is so far up his ass that if he doesn't remove it soon, he's going to blow his ride.

Once we've changed and showered, we head out of the locker room for a few rounds with the sports journalists, while Bugs heads up to the press suites for the TV interviews. I stand with Matt while we're both interviewed for the official Whalers hockey blog, and when we're not needed anymore, we make our way to the player's parking lot. As we approach the double doors leading out into the lot, I see a tiny brunette standing with her back to us. Her small body is swamped in a Landon jersey and her shapely legs seem impossibly long despite her short stature. She's talking animatedly into her cell phone, and as she turns around, I can see it's Lana, her face splitting into a huge grin as whoever she's talking to says something she likes.

"Barry, that's fantastic news," she cries in her light, lyrical voice. "Can we come and see it tomorrow? Perfect. Is ten am too early?"

"It is for me," Matt grumbles beside me as we approach his sister. "For fuck's sake, Squirt. Can't we make it midday? I'm exhausted."

Lana glares at her brother. "Barry, I'm sorry, but my lazy ass brother can't make it until midday. Is that still okay? Promise you won't let anyone else see it before me?" The eager, expectant look on her face is fucking adorable, and I feel my dick take interest, despite Matt being within punching distance of it.

Lana pokes her tongue out and continues her conversation as we all walk through the doors into the lot. "Fantastic. We'll see you then. Bye." She ends the call and barges her tiny body into Matt's side, barely making him lose his stride. "We're checking out the trailer at noon as requested by his Majesty. If he sells it before we can get there, it'll be on you."

"It'll be fine. He promised us first look, right?"

Matt answers.

"Yes, but he could…"

"What are you guys looking at?" I interrupt, feeling the full force of Lana's annoyed stare as I talk over her.

"God, interrupt much?" She snorts, rolling her eyes, but quickly adds, "If you must know, we're going to look at a food truck, so I can start my own business."

"Wow, that's quite a step down from cooking in Paris," I reply, immediately regretting my words because they sound like an insult. From the hurt and pissed off look that clouds Lana's face, I can tell that's exactly how she's taken it, too.

"Well, I'm so happy you've pointed that out to me, Alex," she says through gritted teeth. "I had no idea you were such an expert in the culinary arts." She props her fists on her curvy hips, and I can't help but let my eyes linger there.

"Hey, I'm sure that's not what Thor meant." Matt tries to come to my defense, but the firecracker is lit, and she's about ready to go off.

"Why doesn't he tell me exactly what he does mean, then?" she replies, flashing her angry eyes at Matt and then returning them to me. As she continues to stare daggers at me, I can't help but think she's sexy as hell when she's mad. Angry sex comes to mind, and I'm now also wondering what she looks like when she comes. However, having dirty thoughts about her right now is not going to help me remove my foot from my mouth.

"I just mean it's different being your own boss and cooking what you want, the way you want, rather than other people's recipes," I splutter, hoping I've done enough to ease the situation.

My words seem to be the water that extinguishes the firecracker's fuse, and I visibly see her relax. "That's exactly why I'm doing it," she replies, her face suddenly glowing with excitement.

"Well, there you go." I sigh. *Jeez.* She really is something else. I see Matt chuckling into this fist at our heated exchange as Mila approaches.

"C'mon, let's get to O'Connell's before all the good seats are taken." Matt laughs, pulling Mila in for a kiss, and we walk over to our cars. Lana goes with Matt and Mila, but as she walks away, I can see her looking over her shoulder at me, her eyes still holding some of that fire she just aimed my way. I like it. A lot. And I wouldn't mind getting burned.

She's definitely the most interesting woman I've met in a really long time. Why the fuck does she have to be my teammate's little sister? Fate can be so cruel sometimes.

Lana

O'Connell's is a cool place, a beer-sticky sports bar full of memorabilia and big screen TVs showing constant sports news and footage. It's hard to compare it to the chic Parisian cafes and European nightclubs I've become used to, but it looks like fun.

I'm still on a high from the phone call I took just before I met Matt and the Swedish goalie. I'd just had the news that the amazing, ready-to-go food truck I'd found on Craigslist was still available, and we have an appointment to see it tomorrow.

Once Mila suggested the food truck idea, I felt so

inspired that I stayed up all night writing out all my best grilled cheese recipes. Then I scoured the internet looking for similar food trucks based in Seattle and Washington state. I found one in Olympia but that's it. There are several sandwich trucks that serve grilled cheese, but none of them offer it exclusively.

Over the next few days, I spoke to Zac and ran my ideas past him. His enthusiastic yelling and whooping meant the world to me. It's great to have his support, and he remembered a few recipes that I'd forgotten. I took Mila out on her day off, and we ate at as many food trucks as we could, asking questions of the owners to get some tips and contacts. I expected it to be a difficult task because I may end up being their competition. What I was happy to discover is that the food truck community in Seattle is like a big family and they're more than happy to help. In fact, toward the end of the day, I had so many phone numbers and invites to visit trucks all over the city, my head was spinning. It's one of these contacts that suggested I look on Craigslist for used trucks to get me started.

Of course, Matt offered to buy me a brand new, state of the art truck, but I refused. I like the idea of owning a preexisting truck that's got some history and turning it into my own enterprise. I did, however, accept him as an investor, and we're going to buy and outfit a food truck with his money and my savings. It'll hopefully be ready by the spring, so I can try to get established at some of the outdoor events that happen in the summer.

I'm so excited about this venture that I can almost forgive the douchebag who spills half a pint of beer down my back as we push through the crowds to reach the stairs to the VIP seating.

"Is it usually this crowded?" I yell at Mila as we're let through the velvet rope onto the stairs.

"When the Whalers win at home? Absolutely!" She laughs, grabbing my hand and pulling me up onto the mezzanine level that overlooks the crowds below.

"There you are!" a tiny blonde with red lips and sky-high heels yells as we approach the bar. "I've got us tequila to start!"

"Thanks, Bee," Mila replies, pulling the woman into a warm hug and accepting the shooter, handing me the other one. "You remember Lana?"

"Sure, Matt's sister, right?" She pushes away the hand I offer her and hugs me. "I'm Beth, Mila's bestie and fabulous girlfriend of the hottest Whaler, Nate Halstead." Beth smirks and downs her shot, grimacing and shoving a lemon wedge into her mouth.

"Don't start with that shit again." Mila laughs before taking her own shot.

I look around as the friends bicker about the hotness of their respective boyfriends and see Matt and some of the other players still signing jerseys and autographs at the main entrance. I even see the young winger called Knox signing a woman's ample cleavage! I snort out a laugh as I take my shot, imagining women going crazy over my brother like that. *Ugh, gross!* I'm so glad he's settled down with Mila, especially after all that shit with Delia. I'm convinced that if Matt can survive a woman trying to pass off someone else's kid as his to get a payout, then I can get over Etienne and find my own happy ending.

I'm pulled from my train of thought by loud booming laughter as Matt, Nate, and the annoying goalie come up the stairs and head our way. Why does Thor get under my skin so much? We've met twice, and each time he's riled me to the point of explosion with his stupid, infuriating comments and charming accent. I hate that I can't look away when he fixes me with his piercing blue eyes and ruffles his shaggy blonde hair.

He is the complete opposite of my type as well. I've never gone for athletic guys because they were always linked to my brother in some way, either his teammates or his rivals. I quickly learned that these were not the guys to go for when I became interested in boys. Not only were they mostly assholes, but as soon as I showed any interest in them, or vice versa, Matt would strong-arm them into backing off with threats of violence.

I tended to drift toward the creative, artsy guys who were sometimes confused about their own sexuality, and most times we'd end up as friends. At least I managed to go on some dates without them constantly looking over their shoulder to check my brother wasn't there with a hockey stick aimed at their nuts.

I definitely am *not* attracted to men that are so tall and muscular that if we were to go out on a date, it would look like they're kidnapping me!

"I see you girls have started on the shooters already." Nate chuckles and he puts his arm around Beth's waist, lifting her up to plant a sexy kiss on her red lips. "Is this your influence, Princess?"

"Absolutely," she giggles as Nate deposits her on a high stool, and they begin to make out like horny teenagers.

"Anyway." Matt laughs as we all turn away to give them some privacy. "Who wants another drink?"

While Matt and Mila go to the bar to get a few pitchers of beer, I'm left alone with Alex. I just can't bring myself to call him Thor. I'm a huge Marvel fan and Chris Hemsworth is delicious. Not that Alex isn't attractive because he definitely is, but I'm just not looking for any more romantic complications right now.

I notice he's shuffling uncomfortably in my presence, and I study him carefully—what's his deal?

"Cat got your tongue?" I ask, waving my hand in his face to get his attention. "You had plenty to say to me earlier. Why so quiet now?"

"I'm trying to avoid pissing you off, I guess," he grumbles, stuffing his hands in his pockets. "I can't seem to say the right thing, so it seems easier to say nothing at all."

Shit, have I been a complete bitch to him?

The guy has said some boneheaded things to me, but he doesn't seem mean spirited or vindictive. Perhaps I'm so used to Etienne's poorly disguised barbs and digs that I'm over sensitive.

I suddenly feel bad for the guy, so I decide to try and make peace with him. He is one of my brother's best friends, and if I'm going to be living in Seattle for the foreseeable future, I should at least attempt to get along with his friends. It's not like I'm falling over friends of my own.

"Look, I'm sorry I've been so snippy with you," I offer, stepping closer so I come into his line of vision, which is downcast toward the floor. "I've just had a big upheaval in my life, and I guess you happen to have been there when I've not been at my best."

His cool blue eyes lift up, and when they crinkle at the edges in a smile, I get the strangest feeling of butterflies in my belly. He has the most beautiful straight, white teeth, which for a hockey goalie is like finding a unicorn that poops rainbows!

"Is that an apology, kid?" he asks in a gruff, raspy voice, his eyebrows rising up his forehead in surprise.

I huff out a breath. "It is if you don't call me kid. It's patronizing. I'm a grown ass woman." I cross my arms and wait for his reaction.

To my surprise, he laughs loudly and puts his arm around my shoulders. I flinch slightly at the weight of his arm on me, but after the initial shock of contact, it actually feels comforting. Warm, supportive, kind. I honestly started thinking I'd never be able to enjoy the feel of a man again. During the last few weeks, I came to hate feeling Etienne's hands on my body. It was like I was his property, not his girlfriend or his lover.

"You definitely are that… How about this…" Alex's deep voice brings me back to the moment. "You let me call you kid, and I promise not to insult you or your career of choice for at least a week." He laughs. "Or at least I'll try not to."

I can't help but giggle, turning away so his heavy arm falls from my shoulders. I need to keep him safely in the "friend zone," and I'm enjoying being close to him a bit too much. I'm not ready for this. "Deal." I stick my hand out, and as it disappears into his enormous, rough mitt, I feel like I may have made a new friend in Seattle.

7

Lana

"**O**h my god, this is perfect," I gasp as Barry shows me into the back of the slightly dilapidated food truck that used to serve churros and donuts. I step up the creaky steps into the galley style kitchen space that consists of high cupboards I may struggle to reach without a little step of some kind. One side is made up of counter space, two fryers and a sink, and the side facing the serving hatch has two spider burners and a large hot plate plus preparation and serving space. I'm happy to see large extractor vents that will help keep the cooking smells and heat out of this small space.

Everything is stainless steel, and I can immediately see its potential, even though it's covered in a thick layer of grease and smells terrible. As I walk up and down, I look up at the three skylight windows that will provide much needed air and ventilation and begin to imagine how it will look once it's clean and functioning.

"Jesus, it stinks in here," I hear Matt grumble as he pokes his head through the door, wrinkling his nose, looking around.

"It just needs some TLC." I laugh, lifting the lid to one of the fryers, finding it still half full of very old, dirty cooking oil. "Does everything still work?"

Barry rubs his stubbly chin and makes a so-so gesture with his hand. "The fryers need a good clean and might need replacing and the fridges are totally dead, but the gas, water, electrics, and hot plate are all good and up to code."

"How about the motor?" my brother interrupts. "I want it to be road worthy if she's gonna be driving all over the city."

"Ah, the motor's the newest thing about this little beauty." Barry chuckles. "Replaced it all myself." He digs the keys out of his pocket and tosses them to me. "Go and start her up."

As I clamber excitedly out the back, Matt follows me to the driver's door. "You ever driven anything this big before, Squirt?" he asks, looking slightly concerned as I take two attempts to climb into the seat.

"Sure, it's just like an SUV, right?" I ask, looking to Barry for confirmation.

"Absolutely, you just have more out back so you have to watch your turns," he replies as I put the key in the ignition and turn it over. To my relief, it starts first time and purrs to life—Barry's right, the motor is the best part of the truck by far. The rest will take work, tons of elbow grease, and some more money, but I can do a lot of the cleanup myself.

As I sit in the driver's seat and imagine pulling up to music festivals and carnivals, I watch my brother walk around the truck several times, bombarding poor Barry with questions about permits, warranties, and tips on suppliers to help outfit the truck to get it ready for business.

"So, is this the one you want?" Matt finally asks, making me jump slightly as he appears at the door.

"It is! Is the price okay?" I reply cautiously, knowing Matt is footing the bill for most of the truck.

My brother smirks. "Let's just say Barry and I have come to an arrangement that might involve some season tickets to secure us a decent discount."

I squeal and slap my hands on the horn, effectively startling Matt and Barry, and burst out laughing. I leap out of the cab and hug my brother tightly. "Thank you so much," I whisper.

"It's no problem, sis," he mumbles, putting me down and rubbing the back of his neck, slightly embarrassed by my emotional outburst. "Remember—you're giving me a profit percentage until you pay me back."

I laugh. "I know, but just the fact that you believe I can do this and you're willing to invest in me is amazing enough."

"I'll always believe in you, Squirt." Matt pulls me into a headlock. "Now let's go and sort out the paperwork with Barry and then I'll take you to lunch."

Once we've sorted out the sale with Barry and arranged delivery for a week's time, Matt insists a professional deep cleaning company be allowed to come in while it's still on Barry's lot to get rid of all the grease and grime. He mumbles something about not wanting his new driveway being flooded with an oil slick. Barry is happy to oblige; the Whalers season tickets have obviously kept him sweet for more than just the discount on the price.

With everything signed, sealed, and shaken on, we jump into Matt's Mustang and roar out of the lot, heading back to the city for lunch.

"This is so freaky exciting!" Beth gushes, sipping her champagne. "It's amazing being your own boss. I'll have to bring you to one of my Women in Business networking meetings."

I giggle as the bubbles from my own drink tickle my nose. "Thanks, but I have a slightly rundown food truck and no customers, so I don't think I'm a Woman in Business quite yet."

"Oh bullshit, you just need to start getting word out on social media. Build the buzz so people will be salivating for your grilled cheese when you're ready to open," Beth replies.

I've been invited to Champagne Tuesday with Mila and her friends, Beth and Cam. However, Cam's on sparkling water because she's still breastfeeding. Baby Sawyer is currently sleeping in the car seat next to her mom, hardly stirring even as Beth continues to talk enthusiastically and rather loudly about how to build my social media presence.

"Beth's right," Cam says as she gently rocks the car seat with her foot. "You need to set up your Instagram profile immediately and start posting videos of yourself making each recipe. Perhaps release one every few days in the lead up to the opening."

"That's a great idea." Mila joins in, grabbing some chocolate-covered pretzels from the bowl on the coffee table. "I bet if we got all the guys to follow you and share your posts, you'd have thousands of followers in no time."

"Yes!" Beth cries, pointing at Mila. "We should get them all trying your sandwiches and posting that too. Come on—let's make a plan!"

I'm so touched by the way these women, who hardly know me really, are banding together to help me. I've felt so alone and unsure of my decisions since arriving back in America; did I do the right thing? Should I have given everything up because of a bastard like Etienne? But at this moment, surrounded by these confident, driven women, I'm beginning to believe I made the right decision. Sometimes great things can come from crappy situations, and Paris will always be there so I can go back someday.

We continue to drink and talk about my business plan, Mila jotting down notes on a yellow legal pad while Cam, Beth, and I bounce ideas back and forth and search for things on our phones. First and foremost, we decide a name for the food truck is the most important thing, so that I can start looking into branding and making logos. I'll also need it plastered all over the truck that's currently sitting on Matt's driveway.

"How about 'Sweet Cheezus'?" Beth suggests when we start to bounce names around.

I wrinkle my nose. "I don't think it gives off the right vibe. I mean, I'm not serving anything sweet so it might mislead people." I hate dismissing their ideas, but I have to get this right.

Mila looks up from her phone and reads out the names of other food trucks in the area so we can avoid using any of those.

"Let's make a list of keywords that best describe what your main selling points are and see if any of those suggest a name," Cam says quietly, careful not to disturb Sawyer, who is now nestled at her breast, feeding contentedly.

"That's a great idea, but I think I'll need to sample one of these incredible sandwiches before I can comment," Beth replies, her eyes wide with expectation, a cheeky little smirk on her red lips.

"Yes!" Mila cries, startling the baby who then begins to cry and spit up. "Oops, sorry!"

Cam sighs and stands up. "Can I feed her in your room?"

"Yeah, sure. There's a comfy chair in Matt's office just down the hall," Mila replies, her cheeks flushed with champagne and embarrassment at disturbing Sawyer's meal.

"Thanks babe. C'mon, SJ. Let's clean you up and finish this feed." Cam picks up her changing bag and heads off toward Matt's office with a wailing baby in her arms.

The rest of us head into the kitchen area, and I gather what I need to make a classic French sandwich called a Croque Monsieur. I fully intend to have this on the menu because it was one of the first meals I ate when I arrived in Paris and was always a go-to snack after a hard shift in the kitchen.

While Mila and Beth watch and continue to sip champagne, I make a basic bechamel sauce.

"Now I add some nutmeg and seasoning for flavor," I explain, suddenly realizing that my audience is watching in hungry silence.

Leaving the sauce to cool, I slice the loaf of sourdough into eight thick slices, smearing the cooled sauce into each piece. Then I top that with grated Swiss cheese, Dijon mustard and wafer-thin slices of ham.

"I'm gonna need to hit the gym tomorrow after this," Beth mutters, not taking her eyes off what I'm doing as I add more Swiss cheese to each sandwich and finally another smear of bechamel on the top slices of bread.

Putting the skillet on the burner, I add butter and begin to heat it until it bubbles, the smell of hot butter bringing back so many lovely memories of buying fresh croissants and bread from the bakery down the street.

I carefully add two sandwiches to the skillet, and as they sizzle, I hear Mila and Beth sigh, their reactions giving me a warm gooey feeling in my heart and making me smile. I flip the sandwiches to brown on both sides and then remove them from the skillet, placing them on kitchen paper to drain. As I load up the spatula with more bechamel, I hear Beth gasp.

"More of that?" she giggles.

I laugh as well, as I load up the top of each sandwich with more sauce and grated Gruyere, putting them on a tray and flashing them under the broiler to make the top bubbly and gooey. Beth and Mila are literally drooling by the time I slice the sandwiches in half, load them onto plates and hand them over.

"Oh my god," Mila breaths, holding her plate up to her nose and taking a deep inhale of the cheesy goodness.

As I continue to make sandwiches for Cam and me, all I hear behind me are moans and mumbled compliments. By the time Cam returns with a contented Sawyer nestled against her shoulder, the girls have finished their sandwiches and are frantically jotting down adjectives to describe what they've just demolished.

"Lana, this looks amazing," Cam enthuses, handing a sleepy Sawyer off to Mila, then carefully picking up half of her sandwich and biting into it with a satisfying crunch, her eyes rolling back in her head. "Oh Jesus!"

"I love this sandwich. I really want to make it the signature dish," I explain, taking a bite of my own. "If I add a fried egg on top, it turns it into a Croque Madame."

"Yum, I'd eat these every day." Beth giggles, picking up crumbs from her plate with her finger. "Although my ass would be the size of a Buick if I did."

Cam laughs. "I love that they're so rich and indulgent, totally gourmet." Her mouth is full of bread and cheese that she swallows before continuing. "And the cheese is so gooey." She sighs and continues to munch the crispy bread.

"Oohhh, I've got it!" Mila cries, throwing her hands in the air, standing up. "How about 'The Gooey Gourmet'?" She looks round at us with an expectant look on her face, so pleased with her idea.

As soon as she says it, I can clearly picture the food truck with a huge picture of a grilled cheese sandwich being pulled in half, stringy cheese extending between the two halves.

"I love it!" I yelp, rushing round the kitchen island to kiss Mila's cheek. "It's perfect! I can already see my logo and what the truck will look like."

"This is so exciting!" Beth squeals, hugging me,

pulling Cam off her stool to join us.

"Oh god, I can't wait to get started on this now." I sniff, feeling emotional and overwhelmed but also more motivated than I have in a really long time.

8

Thor

When I have some free time, I always try to make it to the yoga studio for a workout. As I get older, my flexibility and balance are more important than ever and even though I have a specific trainer at the Whalers for this, I always like to fit in extra sessions when I can.

It's pouring down as I pull up to the studio I regularly attend uptown, so I make a mad dash for the entrance, my duffel slung over my shoulder. By the time I burst through the front door, my sweatpants and hoodie are soaked through, and so are my sneakers.

"Whoa there, big guy." The guy behind the reception desk laughs as I slip around on the wet marble floor, quickly regaining my balance, trying to style out my clumsiness.

I laugh and run my fingers through my shaggy wet hair, shaking it off. "Hey Dev, how's it going?" I ask the lean Indian guy who jointly owns the studio with his twin brother Nish.

"It's going great, man. We're always extra busy when it rains and people can't use the outdoor spaces." He chuckles. "You booked in for a private session today?" He begins to scroll through his iPad.

"No, just thought I'd join the next available class if that's okay," I reply, wiping my sneakers on the mat before carefully walking to the reception desk. Last thing I need is to fall on my ass on a wet floor and injure myself.

"Sure thing. We have a Core Power class with Lynn starting in ten and there's a few spaces free," Dev says, typing on his iPad. "Want me to book you in?"

"Sounds perfect. Could do with Lynn's brand of ass kicking today." I laugh, knowing that she always manages to push me to my limit, and I feel like I need that today. For some reason I've been unusually tense this week, and I need to lose myself in the peace and focus of Vinyasa yoga.

I hand Dev my credit card so he can charge the class and then I fill my water bottle from the cooler and make my way back to the locker rooms. I pass a few regulars on my way, and we exchange brief greetings. One of the reasons I keep coming back to this same studio is the chilled atmosphere Dev and Nish have created. Several other athletes from the city's sports teams come here for the same reason I do—we can work out in peace because no one bothers us. The few times I've had people interrupt my low lunge asking me to sign their yoga mat, Dev has made it clear it's not cool and has asked them to back off or leave. Obviously, I catch the sideways glances and the nudges from people who don't know that I come here, but on the whole, I'm left alone.

Once in the locker room, I strip out of my damp

sweatpants and hoodie so I'm just in my yoga shorts and tank top, stuff everything into a locker and take my yoga mat, water bottle, and towel, and make it through to the studio area. There's quite a crowd outside Lynn's room waiting for the class to start, so I hang back and try to relax and concentrate on my breathing. I need to lose some of this tension in my body before the class or I'll end up pulling a muscle. As I wait, I try to pinpoint what's got me so worked up. It could be that I've not got laid for months. Even though I've been out as much as usual, no one is catching my eye lately—other than one very obvious exception. The bunnies that hang around the team pale in comparison and just look more and more unappealing. It's funny that the only woman to pique my interest is the one woman I can't have. After that night at O'Connell's when Lana and I called a fragile truce, I've not seen her but that doesn't mean I haven't thought about her. In fact, the woman seems to haunt my dreams like some kind of sexy spirit, and I'm fed up waking up in middle of the night, covered in sweat and as hard as granite.

"Alex?"

I spin around at the sound of my name and as if my thoughts have manifested her into being, Lana stands in front of me, looking cuter than I remember. Her long chestnut hair is up in a high ponytail, soft tendrils skimming down her elegant neck. She's wearing a matching purple sports bra and yoga pants that hug her dangerous curves and make my mouth water. Her skin has the same lightly tanned tone as her brother's, and I fully take in the sprinkling of freckles on her shoulders and the swell of her breasts for the first time.

I literally have to grip my yoga mat in my fist to stop my fingers from reaching out to touch her, tracing the freckled pattern across her silky skin, and finding out if there are more of them hidden from sight

As I stare dumbly at Lana, Mila appears as well. "Oh hey, Thor. I forgot you come here," she says cheerily. "Are you waiting for Lynn's class?"

I shake my head, so I stop staring like an idiot and train my gaze on Mila. "Yeah, thought I'd fit in a session before the game against the Twisters tomorrow."

"I didn't know you big alpha jocks would do something like yoga." Lana smirks.

"It's not nice to generalize about jocks, you know." That wipes the smirk from her face. "Some of us can be sensitive guys who just happen to need the flexibility for our job and … other stuff."

I'm the one doing all the smirking now, and she's the one standing there, mouth hanging slightly open, looking up and down my body.

"Oh, yeah. Lots of them do," Mila says, after a few seconds go by, surely feeling the tension. "We actually have a yoga trainer at the Whalers, but lots of the players do their own private sessions, right?" She looks at me with her wide whiskey-colored eyes, and I realize I haven't heard a word she's said because I'm transfixed by the length of Lana's eyelashes.

"Huh?" I mumble, dragging my hand across my mouth because I'm sure there's some drool there. Lana seems to snap out of it at the same time.

"Okay, everyone. Come on in!" Lynn calls from the door to her studio, saving me from more awkward staring.

"Thank god. It looks like the big guy is about to stroke out." Lana smirks, commenting on my sudden inability to hold an intelligent conversation. I could comment on the looks she's given me, but I let it slide. She strides past me into the studio, and the sight of her round ass in those yoga pants does nothing to help my moronic state.

"Dude, you need to stop drooling over Lana," Mila hisses as she walks beside me, digging her elbow into my ribs. "You know Matt will kick your ass into next week if he catches you."

"What?" I protest, realizing I've been less than stealthy, and I need to rein that shit in, especially around Mila. "I wasn't… you're insane. I don't have a death wish."

Mila stops me with a hand on my forearm. "I hope not." Suddenly, she looks deadly serious. "I don't know what went on with her in Paris, but I have a feeling someone hurt her. She's not some random girl you can just hook up with. Please, just stay away."

All at once, I find it hard to catch my breath. Did someone hurt her? I want to track down whoever it is and rip them apart. I can feel my teeth grinding and my fists clenching as I try to control the surge of anger that's bubbling up in my chest.

Mila obviously senses my change in mood and squeezes my arm, bringing my attention back to her. "Hey, relax. She's fine. I just think there's more going on than she's letting on. Call it female intuition. But you do need to back off and leave her alone."

I take a deep breath. "Message received and understood." I pat Mila's upper arm, and we go into

71

the yoga studio and set up our mats next to a confused-looking Lana.

"What have you two been whispering about?" she asks, sitting cross-legged and looking at me with her wide blue eyes.

"Oh, just work stuff," Mila replies nonchalantly, rolling out her mat and joining Lana.

She seems to accept that explanation, and as Lynn begins the class, she turns her attention to the pre-session briefing, and I set up my mat so that Mila is between us. Even with her warning still ringing in my ears, I know that if I work out next to Lana, my situation won't get any easier.

Lana

I've never seen a man as huge as Alex Bergman move with such grace and nimbleness. As we move from position to position, I'm finding it harder to concentrate on my breathing and focus on what the instructor is saying. I watch his impressive muscles flex and strain into poses that should be physically impossible for him. He moves effortlessly from mountain pose to warrior pose, his center perfectly aligned so he doesn't even wobble.

I, however, haven't set foot inside a yoga studio for months, so I'm all over the place. My plank is weak, and I can barely touch the floor in triangle pose without tipping over. My body is slicked in sweat and muscles I forgot I had are screaming in protest. I really need to lay off the cheese!

However, the more pressing issue is the heat that's

building in my core as I covertly watch Alex work his body in my peripheral vision. He has this intense look of pure concentration on his face, and as I take a break and watch him stretch his hips up into a bridge, I try to avert my gaze before I embarrass myself. But I can't stop tracking the defined muscles of his huge thighs and muscular calves that power his body up into each position, my imagination going to filthy places that they really shouldn't, especially with one of my brother's teammates.

In any case, I may be on a diet, but I can still look at the menu, right? And what an impressive menu it is.

As I ponder this, I realize my mouth is hanging open and it's suddenly very dry, so I reach for my water bottle, still staring at him like a fool.

"Enjoying the view, kid?" He smirks at me as his hips thrust slowly toward the ceiling again, and I notice the impressive bulge clearly visible in his yoga shorts. *Shit, I'm so busted.* My already red cheeks heat up even more at being caught out ogling his junk, so I take a huge swig from my water bottle and end up choking on it on his next upward thrust.

"Excuse me a minute," I splutter, leaping up from my yoga mat and racing for the door so I can put some distance between me and the hot hunk of man that I suddenly can't take my eyes off.

"Are you okay, babe?" Mila follows me out of the studio and lightly pats my back as I continue to cough up the water that's gone down the wrong way.

"Yeah, I'm fine, thanks," I gasp. "I've just not done yoga for a while and that's a pretty intense class."

Lies! It's actually the blonde Viking doing the

sex positions in the other room that has me all hot and bothered.

"Take no notice of Thor." Mila laughs. "He's a total goofball. You should see how he pushes Beth's buttons."

Great, now all I can think about is Alex pressing my "button"! For fuck's sake, I need to get out of here.

"Can we go and get a coffee?" I suggest. "I think I'm done for today."

"Sure, the class is almost over anyway." Mila's eyes flick back toward the studio. "You stay here, and I'll grab our stuff and tell Thor we're leaving."

"Thanks, Mila," I sigh, happy that I won't have to go back in there and see Alex all sweaty and flexing.

Thankfully the rain has stopped as we step out of the studio, so we walk down the street to a coffee shop and order café au lait and an indulgent chocolate cake to share. As I put the first forkful into my mouth, I moan loudly. It's almost as good as the cakes I used to buy from the patisserie near Etienne's apartment.

"Oooh, this is good," Mila groans. "And I don't feel guilty eating it after that yoga session." She licks her fork clean and goes in for another piece.

"All the cakes are like this in Paris," I recall. "I swear when I first arrived, I put on ten pounds just because I couldn't resist going to the patisserie every day."

"God, I'd be a nightmare." Mila laughs, sipping her coffee. "I have zero willpower."

We eat in companionable silence for a while, but I can almost see the cogs turning in Mila's head as she thinks extra hard about something.

"What's up?" I finally ask, unable to stand it any longer. "You look like you have something you want to say." I put my fork down and wait for her to make a comment about me drooling over Alex at the yoga studio.

Mila also puts her fork down as well and sighs. "Matt always says I have a terrible poker face." She laughs self-consciously.

"It's pretty obvious you're trying to think of a way to ask me something, so just come out and say it." I don't mean to come off as snappy, but I've always been a straight talker and I can't stand people beating around the bush. I'm a big girl. I can own the fact that I was ogling Alex's body.

"Matt's worried about you. He thinks there's more to your return than you're letting on, and it's starting to drive him a little bit crazy," Mila states, crossing her arms over her chest. Suddenly, all the fun has gone from our conversation.

Wow, I wasn't expecting that. The guilt about causing my brother pain immediately crushes the breath out of my chest, and I feel the tears threaten to spill over.

"Oh, Lana. I'm sorry," Mila gasps, reaching over to cover my hand with hers. "I'm sorry. I didn't mean to upset you. But he's really worried about you, and so am I."

"I'm fine," I reply a little too quickly, blinking back tears. "It's nothing, really."

Mila smiles kindly and squeezes my hand. "So perhaps you can explain why we hear you crying and calling out in your sleep."

"What?" I ask, feeling a cold chill creeping up my spine at her revelation.

"We hear you almost every night," she continues.

"You're crying out for help and other stuff that doesn't make much sense, a lot of it is in French, I think."

"Oh," I whisper, my cheeks burning with embarrassment. "I didn't realize I'd been doing that. I'm sorry if I disturbed you."

"Honey, it's not that you're disturbing us. We're worried that you're having nightmares every single night."

I huff out a breath and cover my face with my hands, unable to contain the emotion I've been trying so hard to conceal. Obviously, I've been doing a poor job of it because my subconscious has been letting it out at night.

"Lana, please. Let us help you. Or just me." Mila shifts her chair so she can put her arm around my shoulders. "You can tell me as much or as little as you want, but you might feel better if you let some of it go."

I look up and meet Mila's kind eyes and before I can chicken out, I say, "There was a guy in Paris. Turns out he wasn't a good guy, and he hurt me, so I had to leave." Tears of shame slide my cheeks, and I quickly wipe them away.

Mila's arm tightens around my shoulders. "Oh, I'm so sorry, Lana." I can see her eyes glistening as she imagines all sorts of horrors. "Did he physically hurt you? Was he abusive?"

I want to say he didn't, but I love Mila, and I think she deserves to know.

"He did. I think I'm a walking cliché." I smile, trying to dismiss her concerned look. "The stuff you see in movies, the way women think it'll all turn out okay in the end, and that he will change? I thought so, too. But he didn't. I'm fine now, though. I got out."

"You're obviously not fine, babe. Not if you're dreaming about him every night," Mila states, the muscle in her jaw ticking as her anger builds. "That asshole needs to be dealt with!"

This is exactly what I was scared would happen if I told people what Etienne did.

"No, please, Mila. I'm okay. He's in Paris and I'm here," I plead, grasping her hand. "If you tell Matt, he'll make a huge deal out of it, and I'll never be free. I just want to forget about it and live my life. Please."

Mila looks torn between honoring my request and her loyalty to my brother, her eyebrows knotting in contemplation.

"I don't know, Lana. I need to tell Matt something. He's lying awake at night waiting to see if you're okay, and he's exhausted."

Yet again, the guilt that I'm interfering with my brother's life weighs heavy on my shoulders. I didn't mean to bring all this drama to his doorstep.

I take a deep breath and pull up my big girl pants. "Fine, I'll tell him about Etienne, but I'm still not comfortable giving him all the details."

Mila hugs me again. "Thank you. He only has your best interest at heart, and he loves you. It's killing him that you're hurting, and he can't help."

I laugh bitterly. He always thinks it's his job to save me. Hopefully, this time I've managed to save myself.

When Mila and I get back to the house, I quickly disappear into my room to take a shower and consider how I'm going to bring up the subject of Etienne with my brother. He's a hothead and his first reaction is bound to be anger, so on the drive home I asked Mila to be there when I tell him. She has a very calming energy over him, and hopefully it'll prevent him from going nuclear.

I'm just roughly drying my hair when someone knocks on my door.

"Hey Squirt, you decent?"

"Come in," I call, pulling my robe tightly around my body.

Matt cracks the door open and pokes his head in. "Mila's ordered Thai. You gonna join us?"

"Yeah, perfect. Give me ten minutes," I reply.

Stage One of the plan is in place—order Matt's favorite takeout to keep him sweet.

By the time I get downstairs, the food has arrived, and Mila is opening takeout boxes and handing out plates and napkins.

"Mmmm, this smells amazing," I say, spooning some red curry onto my plate even though my stomach is in knots, and I can't even think about eating.

"Great choice, Red." Matt leans over and plants a sweet kiss on Mila's cheek. They're so cute together that it makes it hard for me not to feel lonely or wanting to have someone special in my life too.

"Actually, Lana suggested it," Mila replies, her eyes widening as if to indicate that this is my moment. I suppose it is because as long as my brother is shoveling jasmine rice into his mouth he won't be growling or threatening to kill Etienne.

Matt grunts his appreciation, grabbing a chicken

satay from a carton and sliding the meat off the stick with his teeth.

"Actually, I wanted to talk to you about something," I say quietly, pushing my plate away, the smell of the pungent curry making my stomach churn.

"Shoot, what's up?"

"It's about Paris."

Matt looks up at me, a spoonful of curry halfway to his mouth, hovering there. His eyes flick to Mila, and she smiles at him and puts her hand on his arm, lowering the dripping spoon back into his bowl.

"Hear her out, baby," she whispers, leaning over to kiss his scruffy cheek. "I'm gonna go eat on the couch, give you two some privacy."

I nod and smile. Mila is so kind and thoughtful, giving us space but staying close enough to intervene if Matt gets too big brothery.

"So, what's on your mind?" Matt also pushes his plate away and folds his arms over his broad chest, leaning back in his chair.

Shit, this is it. It's time to come clean and at least tell my brother some of what went down in Paris.

I huff out a breath and run my hands through my hair, my skin suddenly feeling too hot and too tight.

"I left Paris because a relationship I was in ended, and I needed some space from him," I state quietly, fiddling with my napkin.

"Okay, I suppose that makes sense," he growls. "What happened?"

This is where I need to be careful. If I say too much, my brother will be on the warpath.

"Etienne was ... very intense and passionate," I begin,

my heart thumping against my ribs as I remember the early days of our relationship when his passion used to make me feel like the only woman in the world. "He was a head chef at one of the best restaurants in Paris, and we met at Le Cordon Bleu when he came to give a cooking demonstration. He was so chic and handsome, from a really good Parisian family, and he literally swept me off my feet."

"Ugh, enough with the lovey dovey shit, Squirt!" Matt mumbles, looking deeply uncomfortable at my recollections.

I laugh lightly, always happy to make my brother squirm. "We started dating, and it was wonderful and romantic, and we were so happy."

"So, what went wrong?"

I prepare to tell the half-truth that I hope will satisfy Matt enough that he'll drop it for at least a little while longer.

"What started out as passion soon turned into possessiveness. He wanted to know where I was all the time and to control me." I lower my gaze from Matt's as his eyes begin to blaze with anger. "He put a tracker on my phone and started keeping track of where I went when we weren't together and who I was with. It was pretty scary."

"What the fuck, Lana?" Matt bellows, standing up so quickly his chair tips over and crashes to the floor. "How long did it go on for?"

"We were together for a year, but it got really bad about six months in," I reply. I feel the shame flooding into me, even though I'm not the one who should feel ashamed. He was the one who was wrong; I allowed it to happen, but I won't allow him any more space in my life.

"Six fucking months! You put up with that shit for six months?" He slams his palms into the table and the glasses rattle. Thankfully, Mila chooses that moment to come back to the kitchen and puts her hand on Matt's shoulder.

"Babe, you need to calm down and let Lana say her piece," she coos quietly into his ear, and I slowly see the tension leave his body as he picks up his chair and sits back down.

"I'm sorry," he sighs. "Carry on."

I swallow hard and let out a breath. "I did try to leave him a few times, but he always charmed his way back in. I'm not proud of it. I thought it was better to have him than to be by myself, and I know that's wrong. In the end, I knew I had to leave Paris to put enough distance between us to really cut ties. It was such a hard decision because I love it there, but I was afraid I wouldn't be strong enough to say no to him." I finally let the tears that have been threatening throughout my story fall down my cheeks, and I do feel a little more peaceful having shared at least part of my story with Matt and Mila.

As I sit and cry, I feel my brother's big hands on my biceps as he pulls me to my feet and envelops me in a warm hug. I wrap my arms around his waist and breathe in his comforting familiar smell. We stand like that for a long time until my tears dry on my face and my arms ache from reaching around Matt's thick body.

"You can always come to me. I am always here for you, whatever it is. We both are." Matt's voice is thick with emotion. "Hope you haven't got snot on my shirt, Squirt. It's new." He chuckles, and I know everything will be alright.

I rub my face on his chest, making sniffing noises, and he pushes me away, laughing. "Little brat," he chuckles, kissing my forehead and ruffling my hair.

I slap his hand away and smile, yet again so thankful my brother is such a good and caring man, even if he does bug the shit out of me sometimes.

9

Thor

"Why are we going to Matt's again?" Knox asks as I drive out of the city toward Matt's house.

"We're doing a taste test for Lana's new food truck," I reply, glancing over at the kid who looks like he's been dragged behind my SUV instead of riding in it. His face is covered in ragged scruff and his eyes are bloodshot. His brown skin looks sallow and dull. "Looks like you could do with a good meal, kid."

Knox scoffs and rubs his hand over his face, taking a swig from the water bottle he's been nursing since I picked him up from his condo. After the amount of shots he put away last night after our winning game against the Twisters, I offered to drive him out to Matt's this morning.

Judging by the bedraggled puck bunny he was kissing on his doorstep and the smell of stale alcohol seeping out of his pores, I made the right call.

"I'm fine, dude," Knox grumbles, shooting me a glare. "Just hungover, that's all."

And that seems to be the end of the conversation because no matter how hard I try to engage him, he's not biting. Instead, he pulls his shades down over his tired eyes and appears to fall asleep.

The lack of conversation with Knox gives me time to think about seeing Lana again after her rapid exit from the yoga studio the other day. She was obviously checking me out as I put extra effort into my bridge pose, and I loved the way her cheeks burned red when I called her out on it. However, I was disappointed when Mila came back in to collect their stuff, and I didn't see Lana again. By the time I grabbed my things and rushed out into the reception area, they'd disappeared. The warning that Mila gave me about someone hurting her in Paris rang in my ears, and I regretted teasing her like that. I'm a bit of a joker, but I guess sometimes I take things too far. I don't even have her number to call and apologize, and there's no way I'm going to ask Matt or Mila for her digits.

Hopefully, the fact that I've been invited to this tasting for her new food truck menu means she's forgiven me. Although Mila's invited most of the Whalers, so I won't read too much into it. I've already decided that I'm going to find a quiet moment to apologize to Lana … again. That's all I seem to do these days—piss Lana Landon off and then apologize—but I have to be honest, I just love lighting that little firecracker's fuse. The way her cheeks heat up and the little wrinkle that appears between her eyebrows—I can't get enough of it. I'm quickly becoming obsessed with the idea that she gets the same look on her face when she's in the throes of ecstasy.

I'm so deeply engrossed in my fantasy that I'm surprised when I pull up to Matt's house. There are already several cars and SUVs parked in his large gravel drive, so I pull behind Nate's truck and shove Knox awake.

"C'mon, Sleeping Beauty. Get your ass in gear and try not to look like something I pulled out of my shower drain." I chuckle as Knox grunts and moans, trying to shove my hand away and go back to sleep.

"There'd better be beer on the menu," he grumbles, unbuckling his seat belt and almost falling out of his seat when he opens the door.

"That's the last thing you need, kid. I'll get Mila to make you some black coffee when we get inside," I reply, locking the car and walking with him up the porch steps. "Want my advice?"

"Fuck no, but I'm sure you're gonna give to me anyway."

I stop at the top of the steps and fix him with my most serious expression, pulling his shades off so I know he's looking at me. "I've been there—my bank account full of more money than I dreamed possible, chicks throwing themselves at me, people telling me I'm the king of the fucking universe. But none of it's real, man." This at least earns me a look when Knox fixes me with his green eyes. "This can all be gone in a heartbeat, so while I'm all for living your best life and enjoying yourself, you need to be careful because you're this close to pissing it all away."

"And what the fuck do you know about that?" Knox asks, scowling at me. "You're one of the most successful goalies in NHL history and your career just keeps getting better even though you're old as fuck." He snorts out a laugh, amusing himself. "You've got it made."

"That may be true, but do you see me with anyone

to share it with?" I ask, surprising myself with my own question. "All my linemates are finding their women and settling down, and I'm still fucking about in bars, hooking up with women who have no interest in me beside the size of my bank account."

"And the size of your stick." Knox laughs, slapping my thick bicep and cocking his eyebrow.

"You're a dick," I snort, barging him against the doorframe as we enter Matt's house where the smell of frying bread and cheese hit my nostrils and makes my stomach rumble despite the fact I ate a huge breakfast only a few hours ago.

We follow our noses to the main room where our teammates are milling around, drinking coffee and soda, and a few of the younger guys have beers. Before I can stop him, Knox makes a beeline for one of the rookies to find out where he got his beer, and I decide to leave him to it. However, I do make the decision that if he gets shitfaced, he can take an Uber back to the city.

After greeting a few of the guys, I exchange hugs with Beth, Cam, and Mila and high fives with the guys. Bugs can only offer me a quick wave because he currently has baby SJ draped over his shoulder and is in the process of patting her back, a little too hard if you ask me.

"Hey man, go easy on her." I chuckle, reaching out to stroke her impossibly soft brown hair. "She's tiny and I know the power you've got in those hands."

Bugs just rolls his eyes and smiles, kissing his daughter's head. "I do know what I'm doing. She loves a good hard pat when I'm burping her." And as if on command Sawyer lets out a massive belch and then spits up all over Bugs' shoulder. "Ah shit! Cam, did you pack a spare shirt in the diaper bag?"

I turn around just as Cam appears and hands over the diaper bag, taking the baby so he can change out of the shirt that now smells like puke and sour milk.

"So, how's it going, Cam?" I ask. "Is Cap pulling his weight with the baby stuff?"

Cam smiles as Sawyer snuggles into her neck, her perfect little bow lips making sucking movements against her skin. "He's been amazing," she replies dreamily. "Even when he comes back from the road, the first thing he does is send me off to take a bath or relax while he spends time with the baby." I notice the happy little smile that spreads across Cam's face as she talks about her new family, and once again, I hear my mom's words ringing in my ears. But for the first time I'm not terrified or repulsed by the idea of having what Cam and Bugs have. They seem to have it all, so why can't I?

A loud whistle suddenly interrupts us, and we all look over to the source of the noise. Mila is standing up on a chair so she can be seen and heard over the noise of hungry hockey players.

"Okay everyone, the first round of sandwiches is ready," Mila yells. "Make your way to the table in the dining room, and don't forget to pick up your clipboard with your scoring and comments sheet. It's really important you fill this in. It's gonna help Lana design her menu. So, no stuffing your faces and running." She scowls at a few of the players who are known to be greedy bastards and then Matt lifts her down from the chair and kisses her lips, whispering something in her ear.

"Ugh, thank god. I'm starving." Cam laughs. "Breastfeeding makes me feel like a dairy cow and I'm always hungry."

"I'll take the baby if you want to get yourself a plate," I say, surprising myself with the unexpected offer.

"Oh, that would be awesome," she replies, hardly containing her surprised expression. "Have you held a baby before?"

"Sure," I scoff, reaching out both of my huge hands. "I have nieces and a nephew. I know to support the head."

Still looking slightly wary, Cam eventually hands Sawyer over to me, and I'm mesmerized by how tiny she looks resting on my forearm, my bicep almost as big as her head. "Sawyer, this is your Uncle Thor," Cam whispers to the sleepy baby. "He's gonna watch you while mommy eats her body weight in grilled cheese sandwiches. Be a good girl and don't barf or poop on his expensive shirt."

I laugh quietly as Sawyer tries to focus her big brown eyes on her mommy's face but seems much more interested in nuzzling against my pec. "We'll be fine," I reassure Cam, actually enjoying the feeling of the warm baby in my arms.

"Thanks, I owe you. I'll make you a plate as well so you don't have to line up when I come back." And with that Cam virtually runs into the dining room to attack the table loaded with goodies.

Feeling slightly nervous and a little terrified that I'll crush the tiny baby, I look down at her and try to imagine being responsible for something so precious. Sawyer blinks up at me with sleepy eyes and waves her little arms around, wriggling against my chest. Instinctively, I fit my finger into her tiny palm, and she grips it tightly and something flips in my chest, making it hard to catch my breath.

"That's a good look on you." Lana rounds the corner from the kitchen with a loaded platter of sandwiches.

I look up and notice that sexy smirk of hers firmly in place while she watches me with the baby.

"Just doing a favor for Cam," I reply, enjoying the fact that she likes me holding the baby.

"Did you get some food?" she asks, approaching me with delicious looking snacks. My stomach rumbles again, making the baby startle in my arms. "Judging by that noise I'd say no." She laughs.

I laugh quietly as well so as not to disturb Sawyer further and look over at the sandwiches. "What's in those?" I ask.

"I call these 'The Notorious P.I.G.,'" Lana replies, her whole face lighting up when she talks about her food. "It's pulled pork, Louisiana hot sauce, and apple-wood smoked cheese. Want one before they all go?"

"Abso-fucking-lutely," I say quickly and to my immense surprise, Lana picks up one of the small squares of sandwich and holds it up to my mouth. For a moment, I don't know what to do, but then desire and my hunger take charge, and I open my mouth so she can pop the tasty morsel in. I close my lips over the bread, feeling the explosion of hot sauce, smoky cheese, and soft meat on my taste buds, my tongue sliding over her fingertips. Our eyes lock together as her fingers slowly slide from my lips, her pupils dilated, and her cheeks flushed a pretty shade of pink. Not breaking eye contact, I chew the delicious food in my mouth; the heat vibrating between us is undeniable.

"Are those more sandwiches?" Nate's voice breaks the spell we're both under, and Lana takes a huge step back, shaking her head and turning to him, almost dropping the sandwiches all over the floor in her haste.

"Yes," she squeaks in a weird high voice. "I'm just bringing them through." She scurries off into the dining room and Nate offers me a weird look.

"Dude, what was that?" he asks, flicking his head in the direction that Lana just rushed off in.

"Nothing," I grumble, trying my best to shake off the feeling of her fingers in my mouth.

"Because if you're hitting on Matt's sister, you know he'll end you," Nate replies, stating the fucking obvious. Yes, I do know this. I heard the many warnings Matt issued the team just as loudly as everyone else.

"Nah, man, she was just helping me because I've got SJ in my arms," I shoot back nonchalantly, holding up the baby to drive home my point.

"Sure thing." Nate laughs, rolling his eyes and heading back into the dining room just as Cam reappears with two plates loaded with food and two clipboards under her arm.

"Oh, you got her to go to sleep," Cam whispers, peering at the baby. "Here, let me put her in her car seat so we can both eat in peace."

I look down as well and realize SJ has indeed fallen asleep, so I carefully hand her back to her mom and watch as Cam gently fits her into her car seat and straps her in, all without waking her. She sets up the baby monitor on the table and takes the receiver and her plate, heading for the other room.

"C'mon, let's go join the others," she says, looking back over her shoulder.

"You're just gonna leave her here?" I ask, suddenly feeling very protective of the little baby.

Cam laughs and pats my arm. "She'll be fine. She's so nosy that if I take her in that noisy room, she'll wake up to see what's going on. If she cries, I'll hear it on the monitor." Cam waves the receiver at me.

"Okay, as long as you're sure." I take another look at the sleeping baby and pick up my plate, following Cam.

"You're very cute, Thor," she says sweetly. "Have you ever wanted kids?"

Up until a few hours ago, the answer to that question was a firm hell no, but now I'm not so sure. Seeing more and more of my teammates falling in love and starting families has made me reconsider my life choices.

"Not really. But I feel like the closer I get to turning thirty, I should really consider what I want my future to look like." *Jesus, are these sandwiches or a truth drug?* I've never spoken so freely about relationships with anyone and here I am spilling things I didn't realize I wanted.

"It's as good a time as any to make changes," Cam replies. "I mean, I know what Warren and I have was unexpected, and we did it in totally the wrong order, but I've never been happier. There's something so amazing about committing to another person and trusting them with your whole heart. It took me a long time to realize that, and I know I hurt him in the process, but we are where we were always meant to be."

I notice the dreamy look settle over Cam's face, and

I can tell how much she loves the Cap. She took her time getting there, trying to keep him in the Friend Zone, but everything changed once they found out the baby was on the way. Will it take a massive upheaval in my life for me to commit to someone? Or will I just grow a pair and go after the one woman who I suddenly can't get out of my head?

Lana

I quickly deliver the platter of sandwiches to the table and then rush into the downstairs bathroom, slamming the door. I lean back against it, lightly banging my head to get rid of the feeling of Alex's tongue sliding across my fingertips. I can still feel my hard nipples pressing against the rough lace of my bra, and I have a feeling my panties are less than dry. There's an insistent throbbing between my legs and pressing my thighs together is not making it go away.

What the actual fuck just happened? I innocently fed him a piece of sandwich, and it snowballed into some kind of sexy finger licking thing that made my pulse rate skyrocket. I can't help but let my mind wander; I'm left wondering what that wicked tongue would feel like on my neck, in my mouth, on my nipples, and other forbidden places. I can still feel the warmth of his lips and the slightly shocked look on his face as we both realized what was happening and that it was affecting both of us so strongly.

And the fact that he was holding Cam's baby makes it even worse. He looked so good; such a huge, strong man holding something as delicate as a baby—my ovaries almost exploded on the spot.

Suddenly, I feel the need to wash the evidence of that erotic moment away, so I lunge over to the basin and turn on the faucet, lathering up my hands and rinsing them in water that's just a little too hot. I keep my hands under the water until my skin stings and I hiss with pain.

There's absolutely no way I can get involved with a man like Alex Bergman. Since meeting him, I've indulged in some Google stalking and judging by the articles I found on the sports and bunny blogs, he's a complete man whore. There have been kiss and tells, leaked dick pics and even a suspected sex tape. As far as I could see, he's never been in a long-term relationship. Coming out of the mess with Etienne, he's the last man I should get involved with. Not to mention the fact that he's my brother's teammate. I need to get my life under control, not just let it go. No, absolutely not—hard pass!

I catch my reflection in the mirror, and my flushed cheeks and slightly frantic eyes make me look like a crazy person. Jesus, I have to sort my shit out before I go back out there. I splash cold water on my face and hold a cold washcloth to the back of my neck. This is an important milestone in my journey to opening my food truck, and I can't let that sexy Viking with his wicked tongue distract me.

Once I feel more in control, I make a pledge to myself to stay as far away from Alex as I can for the rest of the day—and perhaps the rest of my life.

"There you are!" I almost collide with Beth as I sneak out of the bathroom. She has a pile of clipboards in her hand. "I have all these feedback sheets for you. The guys are going crazy for the food."

"Oh, that's amazing. Thank you," I reply, reaching out for the clipboards, but Beth just looks at me with narrowed eyes.

"Are you okay? You seem a little freaked out," she asks, tucking the clipboards under her arm, so she can put her other arm around my shoulders.

"Yeah, I'm good," I lie, laughing it off. "I'm just overwhelmed by the way people are responding to the food, that's all."

"Well, you shouldn't be, babe." Beth laughs, steering me back toward the dining room. "The sandwiches are delicious and it's such a great concept. I just checked your new Insta account, and with all the players and the team account following you, you're at ten thousand followers already."

"What?" I gasp, looking at her with my mouth hanging open. Beth and I only set the account up a few days ago, so this is incredible.

"Yeah, those clips of you cooking have gone viral." Beth filmed me cooking this morning and posted the clips, making sure that as all the players arrived, they followed me before they were allowed in the door.

I quickly pull my phone out of my back pocket, open the Instagram app, and see that Beth is indeed telling the truth. In fact, looking at my followers, I now have over twelve thousand because not only have the clips of me cooking got hundreds of likes and reposts, but the players have all been uploading pictures and clips of them trying my food and tagging me.

"Oh my god, I can't believe this," I cry, my nose

stinging with happy tears.

"Well, believe it, baby." Beth laughs. "You're gonna have the people of Seattle lining up around the block to get these sandwiches."

"Won't people think it's bad that I'm using my brother and his connections to help push my business?" I ask, suddenly feeling completely unsure of myself.

"Of course not!" she cries. "Jesus, everyone knows it's not what you know, it's who you know. And the guys do lots of favors like this for friends, so it's no big deal."

I release my breath and smile at Beth. "I really can't thank you enough for helping me. Setting me up with the designer for my logo and doing all the social media stuff, you've been a life saver."

"It's my pleasure." Beth pulls me into a warm hug. "Women in business have to stick together. I see so many chicks trying to tear each other down to get ahead, and I always believe that we're stronger together."

I love Beth's kick ass attitude and again I realize how much I can learn from her and how lucky I am to have made such wonderful friends. But as close as I feel to this crazy gang, it makes me miss Zac all the more. I noticed he was one of the first people to start following me when I messaged him with the link to my new account, and even though he can't be here to support me in person, I know he's cheering me on across the Atlantic.

When Beth and I go back into the dining room, I immediately notice that all the platters are clear and there's an eerie silence. Either I've poisoned the entire Seattle Whalers hockey team, they've all left, or everyone is studiously completing their feedback forms. Thankfully it's option three, and as I begin to clear the table, I notice large hockey players perched on every available chair, table surface, and floor space, scribbling away on their clipboards.

"I've literally never seen them all so quiet." Beth giggles as she helps me carry the empty platters to the kitchen where we load them into the dishwasher.

"Fucking awesome snacks, sugar," one of the players says as he comes into the kitchen with his clipboard. I think this guy is called Ford and his Southern accent and rugged good looks are quite disarming.

"Thank you," I reply, feeling my cheeks flush at the compliment.

"No, thank you." He laughs, patting his hard abs. "That's me in the gym for the rest of the day." With an easy wave, he says his goodbyes and follows several of the other players out the front door.

Over the next hour, my head spins with all the questions and compliments I receive from the players. Looking through the feedback forms, I can already see some firm favorites coming to the forefront, and I decide to start with a small menu featuring these sandwiches and steadily increase the offering as business and my confidence grows. I don't want to be overwhelmed and set myself an impossible task, so this seems like a sensible approach.

Luckily, I'm so busy I don't have to deal with what happened with Alex earlier. When he and Knox say their goodbyes, I manage to busy myself at the sink, shooting a casual "thanks for coming" over my shoulder. It's childish, I know that, but I can't risk him pulling me into a hug or making any kind of physical contact with me. I'm terrified at the way my body reacted earlier, and I absolutely can't allow that to happen in front of people, especially my overprotective brother.

Once a majority of the players have cleared out, I ask Matt, Mila, Beth, and Cam to gather around the kitchen island. Bugs and Nate excuse themselves and go into the main room to play XBox and look after a sleepy Sawyer while we debrief after the testing. We make light work of logging the responses from the feedback forms, and as I suspected, there are four sandwiches that stand out as clear favorites.

"So, it looks like we'll start with Croque Monsieur, Hey Pesto, Sweet Cheezus, and the Notorious P.I.G.," I say, making notes on my iPad.

"I agree," Mila replies. "You're offering two meat and two veggie options, which is good, and your main expense will likely be the pulled pork so you can sell that at a high price point."

"Yeah, but if I can source the pork locally and get a deal for a bulk order, I should be able to keep the costs down," I suggest. I've already got a few leads on suppliers from my local restaurant contacts for cheese and sourdough, so finding a good butcher shouldn't be that difficult.

"Hey, you should get one of those big chest freezers, so you can store the pork and have it ready when you need it," Beth suggests. "I'm sure Matt will give up some room in his garage for it."

The horrified look on my brother's face at the thought of losing some of his precious garage space to a freezer is priceless, and I can't help but laugh.

"I'm supportive, Squirt, but that's a step too fucking far," Matt sulks, folding his arms across his chest.

"Easy tiger, we can put it in the unused outbuilding if you want." Mila giggles, patting Matt on his back and kissing his cheek.

"Whose side are you on, Red?"

"Hey, look I don't wanna create friction here," I say, holding my hands up to stop the bickering. "It's not something I need to think about just yet, so chill."

Before my brother can continue being a baby about his sacred garage space, the doorbell rings. "I'll get it. It's probably one of the guys coming back for seconds." I laugh, leaving Matt and Mila still discussing how much space his cars really need to take up in the garage.

I'm still half listening to the banter as I open the door, and before I can register what's happening, I'm being swept up into a pair of strong, muscular arms. Immediately I begin to struggle and fight, beating my small fists against the broad chest and wriggling to get free, my fight instinct kicking in.

"Will you stop squirming, you little brat, and hug your best friend," a familiar voice laughs as the arms around me tighten.

It can't be... surely not!

I stop struggling long enough to allow certain details to register in my brain; the smell of freshly baked bread and the deep timbre of the voice can only belong to one person.

"Zac!" I squeal, just as my brother comes barreling into the foyer, drawn by my panicked cries. "What the hell are you doing here?"

"I couldn't let my best girl start her own business

without my help." Zac laughs, picking me up again and spinning me round.

"What the fuck is going on?" my brother yells, looking ready to throw off his gloves and fight someone.

"Matt, it's fine," I gasp as Zac puts me down but keeps hugging me from behind, his chin resting on the top of my head. "This is Zac, my friend from Paris. I guess he's come to help me with the food truck?" I phrase it as a question because I still don't really understand what he's doing here.

"Damn right I am," Zac replies, his long arm reaching out toward my brother for him to shake, but Matt just looks at him with suspicion. "Hey man, I'm a huge hockey fan. I played a little when I was younger but didn't have the talent to get out of the juniors."

That seems to relax my brother a little, so he reaches out and shakes Zac's hand, and I release a breath.

"Nice to meet you," Matt says in a tight voice, and I can tell he's still a little unsure about this unexpected house guest. "So, you just came all the way from Paris? Should I be worried that you have my address?"

Zac laughs loudly, his chest vibrating against my back, and I feel a huge smile splitting my face as I realize just how much I missed my friend's carefree laugh.

"When Lana told me she was coming back stateside, I made sure she gave me the address so I could forward on anything she forgot," Zac replies, and I internally thank him for the small white lie he easily tells my brother.

"Where are you staying?" I ask, turning around just in time to see the awkward grin spread over his handsome face.

"Well … I hadn't got that far." He shrugs, looking at me with his best lost puppy dog eyes. "Can I crash here for a while?"

"Jesus, am I running a chef orphanage here?" Matt grumbles, rolling his eyes.

"Come on! You have all these empty rooms," I plead. "And look at it this way: with Zac helping me, I can do twice as much, make more money, and now I have a ready-made roommate to split the rent on an apartment with. Please." I clasp my hands together.

I see the moment Matt caves, and even before the words come out of his mouth, I launch myself at him for a hug. "Thank you," I whisper.

"Sure thing, Squirt." He chuckles. "Make sure he's housebroken."

"Come on," I squeal, grabbing Zac's hand and dragging him into the house. "I'll show you to your room."

10

Thor

I've been on the family video call for thirty minutes, and I'm slowly losing the will to live. My eldest brother Magnus and his wife Astrid update us on the summer cottage they're building on the island of Gotland, Hugo talks about his promotion to Head of Oncology at his hospital, and Ansol shares that he's planning to start his own specialist equine department at the veterinary clinic he owns. Like I said, my brothers are massive overachievers, and as I listen to them talk about their lives and their families, I feel completely inadequate.

"Alex, the Whalers are looking good for another Stanley Cup run this season," Ansol says, snapping my focus back to the conversation.

"Yeah, we're looking solid to win the Conference again," I reply.

"Let's hope you don't choke again, *lillebror.*" Magnus chuckles as he calls me "little brother," stroking his long red beard, a shit-eating grin on his face. We've always been the most competitive with each other being the eldest and the youngest, and he's constantly giving me shit about my shutout record.

"You know your brother sustained a horrible injury, Magnus," my mother scolds, leaning toward the webcam on her laptop. "Don't joke about it. It could have ended his career. Isn't that right, Hugo?"

"How have I been dragged into this?" Hugo grumbles, rubbing his hands over his short blonde hair. "I'm an oncologist, not a sports doctor."

I blow out an exasperated breath and roll my eyes as the bickering continues. I allow my mind to wander to the last time I saw Lana. The feeling of her small fingers in my mouth and the way her eyes blazed with desire have been burned into my brain, and I find it hard to think about anything else. There was no doubt she was as aroused as I was in that fleeting moment, but then she fled, and I hardly saw her for the rest of the afternoon. Every time I entered a room, she managed to slip away, and with so many of my teammates and her brother around, it was impossible to get a minute alone with her.

It's really messing with my head, not to mention the chronic case of blue balls I seem to be suffering from, so I need to know where she's at. She's single, that much I know, but following Mila's warning about possible pain in her past, I need to tread carefully. If I play this wrong, I not only risk upsetting Lana—I risk getting my ass kicked by Matt. That could be a disaster for the team, and if there's one thing I refuse to do, it's fuck up our chances for the Stanley Cup again.

As my family begins to say their goodbyes, I tune back into the conversation, wish my brothers luck in their latest ventures, and promise my mother that I'll keep looking for a good girl to settle down with. I realize I've probably missed a lot of important family news while I've been zoned out thinking about Lana, but I'm sure if I call Hugo later, he'll fill me in. He's always got my back, especially when Magnus is being an annoying dick.

After closing my laptop, I check the time. Shit, I'm going to be late if I don't get my ass moving. At practice yesterday, Matt was talking about the amazing trails around his house, and we made plans to go for a run. I'm already in my workout gear, so I grab my water bottle, phone, and keys, and drive out toward the Sound.

It gives me more time to think about Lana. There's obviously some attraction going on between us, which sucks because Matt's warning rings in my ears like the horn at the end of the period. As much as I want her, I know the bond between brothers is unshakable and to mess with that for a girl, even one as attractive as Lana, is completely against Bro Code.

Fuck! I grip the steering wheel so hard my knuckles turn white, and I fear I might snap the damn thing right off. I either need to get laid in the very near future or find a way to spend time with Lana that won't violate my bond with her brother or my teammates.

By the time I pull up outside Matt's house, I'm so full of nervous energy I bet I could run a marathon in two hours flat. Jogging up the porch steps, I knock loudly on the door and wait, impatiently bouncing on the balls of my feet. I knock again and still get no answer, so I turn the handle, and the door opens just as the sound of Lana's laughter fills my ears.

Jesus, the sound makes the hair on the back of my neck stand on end and my heart rate picks up. It's very quickly becoming one of my favorite sounds.

"No! NO! I swear, you need to stop that right now!" Lana cries from somewhere inside Matt's house, and before I know what I'm doing, I burst through the door like an angry rhino. Charging through the foyer, I follow the sound of her voice, ready to throw down with whoever is doing something she doesn't like. Could she have a guy here who's suddenly getting too handsy and won't take no for an answer? All sorts of horrific scenarios are flashing through my head as I barrel through the kitchen and into the main room, my eyes searching and scanning for signs of a struggle.

The scene that greets me is even worse than I could possibly imagine.

Lana is on all fours on a yoga mat, her small, curvy body shaking with hysterical laughter, which makes her back arch and her round tits jiggle enticingly. A tall, lean man with messy blonde hair stands over her, also laughing loudly, his hands on his trim hips as he rocks with the force of his hysterics. The scene crushes the small glimmer of hope I have that Lana and I can ever be more than friends—of course a woman like her would be snapped up by the first sexy surfer dude who caught her eye.

I must have been standing in there for longer than I thought because the sudden stillness that fills the room attracts my attention. I notice that both Lana and her companion are staring at me with curious expressions, but I notice that Lana's a little pissed off.

"Alex. What are you doing here?" she asks, sitting

back on her haunches, her hands on her curvy hips.

"I ... I'm here to work out with Matt," I reply, trying my best to keep the growl out of my voice as the tall guy drapes a towel around Lana's shoulders and helps her to her feet. *Why does the sight of his hands on her bare skin make me want to rip them off?*

"Okay, but that doesn't explain why you're standing there staring like a creeper." Lana laughs, her eyes flashing to the man who has an irritating, knowing grin on his face that makes me want to aim a slap shot at him.

I guess my confused expression gives away more than I thought because understanding suddenly dawns on Lana's face. "Oh, this is my friend Zac. He's come to stay for a while."

The word "friend" penetrates the mist, and before I know it, the guy steps forward with his hand outstretched.

"Hey man, great to meet you," he gushes, pumping my arm up and down in an enthusiastic shake. "I can't freaking believe I'm in the same room as the greatest NHL goalie since Terry Sawchuk. I mean your shutout record is..."

"Zac! Chill!" Lana snaps. "Stop fanboying over him. I thought it was bad when Bugs came over, but this is verging on pathetic." She rolls her eyes and crosses her arms, clearly annoyed by her friend.

"Sorry, babe," he mumbles, letting go of my hand and stepping back next to Lana, who elbows him sharply in the ribs and scowls at us both.

Gathering my thoughts, I finally engage my brain and ask, "So, is Matt here? We're supposed to go for a run."

Lana looks confused. "No, he went out with Mila about an hour ago. He didn't mention that you were coming over. Sorry." She shrugs awkwardly and crinkles her nose in the cutest way. Suddenly, I'm more interested in counting the freckles on her bare shoulders than being pissed at her dumbass brother for forgetting our workout.

"Okay. Well, I guess I'll drive back to the city and chew your brother out later for forgetting," I huff, trying to conceal my annoyance at a wasted free day.

"Why don't you stay and hang out?" Zac suggests, his brown eyes wide with expectation, a hopeful smile on his face.

Shit, do I really want to hang out with Lana and her "friend"?

I'm still not sure what their deal is—is it a friends with benefits situation or are they purely platonic? I saw how that set up ended for Bugs and Cam, and I'm really not sure I want to get in the middle of that.

"I don't know," I say hesitantly, desperately trying to come up with an excuse. "I have a game tomorrow..."

"You should stay," Lana suddenly says, smiling shyly. "We were just about to cook, and Zac is known for preparing too much food. You're more than welcome."

Well, how am I supposed to say no to that? An invitation from this gorgeous woman and the offer of free food—the words are out of my mouth before I can stop them.

"I'd love to," I reply a little too eagerly, and I don't miss the smug smirk that flashes across Zac's face.

"Great." Lana claps her hands together. "I'm gonna

take a quick shower, so I'm leaving you boys in charge of prepping the Coq Au Vin." With that, Lana spins around, her high ponytail swishing enticingly as she sashays away toward the stairs. As I watch her leave, I suddenly realize I'm now alone with her "friend," who also happens to be my main competition for her attention. I need to spend the time sizing him up and trying to gauge where their relationship is at.

"Okay, we'd better do what Chef Landon says and get the food ready," Zac says, leading the way into the kitchen where he washes his hands, ties an apron around his waist, and starts taking ingredients out of the fridge like he's very familiar with where everything is. That alone worries me—how long has he been here and how long is he planning on staying?

I sit down on a high stool at the kitchen island and accept the bottle of water Zac offers me, wondering how to broach the subject of his relationship with Lana without coming off like a nosy asshole.

"You look like you have something to say," he says as he begins butchering a whole chicken without even looking at what he's doing with the huge sharp knife. I guess I should watch my ass while he's holding it and tread carefully with what I say next.

"How long have you and Lana been dating?" The question comes out in a gruff, tense voice, and I hate that I'm so affected by the fact she might already have a boyfriend.

However, the explosion of laughter that comes out of Zac's mouth makes me flinch and gape at him. What the fuck did I say that's so funny? My shocked expression just fuels Zac's laughter, and he has to put the knife down and wipe his hands on a dishcloth, bracing his palms on the countertop.

"Dude, what's so funny?" I growl, finally tired of being the butt of some joke I'm not in on.

Zac eventually gets himself under control, wiping the tears from the corners of his eyes. "I'm sorry, man," he chuckles, continuing to dismember the chicken. "It always makes me laugh when people think Lana and I are a couple."

"How come?" I ask, still completely confused. "You'd make a great couple." The words are bitter on my tongue, but there's no way I'm going to reveal how saying these words hurt me more than a puck to the throat.

Zac takes a deep breath and fixes me with an intense look. "One, you don't really mean that, and that's obvious. And two," he continues. "Put it this way, big guy. I'd be more inclined to date you than her if you know what I mean?"

Suddenly, the penny drops.

I must still be looking at him in confusion because he smirks and shakes his head, concentrating on preparing the chicken.

"Lana and I have been friends since we met on the first day of classes at Le Cordon Bleu," Zac explains as he starts to brown the chicken, the delicious smell making my mouth water. "She's an incredible talent and a fantastic person, which is why I came back to the States from Paris to help her with this new business venture."

I finally come out of my shocked silence and recover the use of my brain. "That's a big commitment," I comment. "She must mean a lot to you."

Zac looks at me with serious eyes. "She's my best friend—she's family. I'd do anything to help her and make her happy," he replies. And then, almost as an aside, he mutters, "I won't let some asshole hurt her ever again."

I'm not sure he meant to say that last part as loud as he did and just as I'm about to ask him what he means, Lana returns to the kitchen. She's freshly showered and dressed in leggings and a sloppy T-shirt that hangs off one shoulder, showing all that tempting freckled skin. As she passes me, I get an intoxicating waft of vanilla and spices, and I can't help but close my eyes and inhale it like a fucking addict.

Zac notices my reaction and smirks.

"Oh wow, this smells amazing." Lana sighs, joining Zac at the stove as he removes the chicken pieces from the pan and begins to chop vegetables. I'm in awe of anyone who can cook like that; I can only make an omelet and rely heavily on the team nutritionist and food delivery service for my meals. It's pathetic, I know, that a grown ass man can't cook for himself, but I've just never had the time or inclination to learn.

As Lana and Zac move around the kitchen with the grace of dance partners, instinctively knowing where the other one is, I begin to digest the information I've just received. Yet again there's the insinuation that Lana has been hurt in a previous relationship and that shit just kills me. But now I can see how much she means to Zac, and I'm really happy that she has someone like him on her side.

I must be completely lost in thought because I look up to find both of them staring at me with amused looks on their faces.

"What?" I ask a little gruffly, taking a swig of water.

Lana giggles and pours almost half a bottle of red wine into the pot on the stove. "I asked if you cook any Swedish dishes," she repeats. "I went to Stockholm and ate some of the most amazing food of my life."

I cough awkwardly to clear my throat. "Uh, no," I admit, a little embarrassed. "I don't cook."

Zac snorts out a laugh and continues to chop vegetables as Lana just gawks at me. "Seriously?" she gasps. "You don't cook anything?"

I run my hand nervously through my hair, feeling both their eyes on me as I admit to being completely useless in the kitchen. "I just never had a chance to learn," I explain. "I left home at fourteen and moved to Canada, so I spent most of the time either traveling for hockey or moving between billet families. I'm just too busy now and the team nutritionist takes care of everything I eat."

"That's so sad," Lana says, pouting out her bottom lip, making me want to suck it into my mouth. "It's never too late to learn a new skill, you know. You won't have a team nutritionist at your disposal forever. And what about when you start a family—are you expecting your wife to cook for you?" She cocks a questioning eyebrow at me.

Her outburst leaves me a little stunned and slightly on the defensive, so I shoot it right back to her. "Do you wanna teach me to cook?" I blurt before I can stop myself.

Lana blinks in shock and before either one of us can speak, Zac butts in. "That's an amazing idea! You can teach him to cook. You're a fantastic teacher."

"What?" we both cry in unison, both shocked at Zac's ridiculous suggestion.

"I don't have time to teach a complete novice to cook while I'm trying to get my business off the ground," Lana argues, putting the casserole in the oven, slamming the door a little too hard.

"Exactly!" I agree. "I don't have time either between training, traveling, and games."

"Oh, c'mon!" Zac laughs, washing his hands and wiping them on a dishcloth. "How about you make a deal that'll benefit you both?"

Lana and I look at each other and then over at Zac, who's pouring three glasses of wine from the bottle they used for the casserole.

"Explain," Lana demands. I can see by the sexy angle of her eyebrow that Zac has said something to pique her interest. And from my perspective, if I can get some quality alone time with Lana that doesn't get my balls pulverized by her big brother, then I'm down.

"Okay, hear me out," Zac begins, sipping his wine. "Thor is a huge public figure in Seattle, so what if he puts a few shifts in at the food truck when he has the time? It'll bring a ton of business because people will come to see Thor and then stay to eat your delicious food."

Lana looks a little skeptical at Zac's idea, but it actually seems like a really smart suggestion. Hockey fans will come to meet a player and will likely stay and eat her food. Also, from a purely selfish viewpoint, it'll allow me to spend some more time with her without Matt breathing down my neck.

"I think it's a great idea," I say. "And I'm happy to do it when my schedule allows. And you can return the favor by teaching me to cook a few dishes."

"See, that's perfect." Zac laughs, clapping his hands together. But from the look on Lana's face, she's less than pleased that her best friend and I are making all these arrangements for her. She flicks her wide blue eyes between us in astonishment and can't seem to find the words to argue with either of us.

"Fine," she growls through gritted teeth. "But you do at least five shifts at the truck once it's up and running, and I want plenty of posts on your Insta account."

"Deal!" I extend my large hand, and it immediately swallows her smaller one, sending electricity down my spine at the contact, suddenly feeling more excited than I have about anything in a really long time.

11

Lana

I've literally never been so nervous in my life. Not even when I moved across the Atlantic to start culinary school in Paris. That feeling of anticipation and excitement is thrilling. What I feel this morning as I sit in my food truck waiting for Zac to load the last crate of ingredients into the back is pure unadulterated terror.

Today is the first time I take the food truck out in public for real life paying customers. In the last few weeks, one of the Whalers players kindly offered to hire me for his kid's birthday party so I could do a trial run. I needed to check how long it would take me to make each sandwich with the pressure of people waiting and also how Zac and I would work around each other in the tight galley kitchen. There would be plenty of room if it was just me, but Zac is a big guy, so he takes up a ridiculous amount of space. After a few near misses with knives and hot pans, we got into a groove and were soon taking orders and preparing food like we'd been doing it for years. The sandwiches I chose to serve after the tasting were all good sellers,

113

but the Notorious P.I.G. was the most popular by far, so I made a mental note to invest in that large freezer so I could bulk order and make the pulled pork.

After the success of the party, I was hired by two more players and an athletic coach to cater their parties as well, so even before I'd taken the truck on the road, I've had plenty of exposure around Seattle. The Whalers have been amazing at posting on their social media, so I've now got close to thirty thousand followers, and my website is getting hits and email inquiries every day.

And that's what brings me to today: my first official gig that has nothing to do with the Whalers. I managed to secure a pitch at an outdoor Tarantino movie marathon thanks to a cancellation. According to Beth, this event happens a few times a year and has a massive number of visitors, so I've been panicking all night that we'll run out of bread in the first hour and have to close down. But Zac, being the ever-calming presence he is, ran the numbers with me and checked the order I put in at the artisan bakery and the cheese store to check I hadn't under ordered. Everything is in place—what could possibly go wrong?

"It'll be fine. It'll be great," I whisper to myself, gripping the steering wheel so tightly I feel like my knuckles will dislocate. I take a deep cleansing breath just as Zac hops into the seat next to me, looking smart and ridiculously handsome in his Gooey Gourmet polo shirt.

"Are you okay?" he asks as I continue to whisper affirmations to myself.

"Just quietly freaking out." I laugh, glancing over

at my best friend. Thank god he's here. I think if he weren't, I'd run back into the house and hide under my comforter until I came to my senses.

"You've got this, babe," Zac says in his deep comforting voice, reaching over to gently loosen my death grip on the steering wheel. "All the prep is done; we know everything in the truck works like clockwork, we've got enough bread and cheese to sink a battleship, and most importantly, you're an amazing chef. You've totally got this. Now start this jalopy and let's hit the road before we miss the beginning of *Pulp Fiction*."

"Thanks, Zac," I sigh, my voice thick with emotion. "I couldn't have done this without you."

"Yes, you could!" He nudges me with his broad shoulder. "C'mon, let's go before we get all emotional and I say something awkward."

That makes me laugh out loud as I start the engine and head out of Matt's driveway. Zac doesn't like overly gushy emotional moments, so he usually makes an inappropriate joke and laughs it off. But I know what's in his heart, so I let him carry on, glossing over the moment by telling me about his hot Grindr hook up the night before.

We arrive at the park where the huge outdoor movie screen is set up, and we're directed to our pitch, which is at the end of a long line of food trucks parked along a section of parking lot on one side of the field. Several couples and groups of people have already set up picnic blankets and lawn chairs, and toward the back, there are several people having tailgate parties. It's a really chill vibe with music playing over the loudspeakers, and as we unpack the truck and set up the menu boards, several people approach us to ask about the sandwiches. Beth had the great idea of getting customers to tag and post on social media to get a discount on their order, so I make sure the sign with this offer and all our handles is prominently displayed.

Zac and I are so busy that we barely notice the field filling up with people and soon hungry customers are circling the food trucks waiting for the official six o'clock opening time. It gives me a little thrill when I see several people standing next to our social media sign, frantically typing into their cell phones and suddenly the sick, terrified feeling I've had all day begins to subside, replaced by the adrenaline rush I always get before a restaurant service.

"It's a few minutes before six," Zac says, gently placing his hand on my shoulder. "Everything's ready. Shall we say a little prayer?"

I snort out a laugh, knowing full well that Zac only prays to the god of hot men and hockey. So instead of that, I rise up on my tiptoes and pull him into a fierce hug, squealing a little when he lifts me off my feet and carefully spins us in the cramped galley kitchen.

"Thank you," I whisper, my nose stinging with grateful tears.

"You got it, babe," Zac replies in a thick voice, lowering me carefully to the floor, turning away to try and hide the glossy sheen on his eyes. He coughs to clear his throat. "I'll go and open the hatch. Let's do this thing!"

I reach up and tighten my ponytail, and when the hatch lifts, I see a healthy line of people waiting for us to open. Before I have time to freak out, the first customer approaches and orders three Hey Pestos and a Notorious P.I.G. He flashes his cell phone at me to show he's posted a selfie on Twitter by the discount sign, so as Zac starts preparing the order, I ring up his bill and he taps his Smart Watch against my card reader. Wow, I've taken my first dollars as an independent businesswoman! It's almost impossible to hide the massive grin that spreads across my face as more and more people place their orders and show me their social media posts.

Zac and I barely have time to speak besides barking orders at each other, so when *Pulp Fiction* begins to play on the big screen, we have some time when business drops off to a trickle to take stock of what just happened.

"Oh my god, that was crazy." Zac laughs, cracking open a bottle of water and chugging it down in four thirsty gulps. His shaggy hair is held back from his face with a bandana, which he takes off and uses to wipe his sweaty face.

"I know. I think we did a hundred covers already," I reply, hardly daring to believe it. "Let's use the quiet time to do a stock check and make sure we're ready for the rush between the movies."

Just as we begin to do inventory, I spot a group of impossibly huge guys and familiar looking women approach the truck, and I'm thrilled to see them.

"Hey Squirt, poison anyone yet?" Matt laughs, resting his tattooed forearms on the counter, a shit-eating grin plastered on his face. His stupid comment earns him an elbow in the ribs from Mila. The Whalers had a game last night, so they have a few days before an away series to the east coast.

"Ignore him, Lana," she says, scowling at my brother. "I've been following your Instagram on the drive over here, and it's blowing up! Congratulations."

This comment elicits nods of agreement and congratulations from Nate, Beth, Ford, Bugs, and Cam, who has baby Sawyer strapped to her front in one of those baby slings. Everyone comes forward to place their orders and despite suddenly being busy again, I can't help the slight feeling of disappointment that Alex hasn't come along. This wasn't one of the shifts he agreed to cover at the truck, but I would have hoped he'd come to see me and wish me luck.

As if reading my disappointment, Zac leans over and quietly whispers, "Where's Thor?"

I shrug as nonchalantly as I can and press the spatula down hard on the Sweet Cheezus I'm preparing, enjoying the loud sizzle and the smell of melting cheese. Sensing that I don't really want to talk about it, Zac moves away to plate up Matt and Mila's Croque Monsieurs, adding a small bag of organic potato chips and a homemade pickle spear to each paper tray.

Once all the Whalers are happily munching on their sandwiches, Zac and I close the hatch and join them on the group of picnic tables across from the truck. I'm conscious that I'm a sweaty mess, so I don't sit down next to anyone, instead opting to perch on the low wall separating the parking lot from the grass.

"This is so great," Ford mutters through a mouthful

of pulled pork. "I haven't eaten barbecue this good since I left Tennessee."

"Well, there's a huge compliment right there." Nate laughs, wiping crumbs from the corners of his mouth, having just demolished three Hey Pestos. "Ford does nothing but bitch about the lack of good barbecue in Seattle."

The others laugh in agreement as Ford launches into a story about the best barbecue joint in Memphis. I try to listen while I begin to process the deep feeling of disappointment in my stomach because Alex hasn't come along. What the hell is that about? Would I have been as upset if Ford or Bugs hadn't shown up?

And the answer to that question is no. I'm actually disappointed that Alex isn't here and that feeling scares me more than I'd like to admit.

I realize that despite being a bit annoying and goofy, I like Alex Bergman. He looks like he could crush someone my size in one giant hand, but he's got a very gentle soul and I find that oddly comforting. Etienne looked like he should be sensitive and kind, but a monster was lurking beneath his aristocratic good looks. I guess that old adage is true—you should never judge a book by its cover.

As I process this new and slightly alarming revelation that I miss Alex not being here, I'm jolted back to the moment by a loud cheer and catcalls of "About time, man!"

When I look up, I see an enormous figure striding across the parking lot toward us. Alex is wearing a Whalers hoodie and dark jeans that hug his thighs to perfection, his long blonde hair hidden beneath a black beanie. My heart stutters slightly, and I can't help but press my fingers between my breasts to check I'm not suddenly going into cardiac arrest due to the stress of the day and the hotness of the Whalers goalie. As Alex draws closer and my heartbeat increases, I realize it's his appearance that's causing this reaction, and I'm completely thrown by it. My traitorous body reacts as soon as he gets within touching distance; my nipples harden beneath my polo shirt, and my skin breaks out into goosebumps.

"Sorry I'm late," he apologizes. "I forgot to get gas."

He looks around at his teammates and exchanges greetings and fist bumps, but soon his ice blue eyes are fixed on my darker ones, causing a chill to rocket up my spine and settle at the nape of my neck.

"Congratulations, Lana. Looks like you're killing it." Before I can respond, he sweeps me up into his warm embrace, literally lifting me a foot off the ground. The warmth of his body spreads through me, the hard planes of his chest and abs press against my soft curves, and for a second, I wonder what this would feel like without the layers of clothing between us.

"Put her down, you big goon," I hear my brother bark from behind us, and Alex chuckles, lowering me down to the ground.

"Shut up, Matt." My brother means well, but I'm not a teen anymore. "Hi, Alex. Thanks for coming," I manage in a slightly strained voice, adjusting my polo shirt that's ridden up at the front. I don't miss Alex's eyes flicking to catch a glimpse of my bare stomach as I do so.

"Looks like the movie's about to end," Zac

comments, breaking up the sizzle of tension between Alex and me. "We'd better get set up for the intermission rush."

With that, he breezes past me, taking my arm and whispering in my ear, "That hug looked more than friendly. I want all the deets when we're done here."

His comment makes me laugh and I shake my head, but despite this, I too want to get my bestie's opinion on what the hell just happened with the sexy Whalers goalie.

12

Thor

The puck whistles through my five-hole, and I slam my thighs together too late to stop the buzzer sounding, the Toronto fans going crazy. The Titans are now up by three goals to our one, and in frustration, I slam my goalie stick against the goalpost and snap the fucking thing in half.

This is the third game in a five day away series and I'm exhausted. I picked up a stomach flu that had me benched for the second game against the New Jersey Raiders, but I pleaded with Coach Casey to let me play this game. The second string goalie put up a valiant effort against the Raiders, but we lost that game by an embarrassingly huge margin, and I wasn't going to let a little projectile vomit keep me off the blue paint for this game.

"Hold your shit together, Thor," Bugs yells as he cruises past me. Thankfully we've gone to a TV break, so I can quickly skate over to the bench and replace my trashed stick.

"I'm trying, man," I growl. "But Nate left me wide open on that last play, and I didn't stand a chance."

"I know. I've spoken to him about tightening that up, but the Titans' center is so damn fast," Bugs replies, squirting water into his open mouth and spitting it out on the ice. "We've got you, man. No more fuck ups." Then addressing all the players, our captain shouts, "There's ten minutes of the period left. We can get this back, am I right?"

"Yes, Captain!" we yell, slapping gloved hands on helmets and backs. As I skate back to the goal with my new stick, Nate flashes past me and offers me an embarrassed apology, and I feel like a dick for blaming the last goal on him. I saw the damn puck coming; I was just too slow to stop the fucking thing. I squirt water into my mouth and over my face, still feeling slightly feverish after my bout of sickness. Perhaps I shouldn't have played this game. I should have left it to the second string goalie and taken more time to recover.

Well fuck that! That attitude isn't the one that made me one of the most successful NHL goalies of the twenty-first century. As the puck drops for the restart of the game, I suck it up and focus every ounce of energy I have left on keeping that little rubber disk out of my net.

Thankfully, I manage to keep a clean sheet for the rest of the game, and Ford gets one back for the Whalers, meaning the game ends three-two to the Titans. It's the first time they've beaten us in three seasons, and the weight of that rests heavily on my shoulders despite the encouraging slaps to my back and helmet from my teammates as we trudge down the tunnel.

"Thor!" Coach Casey barks as I pull my jersey

off and sling it into the laundry bin. "A word when you're dressed."

"Yes, Coach," I reply, feeling the bile rise in my throat. This could be it—my time's finally come to hang up my skates and retire. Thirty is fast approaching, and I've had just over a decade in the NHL. Not all of us can have age-defying careers like Henrik Lundqvist. My health hasn't been the same since the injury to my throat last season, but I've worked fucking hard to stay on top form.

As I continue to strip out of my gear, I spiral further into a sulky depression until Bugs pulls me aside on my way to the showers.

"Everything okay, man?" he asks.

I huff out a breath and my long hair flips off my forehead. "I've just broken our winning streak against the Titans, and Coach has called me into his office. It doesn't look good."

"Look, you had a stomach flu and should've probably sat this game out. I think Coach just wants to check you're good for the Bull Dogs game tomorrow before he finalizes the roster." Bugs slaps my bicep and leads the way into the showers.

"You're probably right," I reply, turning on the water so it cascades over my aching muscles. "I just feel like I'm about to have that road to retirement talk, you know what I mean?"

"Don't be stupid." My captain laughs, scrubbing shampoo into his hair. "You've plenty of good years left. You're being paranoid. One bad game doesn't mean you're being put out to pasture."

Bugs is a few months older than me, but the career

of a goalie tends to be harder and shorter than any other position on the team due to the fact that we play almost the entire game and not twenty minutes in short shifts. His career could last another five years or more, barring serious injury.

I ponder all of this as I quickly shower, dry off, and put my game day suit back on. The locker room is still buzzing with activity when I knock on the door to Coach Casey's temporary office and wait for Mila to open the door. She smiles kindly at me and that just exacerbates the tight knot of worry in my gut. Was that pity I saw flash across her face?

"He's ready for you." Mila lets me in and then leaves, quietly closing the door. Coach Casey is sitting behind the desk, typing away on his laptop while I stand awkwardly by the door.

"For God's sake, sit down." He laughs, absently waving his hand toward the chair while he finishes what he's doing.

I drop my large body into the chair and count the seconds until Coach closes his laptop and fixes me with his green eyes. He steeples his fingers under his chin and taps them together, a gesture I've become familiar with over the years—he's got something difficult to say, so I brace myself for the worst.

"Hell of a game tonight," he finally states, leaving it open for me to respond with my thoughts.

"Not my greatest performance, I'll admit."

Coach looks at me but doesn't speak, leaving me free to continue.

"I probably wasn't one hundred percent ready after my stomach flu, but I'm prepared to give it my all in

New York tomorrow. Have no doubt, Coach, that I'll be ready to end this series with a win."

I finish my speech and wait for Coach's response. "I'm happy to hear that because you're an amazing goaltender, and it's become clear to myself and the GM that we're not in a position to lose you to injury. You've been a driving force in this team for years, and I think we've got complacent that you'll play forever." Coach Casey looks down at his lap and shakes his head. "With you out of action for part of this series, it's become painfully clear that our back up goalies have been allowed to get lazy and that's entirely on me. I want to apologize to you."

My mouth drops open, and I make some kind of strangled noise. NHL coaches are not known to apologize for anything.

"I'm apologizing because you felt the need to come back before you were ready because you saw there was no other choice. That shouldn't ever be the case. You're a valued member of this team, and I'm sorry you were forced to play sick to cover up the holes in our goaltender roster."

I literally feel like I'm witnessing something no one has seen before, but I can see from the pained look on Coach's face that this is really hard for him, so I don't act like an asshole about it.

"I appreciate that, Coach," I reply after clearing my throat. "I know it was stupid to offer myself up to play tonight when I knew I wasn't ready. I'm happy to put more training hours in with the other goalies to help keep them game ready."

Coach Casey laughs and smiles. "That's just like

you, Alex. Always pulling for the team even if it costs you more of your precious free time."

"It's what we do, Coach," I state. "Anything for the good of the team."

"And that's what makes you a great team player. Thank you, Alex. But I actually brought you in here to tell you that when we get back to Seattle, I'll be hiring another goaltending coach to work with you all."

The relief that floods my system makes me slightly light-headed. I'm not being forced to retire or step down from my starting slot. Thank fuck for that! It would be another thing for my mom to ride my ass about as well as my lack of potential wives.

"Thanks, Coach. I appreciate your support."

"Sure. Go on. You'd better get your ass on the bus. We're due to fly out in a few hours," Coach Casey opens his laptop and fires it up again, essentially ending the meeting and dismissing me.

As I leave, Mila returns and smiles at me again, but this time I return it. This crazy career can end in the blink of an eye, but it looks like I've still got a few more games in me yet.

I walk into my apartment a few days later and throw my duffel on the floor, unable to even comprehend dealing with my laundry yet. I lost my tie and suit jacket before I got into Nate's truck at the airport, so I untuck the dress shirt from my pants and kick off the expensive shoes that hurt my feet. Even though I had them custom made for my ridiculously big feet, they still pinch, and I hate wearing them. I spend most of the time at home in bare feet, so I quickly pull off my socks and fling them on top of my duffel, enjoying the feeling of the underfloor heating as I pad into the kitchen and open the fridge.

Fuck! I forgot that my weekly meal delivery isn't coming until tomorrow, and all I have in the fridge is an out-of-date meal I should have eaten before I went away and a takeaway carton that has something growing in it. I huff out a breath and check my watch—it's only a quarter after five, so if I was so inclined, I could go to the grocery store down the street and pick up something. But the thought of going out now has zero appeal, so I open the drawer that holds the forbidden takeout menus and decide to order something in.

I'm just deciding between Thai and Korean when my phone beeps with a message. Some of the guys were talking about going to O'Connell's tonight for drinks, but I'm really not in the mood, so I pick up my phone intending to sack off the invitation.

To my surprise, when I open the message, it's not from one of my teammates—it's from Lana. Even though we had exchanged numbers so that we could easily arrange my helping out at the truck, we don't talk much. I try hard to brush over the fact that seeing her name on my phone just made my day.

[LANA: Matt said you had a rough trip. Wanna learn how to cook salmon en papillote?]

My mouth waters and my stomach lets out a loud rumble at the mention of food, and even though I'm reluctant to go out with the guys, a night of learning to cook with Lana sounds like perfection.

[ALEX: Sounds delicious but complicated. Can't we start with eggs or cereal? ;)]
[LANA: Hahahahahaha, no we can't. It's very simple. Thought hockey players love a challenge? (thinking face emoji)]

Damn, I can't resist her sassy attitude and I smile as I type out my reply.

[ALEX: Game on, baby. Do I need to do anything?]
[LANA: No, just make sure you have utensils and a tray that can go in the oven]

Thankfully, even though I don't cook, this apartment came fully loaded with everything in the kitchen already, most of which is still in pristine condition.

[ALEX: Got everything you need. Come over whenever you want]

I hit send and leave my phone on the counter, rushing through my apartment, pulling off my shirt and hopping out of my pants and underwear so I can get into the shower. I quickly wash away the smell of traveling from my skin and hair and dress in Whalers sweatpants and my favorite T-shirt that's so old and soft, it always makes me feel comfortable.

I'm just stuffing my smelly duffel in the laundry room and setting up some music to play quietly in the background when the buzzer goes to alert me there's a visitor in the lobby.

I press the Talk button on the intercom and the concierge announces that Lana is downstairs, so I confirm I'm expecting her and bounce nervously on the balls of my bare feet until I hear her gentle knock on my door. Not wanting to seem like an eager loser, I walk in a large circle in the foyer to make it seem like I'm coming from deeper in the apartment and finally open the door.

I have to work hard to control the sharp inhale of breath when I see Lana. Jesus, she's stunning. It seems impossible, but she's grown more attractive and sexier since I last saw her at the outdoor movie marathon. Her chestnut hair hangs in a thick plait over her shoulder and her face is fresh and clear of makeup, her cute freckles dusting her nose and cheeks. Her denim blue eyes light up when she sees me, and then I'm almost floored by her megawatt smile. She's carrying two heavy looking grocery bags.

"Hey," she says in her sweet, lyrical voice. "How are you? Rough trip?" Her brow creases in concern for me.

I regain my senses and step aside, taking the bags from her, allowing her into my apartment, her vanilla scent filling my nose and thickening my cock. I guess sweatpants were a mistake! So as she unzips her jacket and hangs it on a coat hook by my front door, I discreetly adjust myself and wonder if it will look weird if I quickly change into jeans.

"I'm good, thanks," I reply as I show Lana into my kitchen and put the bags on the counter. "It was a hard trip and getting sick didn't help."

"Yeah, Matt said you got sick." Her brow creases again with sweet concern and I have an overwhelming urge to kiss her there. "Are you okay now? We can do this another time if you want."

I laugh and point to the loaded grocery bags. "Looks like you're ready for lesson one now, so let's do this." I squint my eyes and rub my bearded chin, shrugging helplessly. "We're making something with fish?"

Lana giggles and begins to unpack the bags. "Salmon en papillote. It means salmon in paper or parchment and it's a really easy recipe with lots of different variations, so I thought it would be a perfect dish to begin with. I thought we'd serve it with herbed new potatoes and asparagus wrapped in bacon with a hollandaise sauce."

I hold up my hands. "Woah there, firecracker! That sounds a lot more complicated than salmon in a parcel!"

"Don't freak out. You only have to worry about the salmon. I'll do the rest and you can just watch." Lana moves around the counter and begins to open cabinets, taking out utensils, pans, and other things I didn't even know I had.

Once she finds everything she needs, we wash our hands and begin to prepare a marinade for the salmon using ginger, garlic, soy sauce, and rice wine vinegar. Lana seems completely at ease as she shows me how to peel ginger with a small spoon and grate the garlic instead of chopping it. I'm completely useless when I try to slice the zucchini and pak choi, but she's encouraging and patient. She shows me how to hold the knife correctly, keeping my fingers tucked under so I don't accidentally slice one off. The touch of her hand on mine is almost distracting enough that I do exactly that! But she laughs sweetly as I pump my fist in the air when I successfully manage to cut up all the veggies without losing a digit.

"Now we just need to leave the salmon to marinade while we make the hollandaise." Lana finishes covering the fish with saran wrap and gets a large glass bowl out of the cabinet and fills a saucepan with water, putting it on the stove to heat.

As Lana busies herself at the stove, I open the bottle of wine she brought with her, pouring us both a glass.

"How's business been since the movie marathon?" I ask, watching intently as Lana melts an enormous amount of butter in a pan.

"Oh my god, it's been crazy," she replies, glancing over her shoulder as I place her glass of wine on the counter next to her. "I spoke to some other truck owners, and they gave me the names of some upcoming events that might have spots open. So, in the next month I've got a couple of food fairs and a music festival." Lana carefully takes the pan full of melted butter off the heat, and I can already calculate the extra miles I'll have to run after this meal.

"That's so great," I reply, watching as she whisks egg yolks in the glass bowl over the simmering water, adding a splash of vinegar, her lightning-quick wrist movement causing a deluge of dirty thoughts to reel through my head.

"It really is," Lana enthuses. "My Insta and Twitter are so crazy I've had to turn the notifications off and only look at it once a day or else I never get anything done. Your posts have really helped, by the way, so thank you." She flicks her eyes to me and smiles sweetly, and I gulp down the rest of my wine to prevent my hands from reaching out and tucking a loose strand of silky hair behind her ear.

"My pleasure," I stutter, moving away and returning to my seat at the counter. I need to put some space between us before I allow my sexy fantasies to become a reality.

Now that I'm at a safe distance, we continue to talk easily about the truck and my disastrous away series. I even share my feelings about the meeting with Coach Casey with her—she's so easy to talk to while she busies herself whisking ladles full of butter into the eggs until it's a silky, yellow sauce.

"It sounds like Coach Casey has your best interests in mind," she replies as she puts the freshly made sauce to one side. "Will you bring the salmon over? We can start wrapping it in the parcel."

"Yes, Chef!" I laugh, picking up the dish filled with fish and marinade and pulling off the saran wrap. As I approach Lana, she turns unexpectedly, and we end up crashing into each other, the dish tipping between us, covering her in sticky brown liquid. The fish lands with a wet plop on the floor, and we stand there, covered in marinade, our dinner ruined.

I half expect Lana to yell at me for fucking up all our hard work, but instead she shocks me by bursting into hysterical laughter.

"Oh my god, we're such a mess," she gasps between heaving guffaws, holding her arms out to the side as the liquid drips down her shirt and onto the floor. Unfortunately, the dish tipped toward her, so she got the full hit of the mess whereas I seem to have come away mostly unscathed.

"Oh shit, I'm so sorry." I drop down and begin scooping the slippery fish off the floor, hoping we can somehow save it from the trash.

"Don't worry about it." She giggles, grabbing a roll of paper towels from the counter so she can wipe up the marinade from the tiles. "I think it's past saving."

"See!" I laugh. "This is why I stay out of the kitchen. I'm a fucking disaster."

Lana drops the ruined fish into the garbage along with the sodden paper towels and washes her hands. As she turns, I realize her shirt is a complete write-off; she can't spend the night stinking of garlic and soy.

"Let me get you a shirt," I offer, trying desperately not to notice the way the wet fabric clings to the curve of her breasts and the peaks of her nipples.

"Thank you," she replies, trying not to get more of the marinade on her. I lead her through to my bedroom and am immediately thankful my cleaner came by while I was away and there aren't any sweaty workout clothes lying around. Quickly, I disappear into my walk-in closet and dig around in a drawer where I keep my T-shirts. There's surely something that won't swamp her petite figure. I finally pull out a soccer jersey that I've had since I was a teenager and, despite it being too small for me, it'll probably still hang off Lana like a dress.

"Here you go," I say, handing her the shirt. "You can wash up in the bathroom." I point toward the door that's slightly ajar. "I'll go and order some takeout."

Lana smiles shyly and accepts the shirt from me,

our fingers brushing against each other, and I'm positive I feel little sparks of electricity flicker between them. Her eyes hold mine for a moment longer than feels friendly, and then she shoots off into the bathroom, breaking the spell. When the door closes and the lock engages, I release a breath in a long stuttering exhale and press my fingers into my sternum, my heart beating furiously beneath them.

Jesus fucking Christ! I've never had such a visceral reaction to a woman before, and it's beginning to freak me out just a little. It's just my bad luck that the woman my heart seems to want more than any other is completely off the table. I don't know whether she harbors any feelings for me, or if I've been permanently added to the friend list. I can't see Matt ever allowing Lana to date one of his teammates and probably for a good reason, but I don't just want to hook up with her. For the first time, I can actually see a future with someone: dating, moving in together, marriage, children, growing old and fat together, surrounded by grandchildren and maybe a couple of dogs.

Whoa! I need to pump the fucking brakes here. These thoughts are way too intense for me to be having them about a woman I haven't even been on a real date with yet.

I quickly leave my room and go back to the kitchen to order the Thai banquet from my favorite place. I'm just finishing the order when Lana returns, and I forget how to form words. She stands before me in my old soccer shirt that I've only kept for sentimental reasons. It hangs down to her knees and has slipped off one bare shoulder. In her hands, she's holding her ruined shirt, and if I'm not mistaken, I catch a glimpse of black lace which can mean only one thing.

She's not wearing a bra.

Mentally kicking my ass for not taking the chance to change into my jeans, I will my cock to stay down and compose myself enough to finish up the order and give my credit card details. While I finish up, Lana returns to the kitchen and decants the hollandaise into a container which she puts in the fridge along with the other ingredients we didn't get to use.

I hang up the call and ask, "You like Thai, right?"

Lana turns toward me after closing the fridge and smiles, rubbing her belly. "Yum. Yes, Thai's a great choice."

"I'm sorry again that I ruined our meal," I say, stuffing my hands into the pockets of my sweats. "You worked so hard on that sauce…"

"Hey, stop apologizing." Lana laughs, hopping up on one of the high stools at the counter. "I'm not one of those tyrannical chefs who screams at everyone. I've worked for enough of them to know that's not my style."

I join Lana at the counter and pour us another glass of wine. "So, tell me what it was like being a chef in Paris."

She takes a beat and sips her wine, something dark flashing across her face so quickly I almost don't notice it. When she lowers her glass, she captures her plump bottom lip between her teeth and sighs.

"It was amazing. It was a dream come true to learn at the best culinary school in the world, meet some of my foodie heroes and eat in the best restaurants…" She takes another sip. "But it was time to come home." She gives a nonchalant shrug, but I have a feeling that's not all there is to it.

"Sounds to me like you had a great life there," I reply. I want to press for more information, but I'm cautious. I don't want to scare her off. "What brought you back? Especially to Seattle. Matt tells me you lived in Tampa with your parents before you went to Paris."

Lana huffs out a breath. "You ask a lot of questions, don't you?"

"I'm interested, that's all. I know what it's like to move your life halfway across the world to chase your dream," I state, remembering my own transatlantic journey all those years ago.

Lana closes her eyes, and when she opens them again, I can see she's ready to start talking. However, just as she begins to form the words, the buzzer goes to announce the arrival of our food and she clams up again.

Goddamn it!

With my frustration levels at boiling point, I answer the intercom and wait at the door for the delivery guy, cutting his tip in half for fucking up my heart-to-heart with Lana. When I return with the food, she's setting out plates and cutlery and folding cloth napkins that must have been in one of the drawers I never open. We share the food out between us and make small talk while we eat, not returning to the subject of her time in Paris. Instead, we stick to safe subjects like the Whalers cup run, our favorite movies, and current Netflix binges.

By the time we finish eating and load the dishwasher, the wine is gone and there's an awkward atmosphere where neither of us knows what to do next. All I know is that I don't want her to leave yet.

"Wanna watch a movie?" I ask, running my hand through my hair, feeling like a teenager asking his crush out on a first date.

Lana smiles shyly and nods. "Sure. There's a new horror that's been on my watch list for a while if you're in for a bit of a scare."

"Sounds good to me."

She uses the bathroom while I set up Netflix on the large flat screen TV mounted on the wall in my living room, searching for the name of the movie. When she returns, I've got myself a beer and a glass of water for her, and I'm opening a bag of pretzels. Suddenly the room plunges into darkness, and I look up to see Lana making her way carefully to the couch.

"You can't watch a horror movie with the lights on." She laughs, sitting next to me and stuffing her hand into the bag of pretzels. This is suddenly feeling very much like a date, and I'm not sure how she feels about that. I know how I feel, especially with her wearing my clothes. I definitely know how Lana's grumpy ass big brother would feel if he knew I was sitting in the dark with his sister.

The real question is… where do I want this to go, and should I press my luck?

13

Lana

There's a reason this movie has been sitting on my watch list for so long. It's absolutely terrifying. I love a good scare as much as the next person, but this movie is all kinds of fucked up, and before I can stop myself, I'm snuggling into Alex's side and watching it through my fingers. Every time the creepy girl with the long black hair and bloody fingernails crawls out of the TV, I squeak and hide my face.

After a particularly harrowing scene, I feel Alex laughing next to me, his body shaking slightly against my cheek.

"What's so funny?" I ask, a little indignantly.

"Number one, I can't believe you haven't seen this movie. It's really old." He chuckles. "And number two, I thought you liked scary movies, but you've been hiding your eyes through most of it."

"Okay, fair point about the age of the movie, but I do like horror," I reply, sitting up and hitting pause on the remote so I can talk without the creepy girl suddenly popping out of the TV. "I just prefer a good serial killer or vampire. This movie is completely fucked up! I'll never be able to fall asleep with the TV on ever again."

Alex just laughs loudly and pulls me in for a hug, pressing me against his muscular chest. "I'll protect you, firecracker."

I know his words are meant to be comforting, but suddenly I'm finding it difficult to concentrate on anything other than his huge hand resting on my hip, his clean soap scent, and the feel of the soft cotton shirt under my cheek. I never felt this comfortable with Etienne; even when things were good between us, there was always an edge, a tense undercurrent. At first, I put it down to sexual chemistry, but later I realized it was my fear. My fear of upsetting or annoying him to the point where he'd flip out and either verbally or sometimes physically attack me. The physical stuff didn't happen as much as the emotional, but in some ways, that was worse. I could see him gearing up for a slap, whereas the put downs and undermining happened so subtly I almost didn't notice it until Zac held a mirror up to my face and *made* me see it.

"You haven't yelped for a while. Everything okay?" Alex's deep voice brings me back to the moment, and I realize that while I've been lost in thought, the movie has continued and is close to concluding.

I suddenly have an overwhelming urge to share what happened in Paris with Alex. I feel like I can trust him with this shameful secret.

"I left Paris because of an abusive boyfriend," I blurt out, sitting up straight, hitting pause on the remote again. I can see the blank look on Alex's face in the white light from the TV, and I'm afraid I've misread the situation. Perhaps he doesn't like me in the way I hope he does, and he doesn't want to hear why I really left Paris.

But then his blank expression turns into one of compassion with an undercurrent of seething anger. I can see the muscle in his jaw leaping under this beard as he clenches his teeth and his hands ball into tight fists on his thighs.

"Say that again," he growls, staring at me so intensely I feel it everywhere.

"Please don't make me do it," I plead, reaching over to put my hand on his forearm, comforted by his warmth and strength. "You heard what I said. The guy I was with in Paris was an asshole, and the only way I could rid myself of him was to move back to the States. That's the real reason I gave up Paris. It's completely pathetic, I know that. I mean, who allows themselves to be in a relationship with someone like that?"

All of a sudden, Alex reaches out and gently cups my face in his hands. "Lana, stop!"

I clamp my mouth closed and savor the warmth of Alex's hands on my face.

"You did nothing wrong," he whispers. "In fact, it sounds like you did exactly the right thing. You got yourself out of that situation and made a change you knew would be difficult. I think you're the bravest person I know."

"Really?" I ask, feeling tears well up in my eyes, willing them not to slip down my cheeks.

"Yes, baby, you are. You did an incredibly brave thing, and you should be so proud of yourself." Alex's thumb captures the tear that trickles down my cheek when I close my eyes at his kind words. My heart beats loudly in my ears, and I begin to feel a weight lift from my shoulders.

"But I'm such a loser, running away to hide in my brother's spare room. A really brave person would've stayed in Paris, faced up to Etienne, and not let him chase me away," I argue, feeling the shame of what I allowed Etienne to do to me.

"No, I don't believe that." Alex shakes his head. "Starting over is so much harder. Look at you now! You have your own business. That's awesome."

Before I know what I'm doing, I dart forward and press my lips against his, the soft hair of his beard tickling my chin. I feel Alex tense up for a moment, his lips a firm line beneath mine, but then he sinks into the kiss. His fingers slide around my neck and grips the plaited hair at my nape, using it to tilt my head to the side so we can deepen the kiss. Tentatively, I brush my tongue against his, and a deep moan rumbles through him as I press my breasts against his chest. I know this is a really stupid idea, but it feels so good, so right. His huge hand is splayed across my back holding me against him, his tongue is matching mine stroke for stroke, and we begin to devour each other. The heat between us is indescribable, and I become instantly addicted to it.

Suddenly, Alex pulls away, standing quickly and striding over to the floor to ceiling windows. He keeps his back to me and runs both his hands through his long hair, taking in a huge breath.

Oh shit, what have I done? I shouldn't have kissed him. He's one of my brother's teammates, but more than that, he's a really nice guy, and I have no business dragging him into my relationship bullshit.

I stand up, moving closer to him, my chest still heaving with the intensity of the kiss, the massive shirt I'm wearing falling to my knees. "I'm sorry, Alex. I didn't mean for that to happen." When he doesn't move, I come closer. "Alex, I…"

"Are you really sorry? You don't have to be," he replies in a gruff, raspy voice, turning around so I can see the slightly pained look on his face and the clear bulge in his sweatpants. "You weren't alone in the kiss. If I'm honest, I've been wanting to do it all night. Hell, I've been wanting to do it for a very long time."

I look away shyly. "Me too," I admit. "But it's not a great idea to get involved with each other. I mean, I have my business to focus on, and you have the playoff run coming up. Not to mention a two-hundred-pound gorilla who happens to be my big brother."

This makes Alex chuckle and shake his head. "I can take your brother if I need to. If you want me to." He bends his head and kisses my jaw, tilting my head up, and I want to get lost in him.

I laugh, trying to defuse the tense, awkward situation. "I'm sure you can, big guy. But I don't want either of us being put in a position where we have to fight my brother over this."

Alex reaches out to tuck a strand of hair behind my ear. I lean slightly into his touch again, but then pull back, not wanting to get carried away.

"As you wish," he replies. "We can keep things as they were, for now. You can teach me to cook, and I can keep fucking it up!"

We both laugh, and he pulls me into a hug, being

careful to keep the lower half of his body away from mine.

"I should go," I say quietly, pulling out of the hug. "I'll return your shirt when we have our next lesson. Just let me know when you're free." I stumble slightly in the darkened room and make my way back to the kitchen where I hit the light switch, making us both squint at the bright glare.

"Yeah, sure, no hurry on the shirt." Alex rubs the back of his neck awkwardly, making his thick bicep flex which in turn causes my already overloaded libido to do a backflip.

"Okay, thank you." I grab my dirty shirt from the counter and pull my jacket off the hook by the door, backing away from the man who's just given me the sexiest kiss of my life.

"Look, we have an afternoon game on Saturday and then the Annual Charity Auction for the Whalers Foundation. Why don't you come to the game and then be my date for the benefit—in a friendly way, obviously?"

I consider his proposition carefully, weighing up the pros and cons in my head. I'm about to tell him it's not a great idea when he adds, "The whole gang will be there, so it won't be like a 'date' date, more like a group thing. Completely acceptable."

Actually, Mila already mentioned me going with her and Matt to the benefit, but I didn't want to feel like a third wheel. At least this way, I won't be hanging around with them all night.

"Yeah, sure. That sounds nice. It'll be fun to get dressed up and let my hair down."

Alex moves forward so he's standing dangerously close to me, my back pressed against the door. I can see the hungry look in his eyes, and my breath begins to come out in shallow huffs.

I point my finger against his bulging pec and fix him with my most serious look. "It's kind of hard to keep thinking of you as just a friend when you're looking at me like that."

"I'm trying to remind you of how good this can actually be between us. If we let it happen." The cocky smirk tilts his full lips and makes my pulse rate pick up another notch. "Just let that sink in," he adds gruffly, reaching behind me to open the door, accidentally on purpose leaning against me so I get a final whiff of his masculine scent.

"Okay, well, great," I splutter, ducking under his arm and slipping out the front door. "Text me the details, and I'll see you on Saturday. Thanks, bye." I stumble away down the hall toward the elevator and jab at the button, not daring to glance over at Alex's door, afraid that if I see him leaning sexily against the door jamb, I'll run back into his arms and throw all reason out the window.

Why the hell is my life so complicated?

Or am I making it that way, and would it be simpler to just let go?

14

Thor

I'm extra pumped for the game against Vancouver, not only because they're our closest rivals geographically or because Coach Casey and their coach have some kind of long-standing beef. No, I'm brimming with adrenaline because I know the hottest woman I've ever locked lips with is in the crowd tonight. I caught sight of Lana in the team's family section when I skated out at the beginning of the game, and I raised my large goalie stick in her direction, winking as I cruised past. She looks so fucking hot in a Whalers jersey, even if it does say Landon on the back. *Note to self: get her a Bergman jersey as soon as possible, provided she gives in to what this thing between us could be.* There's nothing sexier than claiming a woman like that, putting your name and number on her, even if my brain is still thinking of her as being off limits and all.

It's like my body refuses to believe nothing will ever happen. I'm ashamed to admit that I've jerked off to the memory of our kiss at my apartment the other night more times than I dare to count, recalling the feel of her soft lips moving with mine, her full breasts pressed against my chest and my fingers brushing the line of bare skin on her back where her shirt had ridden up.

Fuck, remembering it makes me harder than ice.

But now is not the time to get a poorly timed hard on. I've got a Vancouver winger speeding toward me with the puck at his stick, and Bugs and Nate are nowhere to be seen. We've got a comfortable three-nothing lead, but that can change in a heartbeat if we take our eye off the game. I make myself as big as possible on the doorstep and try to read the winger's body language—what shot is this kid going to take? At the last minute, he shows his hand, and I lift up on my knees to block his top shelf shot with my shoulder, sending the puck bouncing off toward Nate. He captures it on his blade, drops it to the ice, and skates behind my goal. He shouts his apology for being late and then takes off up the ice, passing to Ford who immediately gets slammed into the boards by a Vancouver enforcer.

I roar in outrage as his head bounces awkwardly off the Plexiglas, and he crumples to the ice, not moving.

Mother fucker! I charge out of my goal toward my injured brother as all hell breaks loose. It doesn't take much for us to drop our gloves against Vancouver, but that check was reckless. The fight that's breaking out between Nate and the offending player is happening way too close to Ford, who still lies up against the boards, trying to sit himself up. When I reach him, I slide to my knees and help him up, glancing over to make sure the wrestling match isn't going to land on top of us and injure him further. As I help Ford to his feet, the team's assistant coaches slide over and begin to check him out.

I look over and see Nate land a crunching round-house on the side of the Vancouver player's head, knocking his helmet off, sending his ass down onto the ice. At that point, the officials step in and send Nate and the dazed player off for a penalty. I smirk when I see Beth pressed up against the glass, screaming encouragement at her man as he skates to the sin bin to serve his penalty. I also catch a glimpse of Lana a few seats to Beth's right. She looks adorably concerned so I smile broadly at her when I skate back to my goal.

"What the fuck was that?" the gruff voice of my Assistant Captain asks as I squirt water into my mouth while the blood is cleaned off the ice.

Matt skates around the back of my net and fixes me with his angry stare.

I think quickly and reply, "Yeah, that was a bad hit. Hope Ford's okay."

"Not that, man," he growls. "Why have you been making puppy dog eyes at my sister all night?"

I laugh loudly despite the fact my stomach almost drops out of my ass. Have I been that obvious with my sneaky looks toward the family area?

"You're insane!" I protest. "We're friends, that's all. You know she's teaching me to cook, and she looked upset after the fight. There's nothing going on."

Matt squints at me and I see his teeth grinding. "That had better be all it is. I know you're going to the benefit together tonight, and I'm letting it slide because Mila thinks it's a good idea to get Lana out of her funk. But I swear to god, if you make a move on her, I'll end you."

Fuck me. He's this angry after a few looks. How the hell would he react if he knew his little sister's tongue had been in my mouth?

I scoff and roll my eyes, pulling my grill down over my face so he can't get a proper look at me in case my guilt is painted all over it. "Of course, that's all it is. We're friends. End of story."

God, I feel like an asshole for lying to one of my best friends, but I want to take Lana to this benefit more than anything in the world. So, I tell the lie that Matt needs to hear to allow that to happen. For a heart-stopping minute, I think he can see right through my deceit, but then he gives me a sharp nod and skates off to back up Bugs at the puck drop. Fuck me, that was close. I can't let my feelings for Lana bubble to the surface tonight, no matter what.

Approaching Bugs' front door, I pull at the bow tie that's currently pressing uncomfortably against my Adam's apple, and I wonder how long it'll need to stay in place tonight. Just like the dress shoes I'm wearing, the tuxedo also had to be custom tailored to fit my huge frame. It fits like a glove, and it should for what it costs, but the bow tie is a pain in the ass. I should've just bought a clip-on, but the tailor almost had a stroke when I suggested it.

So here I am, dressed up like an enormous penguin in this tuxedo, heading out on a non-date with a beautiful, albeit off-limits woman. I huff out a frustrated breath just as Bugs opens the door and greets me, Nate, and Beth with high-fives and hugs.

"Here's the man of the hour!" he announces loudly, ushering me into the house. "Another shutout for the mighty Thor!"

I accept a beer and hold it up to toast the rest of my line who are already here. "Couldn't do it without all of you," I boom, holding up my bottle. "Well, I could do without the kid forgetting that he's there to cover my ass." I tip Nate a wink and receive a good-natured middle finger in return.

As I cruise the room, greeting everyone in turn I notice Matt, Mila, and Lana aren't here yet. My stomach knots uncomfortably as I imagine the worst: Matt didn't believe my denial earlier, and he's decided they won't be coming to the benefit after all.

"You okay, man?" Bugs asks, approaching me with a sleepy baby Sawyer pressed against his chest. "You seem a little out of it."

I laugh quietly so as not to wake the baby. "I'm fine. Just a bit wasted after the game. This getting old shit is no fun."

Bugs chuckles and nods in agreement as Cam joins us and takes Sawyer from him, leaning up to press her lips to his smirking mouth. When they part, she smiles and gazes between her man and their baby and yet again my heart wants what they have. Despite the rocky road, they got their happy ending, and I've never seen either of them so content.

"Oh, c'mon now. You boys aren't old." Cam laughs. "I can tell you for certain that Warren is absolutely in his prime." She lifts her eyebrow and winks, making

Bugs pull her in for another kiss.

"Thanks, Sawyer. It took you long enough to realize that." He smirks, giving her ass a gentle pat.

"Hey, I got there in the end," Cam protests, shaking her head. "I'm gonna put this little lady down so the babysitter can at least have a few hours before she starts demanding attention again."

"Good night, baby girl." Bugs leans in and kisses his daughter's chubby pink cheek before Cam disappears with the babysitter to put her to bed.

We continue to enjoy drinks and shoot the shit as we wait for everyone to arrive. The team has laid on a couple of limos to take us all to the benefit, so we decided to pre-game at Bugs' house as it was big enough to hold us all. Ford still wanted to come despite the hit he took in the game, but I notice he's not drinking tonight, which is a sensible move.

Knox has turned up with yet another random bunny who clings to his arm, eyes as big as saucers as she takes in her surroundings. I've seen her around with a few other players, but if that's the game Knox wants to play, I'm going to leave him to it. He'll soon learn these girls generally want one of two things: to sleep with or marry a pro-hockey player. I've warned him enough times, but the kid has to make his own mistakes.

Nate and Beth stop sucking each other's faces long enough to have a conversation with me, and we make a plan to get brunch tomorrow morning to help with the inevitable hangovers we'll be nursing. The Whalers Charity Auction has a reputation for getting rowdy, and Coach Casey did warn us before we left the locker room that there should be no repeat of last year's streaking incident that landed several members of our second line with hefty fines from the GM.

We're just arguing about whether to meet at eleven or twelve when I hear the front door slam, and Matt and Mila enter the room, looking every bit the happy couple. Matt's arm is slung protectively over Mila's shoulder, and she's laughing loudly at something he's just said.

However, my eyes quickly flick back to the door just as Lana follows, and suddenly my mouth dries out and my throat bobs painfully behind my stupid bow tie. She's an absolute vision in a dark blue evening gown that hugs every one of her banging curves, flaring out at the knee to hit the floor in a fishtail, the neckline plunging dangerously between her breasts. I can feel my fingertips tingling with the desperate need to get my hands on her, so instead I shove them deep into my pants pockets and try not to stare.

I watch impatiently as Lana greets Beth and Cam with hugs and kindly shakes hands with the bunny that accompanied Knox. She fiddles self-consciously with her hair that's pulled into an elaborate twist, tempting tendrils cascading down her slender neck. Fuck me, I'm getting a boner just at the thought of my fingers releasing her chestnut waves from the jeweled clip that holds them in place.

As she approaches, I quickly drink the last of my beer and straighten the cuffs of my tuxedo jacket, pulling them down slightly in order to have something to do with my hands. If I don't, I'm likely to reach out and pull her into a show-stopping kiss.

"Hey," she says in her sweet voice, looking up at me through her dark eyelashes. "Great game today."

Jesus, this is awkward as shit. The sexual tension between us is crackling like static electricity, and I'm surprised my hair isn't standing on end. I'm desperate to reach for her, but I know I can't, especially in the presence of her ever-vigilant brother.

So instead, I take a small step back and bunch my hands into fists in my pockets. "Yeah, it was great. The shutout pretty much sealed the deal on our place in this year's cup run. Just the road trip to Tampa next week, and we'll have our playoff spot secured."

Lana looks a little hurt that I've moved away from her. Her eyes cloud over as she flicks them toward Matt who's drinking a beer with Bugs, side-eyeing the shit out of us. She nods sadly as if understanding why I've put some distance between us and clasps her hands in front of her, pressing her breasts together in a tempting valley that I just want to bury my face in.

Jesus Christ, I need to lock this shit down.

"Right, everyone. The limos have just messaged to say they're five minutes out, so finish your drinks and head out front," Bugs calls, pulling on his tuxedo jacket.

I'm thankful to my captain at that moment because I think if Lana and I have to stand here much longer making awkward small talk, I'll do something stupid.

"Shall we go?" I say instead, ushering her toward the door, unable to resist the need to place my hand on the small of her back. Lana flicks her gaze up at me and can't seem to keep the shy smile from her plump lips. "I thought Zac might be your date tonight?" I ask, desperate for something to say.

Lana laughs and rolls her eyes. "I did ask him, but he's got a hot date. As much as he loves hockey and being in a room with so many of his favorite players would be a dream come true, his need to get laid takes priority."

I join her in her laughter and am just about to ask her who Zac's favorite player is when her cell phone rings in her small purse.

"I'm sorry. I should put the stupid thing on silent, but it could be a booking for the food truck. Excuse me." She takes a few steps away from us, pulls her cell phone out, and looks quizzically at the screen. Instead of answering it, she presses the buttons on the side to silence the call and shoves it back into her purse, returning to my side just as the limos pull up onto Bugs' sweeping driveway.

"Everything okay?" I ask, noticing the crease that appears between Lana's eyebrows when she's thinking hard about something.

Her head snaps up to look at me as if she was lost in thought and she smiles. "Sure, just an unknown caller. I never answer those; it's usually a telemarketer. If it's someone for the food truck, I'm sure they'll leave a message."

"Okay, if you're sure it's nothing more?" I ask, her revelation from the other night about her abusive ex still fresh in my mind.

"No, it's fine." She brushes my concern away and smiles. "C'mon, let's get in the limo that doesn't currently contain my brother." With that, she grabs my hand and pulls me toward the opposite limo to the one Matt is getting into.

15

Lana

That's the third call I've had from an unknown caller in the last week.

At first, I thought it was linked to my business. I've had the calls from my business number diverted to my personal cell phone because I don't want to carry around two cell phones all day. The first time it came up, I answered it, excited that it might be an inquiry about the food truck. But all I heard at the end of the line was silence and then the connection ended, and I just put it out of my mind. However, a few days later the same thing happened, and it made me kind of nervous. And now this latest call has just caused the butterflies in my stomach to soar again.

I'm putting the butterflies down to that and not the fact that my leg is pressed very firmly against the thick, muscular thigh of the Seattle Whalers goalie. In order to avoid the limo my brother is taking, we've inadvertently ended up in the "party" limo with Knox and his girl and Nate and Beth. The champagne has been popped open and the music is loud, and the reason I'm pressing myself so tightly against Alex's side is because

155

Knox and his girlfriend are dry humping each other on the seat next to me. I hear Alex grumble about him being a disrespectful little shit, and before I know what's happening, he's lifting me over his lap to the safety of the free seat next to him.

Holy muscles, Batman! He lifted me like I weigh nothing, and I can assure you that with the amount of cheese I eat, I'm definitely on the curvy side of plump these days.

"Sorry about the kid," Alex growls in my ear, making the hair on my bare arms stand on end. "He needs to check himself and learn some respect." I can see the tick in Alex's jaw going berserk as he tries not to scold Knox for his behavior.

"It's okay." I laugh. "He's young. Let him have his fun."

Alex huffs out a breath and continues to glare at Knox and his girl the entire ride. When we finally reach the plush downtown hotel, he kicks Knox's leg, causing the kid to grunt and look up from sucking on his date's neck. "Time to come up for air, Romeo. Put the girl down and make yourself look respectable. This is a charity event, not a frat party."

"Take it easy, Grandpa." Knox smirks, sitting up and not so suitably adjusting his pants while his date tries her best to salvage her ruffled hair and smeared lipstick.

"Fucking kid," Alex growls again as the door to our limo opens, and he moves ahead of me so he can help me out. I didn't really consider the practicality of this dress when I went shopping with Mila—the fishtail design is stunning and makes my butt look amazing, but my knees are pressed together by the tight fabric, and I can only move in a teetering shuffle at best. Pair that with the high heeled strappy sandals, and I fear I'll fall flat on my face at any moment. However, there's a man mountain standing next to me with his arm held out for me to take, his beautiful ice chip eyes drinking me in, making me hot in all sorts of forbidden places. He looks so incredible in his tux. I had no idea you could get one to fit someone his size. But fit him it does, like it's been sprayed on in fact. The black material makes his blonde hair shine even brighter and the expensive Rolex on his wrist is just perfection. I have a real weakness for a man in a sexy watch.

But as much as I admire Alex's rugged good looks, I know there's no way I can enjoy them like I want to. Matt made it clear to me in the brotherly speech he gave before leaving for Bugs' house that all his teammates, especially Alex, are off limits. I just rolled my eyes and tottered out to the awaiting Uber while I let Mila scold him for being an overprotective jerk. Although I can appreciate my brother looking out for me, he doesn't get to tell me what to do with my life or who to date.

As I take Alex's strong arm and allow him to lead me up the red carpet under the flash and glare of the cameras, I know it's going to be harder and harder to resist him as the evening progresses. I thought after Etienne it would take me forever to feel comfortable with a man again, but with Alex, it just feels so natural. Despite his size and the aggression involved in his job, I know he'd never intentionally hurt me.

Suddenly, the photographers go wild as we pass, and I look back over my shoulder to see Knox dipping his date back, kissing her passionately for the paps.

Alex sees this as well and finally sees the funny side of the kid's antics, and I feel him relax next to me.

"You're very protective of him, aren't you?" I ask quietly as we enter the foyer of the hotel, following the crowd into one of the opulent ballrooms.

"He's a troubled guy," Alex replies sadly. "And I don't think he has many people looking out for him. He never talks about family, and I know he's signed up with one of the sleazier agents, so I feel like he needs someone to watch his back."

My heart swells at his kind words, and I squeeze his bicep a little tighter. "You're very caring."

Alex snorts out an embarrassed laugh. "Nah. I just don't wanna see him ruin a promising hockey career or drag the Whalers name through the mud."

"I don't believe that. You're always looking out for him. I saw it the day you brought his hungover ass to my food tasting." I laugh. "You were constantly checking he was okay and not getting too hammered."

"Yeah, well. It's my responsibility as one of the older guys on the team to do that so there's no need to make a big deal out of it." I notice the pink tinge of a blush on Alex's cheeks, and I know my words are embarrassing him.

"Well, whatever your reason, I think it's very sweet. You're a kind man, Alex Bergman." I smile up at him, and after a beat he returns it, patting my hand and leading us through the doors into the ballroom that's decorated in the Whalers team colors of navy and gold. It looks incredible and the room is already overflowing with people, mostly players and members of the team staff, but also donors and celebrities. I feel completely out of my depth, but Alex makes sure to never leave my side as we greet several players, Coach Casey and his wife, and the Whalers General Manager. He introduces me to everyone, and soon I'm giddy in a sea of expensive tuxedos and glamorous ball gowns.

"Do you want to go and take a look at the auction lots before dinner?" Alex suggests once we've done a circuit of the room and gotten a drink from the bar.

"Yeah, although I doubt there's anything there in my price range." I laugh, remembering the sorry state of my checking account when I looked this morning.

"I'm sure we'll find you something." Alex chuckles, with a wicked glint in his eye.

When we reach the long table holding the auction lots, I can see plenty of items I'd love to bid on, but none that I could ever afford. For instance, the wine tasting experience in the Napa Valley or a helicopter trip over the Grand Canyon. As we move down the table, commenting on the items for auction, I see the one I'm actually looking for.

"Oh good! They included my lot," I say pointing to the card with my picture on it. I'm wearing my chef's whites and holding a whisk and a spatula.

Alex looks at me and then to where I'm pointing, picking up the card to read what it says.

"You donated a night as a private chef to cater a dinner party?" he asks, his eyebrows shooting up his forehead.

"Yes. When Mila invited me and said the tickets were complimentary, I felt like a bit of a freeloader, so I asked Cam if I could donate something instead," I explain.

"So, you're just going to go to a random stranger's house to cook for them?" Alex asks again, this time a look of concern on his face.

I laugh. "That's the idea."

"But what if the person who wins the auction is a serial killer?"

This time I double over with laughter at his ridiculous comment. "Yeah because so many serial killers lure their victims to their lairs by donating money at a charity auction." I giggle, carefully wiping underneath my eyes to save my mascara.

"Hey, it could be the perfect crime!" he protests, looking somewhat put out by my reaction.

"Okay, Sherlock. How about you come with me as my assistant and then if I am being lured to my doom, you can protect me?"

"Deal!" Alex sticks his hand out, and even though I think he's insane, I shake it anyway, still laughing.

"You're ridiculous." I giggle, shaking my head but loving the fact that he's looking out for me.

"I think you're mistaking ridiculous for charming, handsome, and sexy." He smirks, leading me again by placing his warm hand on the small of my back. Every time he does this, I feel heat spreading all over the lower half of my body, and I'm almost thankful that my dress is pressing my thighs together.

After another tour of the room, we make our way to our designated table, and Alex introduces me to the donors and other guests who have already taken their seats. Ford and one of the second line wingers are also already seated, so we quickly take our place just as the appetizers are brought out.

I was worried it would be a bit awkward. I've seen several of these events from the service side of the table, having worked my way through college doing silver service waitressing at a hotel like this one. Some of these benefits can be so stiff and boring with no one making conversation with people at their table. However, Alex does an amazing job at keeping the energy levels high and the people laughing. It's also good to see the Whalers players spread out among all the tables. Again, I've seen some of these events when the people everyone has come to see are kept separate. However, glancing round the room, I can see all the Whalers players and their significant others are doing as good a job as Alex at entertaining their tables.

"So, as a professional chef, what's your verdict on the food?" one of the female guests asks me just as we finish up an exquisite lemon souffle that's lighter than air.

"The food has been outstanding," I reply honestly, wiping the corners of my mouth with my napkin. "I haven't tasted a souffle that good, even in Paris."

"Alex tells us you have a food truck business," she says, looking genuinely interested. I learned from earlier conversations that she's a lifestyle blogger and has something like a million Instagram followers who eat up her recommendations for pretty much anything from skincare and makeup to books and food.

I flick my eyes to Alex, who's sitting next to me with a happy smile on his lips, giving me the nod that I should go ahead and tell her more. If this had happened with Etienne, he would have immediately monopolized the conversation and turned it back to him and his restaurant. That's another thing I'm beginning to realize about Alex; he's kind and selfless, happy to put other people before himself. As I talk to the woman, whose name is Carly, about my food business, I feel Alex's hand gently rubbing small, reassuring circles on the small of my back. It's comforting because I always get a little self-conscious when I have to talk about myself. But more than that, it's turning me on more than if he were touching me in a more intimate place. I feel it everywhere from the roots of my hair to the soles of my feet, and I have an uncontrollable urge to just slide over onto his lap in front of all these people and kiss him like there's no one watching.

However, what Carly says next brings me back to the moment with a crash.

"I'd love to feature your truck on my Instagram and blog," she says. "I'm always looking for new places to feature."

I shoot my eyes over to Alex, and his smile is literally splitting his face in half. I can't help but mimic him, my heart swelling and my stomach flipping with nerves and excitement.

"That would be amazing! Thank you." I gasp, trying to sound as professional as I can while I secretly do a very uncool happy dance on the inside.

We exchange Instagram handles and cell phone numbers with promises to make contact in the coming days. I'm so excited I feel the need to excuse myself to gather my thoughts for fear of completely losing my cool. I whisper my intentions to Alex, grab my purse, and quickly make my way around waiters serving coffee and petit fours, leaving the ballroom to find the nearest bathroom. When I enter, it's thankfully empty, but just to be safe, I quickly check all the stalls before letting out a little triumphant squeal and finally doing my uncool happy dance. Exposure on Carly's blog and Instagram feed could be massive for the business, and all the possibilities of what this could lead to flood my brain. I'm so busy fantasizing about one day owning a whole fleet of Gooey Gourmet trucks that I crash straight into Alex, standing outside the bathroom like a big tree. As I bounce backward off his broad chest, I feel his hands grip the top of my arms to stop me from falling.

However, the firm press of his fingertips on my skin triggers a memory of Etienne and the time he had me cornered in the walk-in closet after I'd had the audacity to comment on the less than favorable review his restaurant received in a prominent food magazine. He'd grabbed me by the arms and shoved me back into the closet, pressing me painfully against the shelves, screaming in my face. When he was done, he released me, and I crumpled into a crying heap, my shoulder blades, ribs, and arms remained bruised for a week and my self-esteem for longer still.

I'm so lost in the traumatic memory that consumes me I don't even realize that Alex has pulled me into his arms, and I'm heaving out desperate, strangled sobs into the lapel of his tuxedo. Through the fog, I can hear him humming quietly, and I eventually slow my breathing, so it doesn't feel like my heart is about to burst free from my chest.

"What happened, baby?" he asks gently, ushering me into a quiet corridor away from potential spectators.

I make a wet sniffing noise and shake my head

against his chest, not ready to talk about it yet.

"Do you wanna get out of here?"

To that question, I nod my head, and it takes no time at all for Alex to whisk me away into a cab, his arms around me the whole time. I know he'll probably get into trouble for leaving the benefit early, but he didn't even give it a second thought.

In the car, Alex continues to hold me with no request for information as to why I've suddenly turned into a sniveling mess. I feel like I owe him an explanation, but I'm not prepared to do that in front of our cab driver. So, I continue to look out the window and breathe steadying breaths as the city whizzes past, realizing that we aren't heading out toward the Sound. We're going in the direction of Alex's condo instead.

It's clear by the tingle of anticipation that zings up my spine that I'm completely okay with that.

16

Thor

I take the glass of whiskey over to Lana, who's been curled up on my couch since we arrived back at my condo. She didn't ask why we came here and not back to her brother's house, but I thought she could do without an hour-long cab ride out to the Sound.

"Here, sip this, baby," I say softly, placing the cut crystal tumbler into her cradled hands, not letting go until I feel her grip close around it. I go back to the kitchen to collect my own glass, mine containing vodka, and quickly shoot off a text to Mila to let her know that Lana took ill, and I've brought her to my place because it's closer. Hopefully, if the message gets to Matt via his girl, he won't be banging my door down in the middle of the night to retrieve his sister. And I have every intention of putting Lana in an Uber once she's feeling better. I'm pretty sure I do.

As I return to the lounge, Mila texts back and confirms that she'll smooth things over with Matt. So, all that dealt with, I shut off my phone and join Lana on the couch, keeping an arm's length between us so as not to trigger her again.

I'm such a fucking meathead.

After everything she told me about her ex, of course grabbing her like that would make her freak out. But all I could see was her tumbling backward and landing on the floor, so my goalie instincts kicked in and I reached out to stop her. I had no idea the effect this would have on her, and I feel like shit about it. I can still see her eyes open so wide the whites were visible all the way around her denim blue irises, her mouth open in a silent scream, and her fists balled in defense. It felt like slow motion as her tiny fists began to beat on my chest, her body squirming and struggling to free itself from my grip. But I didn't want to let her go—she could beat me all she wanted—so instead I pulled her against me until she calmed and relaxed into my embrace.

I've faced a lot of scary shit in my life, but that was by far the scariest. I had no idea I could feel someone else's pain as viscerally as I felt Lana's in that moment. The terror etched on her face was more than my heart could bear, and I realized that I would do anything to protect her from ever feeling like that again.

"Thank you, Alex." Lana's sweet voice snaps me out of my reverie, and I turn to find her looking at me, her drink still cradled in her hands, untouched.

"For what, sweetheart?" I scoff, taking a healthy swig of vodka, welcoming the burn of the liquor in my throat. "I'm the one who made you feel like that. I'm so sorry I put my big paws all over you..."

Before I can finish the sentence, Lana has deposited her drink on the coffee table and is sliding across the section of couch that separates us.

"I like your hands on me," she whispers in a husky voice. I watch, transfixed, as she captures her plump bottom lip between her teeth and looks up at me, something different in her eyes now. I no longer see the fear and confusion of earlier. What I see now is a hunger that I also feel. A hunger that's making my dick uncomfortably hard in my dress pants.

"But I hurt you…" I argue, trying so hard to be a gentleman and not a dirtbag who just wants to push her back on the couch and devour her sweet mouth.

"No, you didn't," Lana replies firmly, her chin tilted in determination. "Etienne hurt me. You are nothing like him, and my reaction had nothing to do with what you did. Zac once grabbed my arm to stop me from stepping in front of a car while we were leaving the bistro, and I had a similar reaction. It's not your fault I'm all kinds of fucked up."

"Lana, I don't want to see you that scared ever again," I whisper in a rough growl, my whole being primed to protect her from anything.

Her eyes become glassy with tears, and she reaches her small hands out and places them on my chest, grazing them up and under the shoulders of my tuxedo jacket, pushing it off. My heart is absolutely pounding as I shrug the jacket off the rest of the way and let it fall behind me on the couch. Keeping my hands bunched in my lap, I allow Lana to continue exploring my body with her inquisitive fingers. They slowly loosen my bow tie, so it hangs around my neck and then she gets to work on the shiny buttons, flicking each one open, her pretty pink tongue poking out of the corner of her mouth in concentration.

"Baby, we don't have to…" I say as her fingers get to the bottom buttons and come dangerously close to my hard dick.

But instead of replying, Lana stands and reaches behind her, dragging the zipper down the back of her dress, fire burning in her eyes. When the dress is loose, she shimmies her hips, it drops to the floor, and my whole world implodes. She's absolutely stunning: rounded hips and belly, tiny black lace panties that are sheer and hide none of her bare beauty. Her luscious tits are encased in black lace as well, her hard nipples straining against it.

"I want you, Alex," she breathes, reaching her hand out to me, imploring me with her eyes. "I know it's not supposed to happen, but it feels right, so I don't give a crap about Hockey Code or my brother. I want this for us. I know you want me too, so please take me to your bed and show me how much."

Now, I'm a simple man, and you don't have to tell me twice, especially when a beautiful sexy woman is standing in front of me in her underwear. With a growl, I push to my feet and reach out my hand to gently take hers, lifting her delicate fingers to my lips to kiss them.

"I don't want to hurt you, so you need to tell me if I'm doing anything you're uncomfortable with," I say, fixing Lana with a serious look. The last thing I want to do is ruin the moment by scaring her somehow.

In reply, Lana reaches up and places her hands on my shoulders, leaping up my body, wrapping her legs around my waist, her gorgeous tits bouncing enticingly close to my face.

"There's nothing you can do to hurt me, big guy."

And with that green light, she leans down and kisses my mouth with so much passion it almost knocks me off balance. But I quickly recover, grabbing Lana's peachy ass in both hands and matching the movement of her tongue stroke for stroke, walking her toward my bedroom. I barely make it into the room because she's grinding her hot little pussy on my hard rod, and it feels so good I don't ever want her to stop.

"Too many clothes," Lana gasps, pushing my unbuttoned shirt off my broad shoulders and sliding down my body so she stands in front of me. As I release my cufflinks and they drop to the floor with a metallic clink, Lana begins to work at my belt buckle and then my button and zipper. We're both so frantic at this point, I almost miss the little giggle that escapes her when she shoves my pants down.

Now, I'm a confident guy, but no one wants a new lover to laugh when they take your pants off. It takes me a second to understand what Lana's giggling about, and thank god it's not my manhood.

"Oh shit, yeah. Forgot I put those on." I chuckle, looking down at the flamingo patterned boxer briefs I'm wearing. I'm usually a plain black or white guy when it comes to my choice of underwear, but for some reason that now escapes me, I thought I'd wear these. I'm hoping the sizable bulge tenting them at the front is enough to restore my masculinity.

"They're adorable," Lana whispers, running her fingers under the waistband, making my abs twitch with anticipation.

"They were a stupid novelty gift from my brother Magnus." I laugh, gently putting my fingers under her chin to tilt her eyes up to meet mine. "We like to bust each other's balls by getting the most ridiculous gift we can find. He won that year."

"Well, flamingoes happen to be my favorite bird, so I guess it's my lucky day." Lana cocks her eyebrow and before I can catch my breath, she's pushing her fingers into the waistband and dragging my underwear down my muscular thighs, dropping to her knees in front of me. My throbbing cock is so hard it springs free, and I see Lana's pretty eyes widen, her tongue once again peeking out between her lips.

Holy shit! There's no way I'm letting this goddess suck my dick before I get a taste of her, so I quickly duck down, wrap my arm under her ass and hoist her over my shoulder. Lana lets out an adorable little squeal and laughs as I march her over to the bed and deposit her there.

"Was that okay?" I ask, suddenly unsure about handling her like that.

The hungry look in her eyes answers my question better than words. "I'm not gonna break, Alex. I know what I want, and I want you. It's fine when I'm expecting physical contact; it's the unexpected kind that throws me. So, will you stop treating me like a China doll and fuck me like I know you want to?"

Goddamn it, that's like a red rag to a bull. I can't help the growl that rumbles out of my chest as I pull off my socks and take Lana's slender ankles in my hands, pulling her to the edge of the bed. I love the breathy gasp that escapes her as I drop to my knees and hook my fingers into the edges of her panties, sliding them down her thighs, flinging them over my shoulder. The heady scent of her arousal hits me, and I feel my mouth water at the thought of getting to slide my tongue through her slick folds.

"Oh baby, you're so beautiful," I moan, lifting her knees and draping her legs over my shoulders, sliding my palms up the impossibly soft skin of her inner thighs. I follow my hands with my lips, pressing firm, wet kisses along her thighs, using my hands to hold them open so I can fully appreciate the beauty of her wet pussy. Lana gasps with frustration when I reach the junction of her thighs, but I don't press my lips against her. Instead, I flick my eyes up to lock our gazes, smiling mischievously as I continue to kiss down the opposite thigh.

"Oh, it's like that, is it, big man?" She laughs breath-lessly, squirming under my touch as I continue to tor-ture her sensitive skin with my lips, tongue, and teeth.

"Just making sure I do a thorough prep job." I chuckle, sliding one of my thick digits between her swollen, glistening lips, making her suck in a breath and arch her back. "This chef who's teaching me to cook told me that preparation is everything."

"Well, in my honest opinion, that chef is a fucking idiot," Lana moans, grinding herself against my finger to gain more precious friction. "I'm all for instant gratification."

Her sassy attitude is such a turn on, and I feel compelled to give her everything she wants. I want her to have it all. So, with one final grin and a cheeky cock of my eyebrow, I lower my head and glide my tongue through her slit and the taste of her explodes like fireworks. I'm instantly hooked, and when I find her hard little clit, I begin to circle it with the tip of my tongue, using her moans and sighs as a barometer for my actions. As I pick up the pace, Lana's fingers run through my long hair, and she grips it hard, guiding my head in the direction of her building pleasure.

"Oh god, Alex," she groans, her thighs quivering beneath my palms. "You're so good at that. Oh yes, right there."

At her command, I increase the pressure of my tongue and add another finger to her tight hole, slipping it in and curling it up to rub that rough spot inside. This action makes her squeal, and her hips shoot up, pressing her delicious pussy against my face. Syncing the movement of my fingers and my tongue, I increase the tempo of my ministrations and soon Lana is gasping and panting and coming all over my face, soaking my bearded chin with her juices. Her fingers grip my hair tightly as she rides out her orgasm, and I gently lick her back down to earth.

"Oh wow," she sighs as I grab my shirt from the floor and wipe my chin, pushing up onto the bed to lay beside her. She's boneless and panting, her cheeks flushed and her eyes hazy with satisfaction. On the other hand, my dick is about ready to rocket right off my body, so I reach over and flick the front clasp holding her bra together and moan as her bountiful tits spring free.

"You're so beautiful, baby," I growl as she shrugs out of her bra and presses her breasts against my chest, dancing her fingers down the center line of my abs and through the dusting of reddish blonde hair on my stomach. My cock twitches with interest, and I suck in a shaky breath when her fingers enclose it in her warm grip. Once again, I can feel the rough little calluses on her fingers from hours in the kitchen and that added friction has me on the edge at an embarrassingly quick rate. Her lips find the sensitive skin of my neck, and she trails her tongue along my collarbone and between my pecs. I can see where she's heading and even though the thought of her plump lips around my cock makes me want to blow my load, I need to be inside her first.

I decide to take control of this situation, so I run my fingers down her arm and gently circle her wrist, easing her hand away from my cock, which is liable to let me down if she continues to stroke it like that. Instead, I roll my big body over so she's beneath me, my muscular thigh between her legs, feeling her slickness there. I hold her wrist above her and lower my head so I can gently nuzzle her neck, scuffing my beard on the sensitive spot behind her ear. Lana giggles and squirms, and I continue to kiss my way along her jawline and finally find those luscious lips. She's so ready to accept my kiss, and it takes no time for us to start devouring each other, tongues lashing and searching. She grinds her hungry little pussy against my thigh, seeking another release before I finally get inside her. And who am I to deny her anything, so I brace my leg and allow her to find her orgasm again, groaning and bucking beneath me.

Watching her fall apart yet again is too much. I need to be inside her now. So, I roll away while she catches her breath and dig around in my nightstand for a condom. Laying back on the comforter, I smirk as Lana watches me sheath my cock in latex, her naughty little tongue poking out of the corner of her mouth, a sure sign she's concentrating hard on what I'm doing. I make a promise to myself to make full use of that tongue and mouth when we go for round two later tonight.

But for now, I just need to bury myself in her as deeply as I can. I need to feel the warm grip of her pussy around my cock more than I need my next breath.

However, before I can roll back on top of her, Lana is up, straddling my thighs. She's obviously a woman on a mission—*and who the fuck am I to stop her?* So, I simply fold my hands behind my head and give her a nod.

"Is this okay?" she asks, biting her lower lip, suddenly unsure of her bold move to take control.

"I love you taking control, baby," I growl, flexing my hips beneath her so she bounces slightly up and down. "You can do whatever you want to me, just so long as it involves my cock in your pussy in the next ten seconds."

Lana laughs huskily, her breasts gently swaying with the movement. I make a mental note to make sure those little pink nipples find their way into my mouth while she's riding me.

As if my consent is all she needs to hear, Lana presses one palm to my hard abs and raises herself up, gripping the base of cock with the other hand so she can guide it into her. Even through the latex, I can feel how hot she is. As she works my dick inside her, I have to list my career shutout games in my head in order not to blow my load as soon as she bottoms out. The look on her face is even hotter than finally being inside her—her eyes half closed with lust, her lips pursed together in a perfect little O, her cheeks flushed pink as if she's also holding on by a thread.

Carefully, I move my big hands to her hips and start to slowly guide her movements, loving how tiny she looks with my hands all over her. After a few encouraging pumps, Lana takes control again and begins to roll her hips in the most enticing way, pressing her palms on my thighs behind her so her breasts jut upward. Before I can stop myself, I rise up and capture a pink peak in my mouth and suck deeply, feeling Lana's pussy clench around my shaft.

As she rides me at a tortuously slow pace, I can't keep my hands off her body, cupping the globes of her ass, holding her waist, gliding my fingers up and down her thighs, gripping her hair that's now gloriously disheveled and falling out of the fancy style.

Fuck, it's everything I can do to hold on to my self-control. Every graze of her skin or lips, every roll of her hips, every clench of her inner muscles is causing my orgasm to hurtle to its conclusion.

"Baby, I'm close," I groan through gritted teeth as she begins to pick up the pace. "I need to know what you need. I want us to come together."

Lana's gorgeous eyes open and her pupils are so blown out with desire they look almost black. But the look on her face is unsure, as if she doesn't want to ask for what she needs.

"Anything you want. Tell me what you need," I press. "You're safe with me, Lana."

As if my words give her courage, she says, "I want you on top, and I want you to really fuck me hard. You won't hurt me. Just do it."

I know that now isn't the time to unpick this request, so I do as she asks. With a squeal, Lana is suddenly beneath me, her eyes blazing with lust. Still inside her, I sit back on my haunches and grab the backs of her legs so that they're pressed up against my chest, her ass resting on my thighs.

"I'm gonna make you feel so good, baby." I chuckle. "Better hold on."

With that, I pull out and thrust back inside, causing her whole body to jolt with the power of my thrust. I look down with a questioning expression to check that she's okay, and Lana just moans deeply and nods up at me to continue.

So I do.

I pound her like she asked me to, using her enthusiastic moans and yelps as a guide to her pleasure.

"I'm close, Alex. Please..." she gasps, her body slick with sweat, her gorgeous tits jiggling with each thrust.

I'm close as well and I know it'll only be a few more pumps before I blow, so I lurch forward and cover Lana's sweaty body with my own. She wraps her legs around my waist as we ride out the end together, and I only just hold on long enough to feel her pussy grip me and her fingers squeeze my biceps. The sounds of our mutual pleasure fill the room, and I empty my release into the condom. The feeling of my orgasm seems to go on infinitely until we both slump into a sweaty heap, breathing in short, shallow gasps.

"Oh, wow," Lana gasps beneath me.

It suddenly occurs to me she has almost two hundred and thirty pounds of hockey player on her tiny body, so I raise up on my forearms and look down to see her smiling and laughing.

"Was I crushing you?" I ask, confused by the laughter.

"No," she giggles. "I was just amazed that sex could feel like that."

I squint my eyes at her and gently sweep her damp hair from her face. "I hope you mean it felt awesome and not terrible." Shit, that would be the worst.

Lana gently cups my face in her hand, and I lean into her touch. "It was the best I've ever had. It was sweet and sexy and perfect. Thank you." She leans up and presses her lips to mine and that moment feels almost as good as the orgasm I've just had.

I roll to the side, pull Lana into my arms, and stroke my fingers down her back, gripping her round ass. "It felt perfect for me, too. You're not just a firecracker in the kitchen it seems."

She laughs throatily into my chest and looks up at me. "I mean it—it's never felt like that with anyone before, not even..." Her eyes dart away from mine, and she snuggles down farther into the crook of my arm.

"Hey, it's okay," I say, shifting so I can look into her eyes. "You don't have to worry about comparing me to Le Douchebag. I know I'm a far superior lover."

This thankfully makes Lana laugh. I wasn't sure how she'd take the nickname I've given her asshole ex.

"I could never compare you to him," she replies, suddenly serious.

With her words, my heart sinks and I realize she must still be hung up on him. Why else would she bring him up after we've just had sex for the first time?

"It's okay. I'm sure the sex with him was incredible..."

I say in a sulkier voice than I intended. I gently slide Lana from my arms and sit up, swinging my long legs over the edge of the bed.

"No, you don't get it," Lana cries, jumping up and standing in front of me, gloriously naked, her hands on her hips. "All I meant is I thought sex with Etienne was the best it could get, but I realize now that a lot of what I felt with him was fear." She moves forward and straddles my lap, holding my face in her hands so we're looking directly into each other's eyes. "You are the kindest, sexiest man I've ever met, and that's what made it better than it's ever been with anyone."

Well, fuck me. I don't know if I've ever been anyone's best ever before.

Unsure of what to say, I do the next best thing, lifting Lana up so we can fall down onto the bed for round two of the best she's ever had.

And if I'm honest, she's the best I've had as well.

17

Lana

"**G**irl, there's a Hey Pesto getting a touch too crispy on the griddle. Might wanna take care of that," Zac whisper-shouts at me from the serving hatch.

"Huh?" I ask, coming back from the sexy daydream I'm deeply embroiled in, the acrid burning smell suddenly filling my nostrils. "Oh, shit!" I manage to flip the sandwich off the griddle just in time to save me from having to make a replacement.

Damn it, that's the second time today that I've slipped into a sex replay and lost track of what I'm doing. The blue caterer's band aid on my finger is testament to that little lapse in concentration.

Quickly, I plate up the customer's sandwich with a bag of organic chips and pickle, handing it off to Zac, who has the rest of their order. Thankfully, they're the last people in line, so I can take a breath and get my head back in the game.

It's been a few days since my amazing night with Alex. Well, the amazing night and most of the next day, too. We just couldn't get enough of each other—all over his apartment in fact. In the shower, on the couch, on the kitchen counter where he smeared my breasts with whipped cream and ate hot fudge sauce off my stomach. In the shower again while we tried to clean up after the food sex. When he finally let me sleep for a few hours, he slipped his hard cock into me from behind while he spooned me.

By the time I crept back into Matt's house, I'd been MIA for twenty-four hours. Of course, Mr. Overprotective was standing like a sentry in the living room, his thick tattooed arms crossed over his chest, a look of thunder on his face.

"What the fuck, Squirt?" he roared when I tried to creep past him, my strappy sandals in my hand. "I've been going out of my mind. If it weren't for Mila assuring me you were safe at Thor's, I'd have been checking all the ditches in Seattle for your dead body."

"A bit dramatic, don't you think, Dad?" I scoffed, trying to secretly check that my hair didn't have that "I just had the best fuck of my life" look.

"Matt, she was fine," Mila said in her best calming voice, placing a reassuring hand on Matt's shoulder. "She was with Alex. He took care of her when she got sick, right, Lana?" I could tell by her wide-eyed expression that this is the story my brother has been told and that I should stick to it.

"Yeah, sure," I agreed, nodding enthusiastically. "I got sick after eating a canape with prawns hidden inside. You know what prawns do to me." I made a gagging gesture and watched my brother's face scrunch up. If there's one thing the big bad Matt Landon can't stand, it's vomit. Even the mere mention of it makes him want to hurl.

"Okay, enough with the deets." He sighed, looking slightly nauseated, waving me past him towards the stairs. "Just check in next time."

"Sure thing." I mouthed a thank you to Mila before I disappeared upstairs to get some much needed sleep.

I haven't managed to see Alex again since that night, but we've been texting constantly, and from the sly looks Zac gave me this morning, he definitely knows something's up.

"So, what's going on with you?" he asks, opening a bottle of water now that we have a break in customers. We're at a music festival and the main act has just taken the stage, so hopefully we'll have a little longer to stock check and clean down before the next rush.

"Nothing," I reply, concentrating way too hard on counting bags of potato chips.

"I call bullshit, babe." Zac laughs. "I know a sex haze when I see one. So, tell me, how was the Viking? Does he have a huge hammer?"

I spin around, my mouth hanging open in shock at Zac's crude comment, to find him leaning smugly against the fridge with a smirk on his stupid, handsome face.

"What?" I ask, trying my best to keep my face indifferent so as not to give away what I've been up to.

"C'mon, you've been in a trance all day." Zac points at my injured fingers. "You never cut yourself, so spill the beans."

"You're insane," I scoff, wiping down the counters. "Alex and I are friends, and he helped me when I got sick at the benefit. That's all there is. I'm a bit spaced out because we have the big trip to Tampa in a few days, and I'm a bit anxious about seeing my parents."

Zac nods and seems to accept my explanation. I haven't seen my parents since I returned from Paris, and I know my mom will have a lot of questions that I've so far been able to avoid. So going down to Tampa for my birthday, which happens to coincide with the Whalers game, could be more like a CIA interrogation if my mom has anything to do with it.

I feel a bit shitty hiding what happened between Alex and me from my best friend, but I know for a fact he'd not be able to keep it to himself. So, for the time being, I'm keeping it quiet. And even if I wanted to share this with Zac, I wouldn't quite know what to say about what happened anyway. As amazing as that night was, Alex and I didn't once discuss whether this was a one and done to scratch an itch or whether we want to keep seeing each other and perhaps date.

The Whalers left for an east coast road trip yesterday that will culminate in their game against the Tampa Tiger Sharks, so I haven't had a chance to properly talk to Alex, other than exchanging flirty texts. I doubt there'll be much opportunity in Tampa either, not with Matt, the team, and my parents around.

"Well, you've got better self-control than I have." Zac laughs, bringing me back to the moment. "I couldn't spend the night under the same roof as that hunk of man meat and not tap that."

I laugh at how ridiculous my best friend can be sometimes. "I still don't think you're his type, babe."

Thankfully, we begin to get busy again, and the steady stream of customers doesn't let up enough for Zac to interrogate me further. However, I have a feeling this trip home will be filled with questions and not just about Paris. If Alex and I are as hot as we were the other night, I think it'll be plain for anyone with eyes to see that we're into each other.

This trip could be very awkward, and suddenly I feel very nervous about the whole thing.

Two days later, Zac, Beth, and I catch our flight to Tampa for some blessed sunshine and relaxation after a week of non-stop rain in Seattle. Even though I tell them not to, my mom and dad are waiting to pick us up at the airport. My mom has made an embarrassingly large cardboard sign with my name on it, and I can tell from a hundred feet away that she's raided her arts and crafts room to adorn the sign with glitter, ribbons, and all sorts of other shit I don't even know the name of.

"Your mom is the best," Zac sniggers, elbowing me in the ribs as we reach them, my cheeks burning.

"Here's my favorite daughter!" Janice cries, shoving the banner at my dad and pulling me into a huge hug, which I have to admit feels amazing. She's ever so slightly shorter than I am, which means she's tiny, her salt and pepper hair pulled into its usual ponytail.

"She's your only daughter, Jan." Zac laughs, joining in the hug completely uninvited. "But I'm definitely your favorite adopted gay son."

My mom just laughs and squeezes Zac extra tight. "Of course, you are, honey. You'll always be my favorite."

I roll my eyes at Zac's smug grin as we untangle ourselves, and I'm pulled into yet another fierce hug, almost disappearing into the huge arms of my dad. Matt definitely got my dad's build, all thick muscular arms and broad chest. His kind, weather-worn face is one of my favorite sights, and I realize as I take in his scent of wood and sand that I've missed him so much I feel tears pricking the backs of my eyes.

"Missed you, Squirt," he says in his gruff voice that rumbles through his chest as I press myself against it.

"Missed you too, Daddy." I pull away for fear of bawling like a little kid and introduce Beth to my parents before we head out to the parking lot. We only brought carry-on luggage, so we make a quick exit and drive through Tampa to the Whalers hotel.

We drop Beth off so she can settle into Nate's room and then we drive out to my parent's beachfront house in Siesta Key. We lived in Detroit for most of my life, but when Matt made it to the show, he made sure to retire my parents out here. And I can tell you one thing: I don't miss those freezing Detroit winters. Coming to Florida is amazing and I love this house. It's right on the beach with its powdered sugar sand and turquoise water and has a definite beach shack feel. However, inside, it's decorated tastefully in grey, soft blue, and white with hints of my dad's carpentry in everything from the shoe rack to the hand-built kitchen.

After Zac and I have settled in our rooms, mom has put on a huge spread of cold cuts, pickles, homemade bread, and salads.

"You know the Whalers eat at the arena before they play, right?" I tease as we fill up our plates from the vast array of food.

"Very funny, smart ass." My mom chuckles, giving

my butt a good-natured smack. "I can't help it if I over-prepared. I figured everyone will be ravenous when they come back here for the party after the games."

"I think the whole of Tampa could come back here after the game, and you'd still have left-overs," Zac sniggers, biting the end off his pickle spear and grinning broadly at my mom.

"That's enough from you, mister." She laughs, trying her best to scowl at him while adding extra corned beef to my dad's plate.

We continue to talk light-heartedly over lunch, eating out on the terrace that overlooks the beach. I can already feel the sea breeze blowing away the dreary feeling I sometimes get living in Seattle with all that rain. It even blows away the knot in my stomach put there by the four Unknown Caller calls I've received on my cell since the charity benefit. I'm still putting it down to a business call, but part of me also thinks it could be Etienne. He's been ridiculously quiet and must know by now that I sent my cell phone on a solo journey across France to put him off my scent. He's also smart enough to know that I'd either go to Seattle to be with my brother or Tampa. And with all the social media attention my food truck is getting, it would only take a few clicks on Matt's Instagram to find out about my business. I probably should have thought a bit more carefully about that, but then again, fuck him! Why should I be afraid of him seeing my success? He's all the way in Paris, and if making some creepy ass phone calls makes him feel like a big man, then he can carry on.

I'm done being afraid of him. I've moved on. Maybe

in more ways than one.

End of story.

Even so, I'm still slightly unsettled and wonder if I should mention it to someone, possibly Mila. I'd feel weird mentioning it to Matt because of course he'd fly off the handle. But Mila has always been good at giving me advice, so I might consider it if the calls continue.

After we help Mom pack away the mountains of food, we get washed up and change into our Landon Whalers jerseys, ready for the afternoon game. Matt kindly arranged for us to have a suite, and Zac is so excited he's bouncing up and down in the back seat like a toddler on the way to the circus.

This is going to be a hard-fought game because Tampa is set to win the Eastern Conference and losing this game will mean that the New York Bull Dogs take it from them. So, I expect there to be plenty of blood and sweat on the ice at the end.

The arena is buzzing, and after sitting in traffic for half an hour, we eventually make it to the VIP parking lot. From there we're taken in a private elevator to the Executive Level and shown to our suite. It's so fancy. As a family, we always sit with the fans when we watch Matt play, but he wanted it to be a special occasion because of my birthday. So, when we enter the suite, it's decorated in Whalers colors with streamers and balloons everywhere, a huge Happy Birthday banner draped above the glass doors leading out onto our private seating area.

Zac and I let out squeals of delight and race around the suite like little kids, exploring the table laden with booze, sodas of every type, and even more delicious canapes. On a separate table is an enormous three-tiered birthday cake covered in white chocolate curls and thick dark chocolate ganache. I can tell immediately it's from my favorite patisserie in Paris, and I turn aghast to everyone, pointing at it, completely dumbfounded.

"How?" I splutter, flicking my eyes between Zac and my parents.

"Zac arranged it after your brother asked him what your favorite type of cake was," my mom explains, clasping my dad's hand, her eyes full of tears.

"Oh my god, you guys!" I exclaim, flinging my arms around my best friend and then hugging my parents as well.

"It's your brother and Mila you should be thanking. They arranged all of this," my dad replies, kissing the top of my head.

I know he won't be looking at his phone with puck drop a short time away, but I fire off a thank you message to our Whatsapp chat and join Zac at the bar table where he's fixing me a gin and tonic.

Shortly before the players take to the ice for their warm-up skate, Beth and Cam enter the suite, along with a sleepy baby SJ in her car seat. Hugs and introductions are exchanged, my mom manages to get her hands on the baby and starts up her speech about how she'll be too old to enjoy her own grandbabies if we don't hurry up and give her some soon. My dad rolls his eyes, but I also catch him looking longingly at baby Sawyer as she sucks contentedly on her chubby fist.

Just as the players take to the ice for warm-ups, Mila pays a quick visit to the suite. I pull her into a hug and thank her profusely for all her hard work arranging the suite and everything.

"My pleasure," she replies shyly, blushing a deep red that matches her hair. "It meant a lot to Matt and me that you'd have a good birthday. I just dropped in to check everything was okay, but I have to go back. We'll all come up after the game and have a drink and some cake before we go back to the house."

"Sounds perfect," I gush, feeling like the luckiest girl in the world.

It's then I notice a Whalers merchandise bag in Mila's hand. She catches me looking and her blush deepens.

"What is it?" I ask, hoping it's not some horrible gag gift from my brother.

Mila gently takes my arm and leads me over to a quieter part of the suite and hands me the bag. "Thor asked me to give this to you. He said he understands if you don't want to wear it, but he wanted you to have it anyway."

Slightly confused, I open the bag to see the navy and gold of a Whalers jersey inside and understanding dawns on me. Alex has sent me a jersey with his name on it, and he wants me to wear it for the game. It's incredibly sweet and sexy, and I know exactly what it means to wear a jersey bearing the name of the man you're sleeping with. Unfortunately, everyone else in this room knows the significance of the gesture as well. So, unless I want to out what Alex and I are to each other before I even know it myself, it's probably safer if I stick to my Landon jersey. Even though … maybe I can tell what we are from his gesture alone.

I quickly grab a napkin from the bar and a pen from my purse and scribble a note to Alex, which I fold up and press into Mila's hand.

"Can you make sure Alex gets this? But don't let Matt see it," I whisper, giving Mila a kiss on the cheek when I see the knowing look she gives me.

"Sure thing, honey."

With that, she flits around giving everyone hugs and kisses goodbye before heading back down to the locker room in time for Coach Casey's pre-game talk. I hold the bag containing Alex's jersey tightly in my hands, pressing it to my chest and feeling an ache there because I can't wear it.

"C'mon, Lana. It's almost time for puck drop," Zac calls from the seating area where he sits with his ridiculously large foam finger and a huge cup of foamy beer.

I laugh, loving my best friend more than life itself. I quickly stash the bag under my jacket and join my family and friends for the hockey game.

18

Thor

*T*hank you for the gift. You understand why I can't wear it in public just yet but bet your ass I'll wear it in private for you later, big man. Lots of love, L xxxx

The words from her note are burned into my brain. And they have to be because as Mila pressed the napkin into my hand, she told me with a wink that I'd better eat the evidence when I've read it.

Fuck, just the thought of Lana in my jersey is giving me a semi chub even as I haul on my heavy shoulder pads and secure them in place. It's been a ball busting few days since we were together, and I'm craving her like a fucking addict. And not just the sex stuff, although I have to admit I've rubbed my dick more times in the last week than I have since I was a teenager. No, I miss the way she smells like she's just been baking cookies—all vanilla and sugar and how her hair is so soft it just falls through my fingers.

Jesus, who the fuck am I? I'm waxing lyrical about a woman when I'm usually the one-and-done type of guy. My head is spinning with thoughts of seeing her after the game, and I don't even notice when Coach barks at me to get my grill on and head out for the game.

"What's wrong with you, man?" Nate asks as we trudge up the chute, the arena vibrating and thrumming with the sound of the Tampa fans. "You've looked like you're on another planet this whole trip. And you're constantly looking at your phone."

"It's nothing," I scoff, barging the big defenseman. "Just got some shit going on. Nothing to worry your pretty little head about."

Nate laughs and barges me back. "Good to know. We need you one hundred percent on your game, man. No distractions."

We stop in the tunnel and do a few chest bumps and rallying warrior cries to pump ourselves and all the other guys up before taking to the ice. This is the most exciting sport in the world, and I can't believe that I get to play it for a living. I'm one lucky son of a bitch.

I guess I'm just missing one thing, and she happens to be sitting in this arena right now. I just have to find a way to make her mine without being murdered by her brother.

"A career defining shutout for the Mighty Thor, and we're definitely on the road to another Cup campaign," Coach Casey bellows over the sound of rowdy hockey players. He's standing on top of a cooler, his beer raised high in the air, and I fear he's going to fall on his ass at any minute. I've never seen Coach let loose like this before, and I'm really enjoying it.

We've been back at the Landon's beach house for

a few hours now, and the drinks are flowing as the sun sets over the Gulf. Everyone cheers and I get a few cups of ice and beer dumped on my head for good measure.

"I'd also like to thank our hosts for inviting a group of pumped-up goons into their home to help celebrate their daughter's birthday." Coach tips his red solo cup toward Lana, who's standing next to Zac, wrapped up in his arms. "Happy Birthday, Lana. Welcome to the Whalers family. And can I say that you're a lot prettier than your ugly ass brother?"

That causes everyone to laugh loudly, and Matt gets several jabs in the ribs from our teammates as Coach jumps down from the cooler and shakes Mr. Landon's hand, thanking him again for allowing most of the Whalers to descend on his house.

It's been a fantastic day—a win over Tampa and another shutout for me, the sight of Lana up in her suite jumping around like a lunatic at the end of the game, the warm welcome we all received from the Landon's when he shuttled over to their house for the party. Coach was gracious enough to arrange a bus to get us all here and back to the hotel safely and in time for our flight home first thing in the morning.

The only problem with that plan is: how the hell do I get to spend any alone time with Lana?

At the end of the game, I was hustled into the locker room to change, so I could do press and then had to shower quickly and dress in order to catch the bus to the party. Other than a few fleeting glances, she's been frustratingly close but out of reach all at the same time.

"Alex, you look big and strong," Janice Landon

says to me, bringing me back from gawping at her daughter. "Would you bring another case of beer down from the kitchen?"

"Of course, Mrs. Landon," I reply, putting my solo cup down.

"Now, now, none of that," she tuts. "It's Ma or Janice. If you bring down the Bud Light, that would be awesome."

"Sure thing, Janice." I jog off up the beach and shake the sand off my feet before entering the back of the house through the mud room. Heading up two flights of stairs, I come into the main living area and see the cases of beer stacked up by the kitchen island.

Just as I bend down to pick up a couple of cases, I feel a pair of hands cover my eyes and the lyrical sound of a giggle I know very well. I quickly stand and turn to find Lana standing in front of me wearing just my jersey, her shapely legs completely bare. Fuck, if she's naked under there I'm likely to die a happy man.

"What are you doing?" I growl, my eyes darting to the stairs, where a member of her family or my team could appear at any moment.

"I've been desperate to see you and thank you for the gift," Lana replies in a slightly breathless voice, tugging the hem of the jersey away from her body so I get a quick flash of lace. I can tell by her eyes that she's aroused and just the sight of that gives me a hard on.

"But everyone's here," I protest weakly as she grabs my hand and pulls me toward the staircase that leads to the next floor. "Baby, we can't."

"Oh, don't be such a scaredy cat," she taunts, jogging up the stairs ahead of me, giving me an enticing view of the lacy thong she's wearing under her jersey.

I chuckle darkly and charge up the stairs after her. "You've asked for it now, baby."

When we reach the top of the stairs, Lana pulls me in the direction of what I hope is her room and then shuts the door quietly, flicking the lock. With a quick switch of positions, I've got her pinned against the door, devouring her lips and tongue with my own. I've been aching to taste her again, and it's like a tonic to have her sweetness on my tongue again. As we kiss, I push my thigh between her legs, and she immediately starts grinding and rocking her hips, moaning into my mouth.

"Oh god, I want you to fuck me, please Alex," she groans as I palm one of her juicy ass cheeks and lift her leg up around my waist.

"Anything for the birthday girl." I laugh, moving my hand between her legs to test her readiness. There really is no need. My fingers come away soaked, and I suck them into my mouth because there really is no time to eat her out like I'm desperate to. Lana's eyes go wide at my actions, and her breath hitches in her chest.

"Oh wow, you're so naughty," she gasps, quickly wiggling out of her panties while I pull a condom from my wallet and undo my belt and zipper.

"If we had time and privacy, I could show you just how naughty I can be, baby," I reply, rolling the condom onto my throbbing cock, loving the way Lana looks at it and licks her lips. "No time for that, firecracker."

I laugh as Lana pouts, but the pouting doesn't last long when I lift her up and press her against the door, urging her to wrap her legs around my waist so I can notch my cock at her dripping entrance.

"This is gonna be hard, fast, and quiet, so hang on." I push my hips forward, and we both gasp as I sheath myself in her warm pussy. I give her a moment to get used to having me inside her again, then I kiss her gently on the nose and go for it.

Lana's fingers are laced around the back of neck, her thighs clamped around my waist as I pound her against the door, feeling the fucking thing rattle in its frame.

"Change of location, baby," I moan, pulling away from the door, still joined. With my pants bunched around my ankles, we stagger over to the bed where we fall in a heap with Lana on top. Immediately, she begins to ride my cock with vigor, thrusting her hips in time with my flexes, and soon I can feel her pussy clamping down, milking an orgasm out of me. As we both come, she presses her fist into her mouth to mask the desperate moans and sighs that she's making. Watching her come gloriously apart on top of me is almost too much for me to contain, so I turn my head and stuff a handful of her comforter into my mouth to muffle my own cries of pleasure.

"Oh fuck," Lana moans, flopping down on my chest, nuzzling my bearded chin. "That was the best present ever."

"I'll expect a very nice thank you card then." I laugh, stroking loose hair out of her face. "Perhaps a fruit basket of some kind."

Lana laughs huskily and swats at my chest. "Fool."

"I've been gone a while now. I should zip up and get back downstairs with the beer before your mom comes looking for me."

Lana rolls off me and I take care of the condom, quickly washing up in her bathroom and pressing a lingering kiss to her pouty lips.

"I wish you could just stay here with me tonight. It's not fair," Lana says in an adorable sulky voice, sitting cross-legged on her bed, looking much younger than her years.

"I know, baby. But we need to play this smart. I don't want your brother on the rampage just as playoffs are about to begin." I press another kiss to her lips. "We can tell him once the cup run is over. It's not ideal, but I think it's the best play. I'm in this for the long haul. We have time."

As I pull away, I see the change in Lana's expression, going from sulky petulance to a huge happy smile that lights up my fucking heart.

"You want us to date properly, like out in the open?" she asks quietly, chewing on her thumbnail.

Oh fuck, she thinks we're just messing around here. So, I quickly step forward and cup her face in my hands, lifting it so she can see I'm as serious as a fucking heart attack.

"Yes, baby. I want us to date, but we just have to be smart about the timing," I reply, pressing a reassuring kiss to her lips.

I feel like a dick asking Lana to hide our budding relationship from her family and friends, but it's the sensible move which will cause the least disruption. I know what it's like to have teammates distracted during the playoffs—look what happened last season with Cam and Bugs. I'm not blaming our loss on that, but it sure as shit didn't help that our captain was having baby mama drama.

"I'll see you out there." I blow her a kiss, unlock the door, check the coast is clear and slip out of the room and back downstairs, remembering to grab the cases of beer Janice asked for.

19

Lana

Oh my god, sex with Alex just keeps getting better. I flop back on my comforter and press my fingers to my swollen lips, reliving the hot encounter we just had in my bedroom. I know it was risky propositioning him like that, but we've been eye-fucking each other all afternoon, and I couldn't stand it anymore.

There's no way I'd be able to sneak back to the Whalers hotel tonight without someone noticing, so I had to grab my chance when I could.

But even better than to mind-blowing sex was his declaration afterward. I was afraid that Alex just wanted to fool around, but he's made it clear that he wants more—eventually. That's the part that stings a little and takes to shine away. I completely understand his reasoning behind keeping us on the down low during the playoffs. I grew up in a hockey family and get that this is a stressful time and team dynamics are paramount. No one wants to be the guy who causes a rift in the team. However, I still feel shitty sneaking around behind my brother's back.

Snapping out of my contemplation, I sit up and

quickly pull off the rumpled jersey and stuff it back in my suitcase. I dash to the bathroom and clean up, pulling on my underwear and the sundress that I had on earlier so as not to rouse suspicion with a costume change.

When I open the bathroom door, I let out a startled yelp. Zac is sitting on my bed with his arms folded and a serious expression on his face, tapping his chin and looking like he's thinking really hard about something.

"Now, a less observant person wouldn't have noticed the birthday girl disappear into the house just before the sexy goalie is sent on an errand to the kitchen. They also wouldn't have noted the time it took the goalie to return to the party with the beer. It was ten minutes and fifteen seconds in case you're curious."

I stand in the doorway to my bathroom and listen to his smart-ass comments, feeling my cheeks burning hot and praying to god it doesn't smell like Alex and sex in my room.

"So, my question to you is are you or are you not fucking Alex Bergman?" Zac asks, a cocky smirk tilting the corner of his mouth as he tries to keep his serious expression.

"Easy there, counselor." I laugh, grabbing my hoodie off the back of the chair because once the sun sets, the beach can get kind of chilly. "There's nothing going on."

Zac stands up and comes toward me, putting his hands on my arms so that I'm forced to look up at him. "Be very careful, Lana. You've just come out of a relationship that was built around secrets and lies. Do you really wanna get involved with a man whose too chicken shit to stand up to your brother and be with you in the open?"

"Hey, that's not what this is!" I cry, glaring at my friend.

"Ha!" Zac, steps back and points his triumphant finger at me. "I knew you two were fucking!"

I huff out a breath and roll my eyes. "Okay, fine, we are. But we both want it to be more. He just thinks getting the playoffs out of the way first is the best thing. He doesn't want Matt to be a dick about it and mess up the team dynamic."

"Babe, I've gotta say that sounds like he's stalling for time. If he really wanted you, he wouldn't give a shit about that."

"No, it's not like that." But even as I say the words, I hear the truth behind them. If Alex won't fight for us to be together no matter what anyone says, will he ever have my back?

"All I'm saying is be careful. Have all the hot sweaty fun you want with him, but please protect your heart." Zac pulls me into a hug and my high from being with Alex quickly wears off, and I feel unsure all over again.

Being back in Seattle also takes the shine off my birthday glow. It's still raining, and I miss the warmth and sunshine of the Gulf deep in my bones. As I sit at the kitchen counter waiting for my pulled pork to cook, slicing the gherkins for my homemade pickles, I think back to Zac's words and how they dumped a whole bucket of iced water over my feelings for Alex.

After our encounter in my room, we spent the rest

of the party staying a respectful distance from each other. However, it did start to look like we were purposefully avoiding each other which looked even more suspicious. So, every now and again, I would join a group that he was part of, and I tried my best not to look at his strong, thick thighs that felt so good between my legs. And I could tell by the way he kept licking his lips that he could still taste my pussy. It was all too much at one point and I had to retreat to the bathroom to splash water on my face.

But despite all the heat we were generating, Zac's words still played on my mind.

At midnight, Coach Casey called time and started to herd the players onto the bus, all of them hugging and thanking my parents for the party and hospitality. I received cautious hugs from them as well, especially when Matt was nearby. And when it came to saying goodbye to Alex, I felt my heart stutter in my chest and my lips tingle with the need to kiss him. Instead, we exchanged an awkward hug, and when we parted, I noticed Zac rolling his eyes.

Thankfully, Matt and Mila went back to the team hotel on the bus, so once the party was cleared away, I headed straight to bed. I think Zac could sense that I wasn't in the mood to talk, so he went to his room and left me to it. Just as I was about to shut my phone off and get into bed, a message pinged in.

[ALEX: Happy birthday, baby. Can't wait to see you once we get back home. Sleep well xxx A]

I read the message several times, tears stinging my

eyes and confusion swirling around in my head. Why did I have to admit what was happening to Zac so he could put all this doubt in my heart?

With a huff, I turn my phone off and put it on the nightstand. It would have to wait until morning. I couldn't deal with it right now.

And it's been a day since we returned to Seattle, and I still haven't replied. Alex sent one more text to confirm he was home because the team plane left before our commercial flight, but I've ghosted that message too. And to help matters more, Zac has been AWOL with his new hook up since we got back, so I don't even have my best friend to talk to about this whole thing.

The sound of my cell phone ringing makes me jump, and I quickly grab it, thinking it could be Alex. But instead of his number, I see Cam's.

"Hey, Cam."

"Hey Lana, how are you?" she asks quietly. "Sorry for the whispering, but I've just got the baby to sleep, so I thought I'd do some work while I have five seconds."

I laugh quietly as well, even though I'm sure SJ can't hear me. "What can I do for you?"

"I just wanted to catch up with you about your donation to the Whalers Foundation Auction," Cam begins. "I know you left before the auction, but your lot went for a great deal of money, and I wanted to give you the details for the dinner party."

"Oh wow," I gasp, shocked that anyone actually bid on it because I'm basically an unknown chef in Seattle. "Can I ask how much it raised, or is that inappropriate?"

"Hell no! Of course, you should know. Hang on." I hear Cam typing on her keyboard and then she's back.

"The donor bid ten thousand dollars."

My mouth drops open, and I'm sure I've heard her wrong. "Did you say ten thousand dollars?"

Cam laughs again. "That's right. Ten grand. Well done you. You should be getting a thank you card and gift basket from the Foundation because they said no one has ever paid so much for such a low-ticket item. No offense meant, but people usually pay that for a trip to the Caribbean or an all-access VIP experience with the Whalers."

"Well, I can't believe it," I gasp. "Who was the donor?"

"A woman who lives in Denny-Blaine, a very exclusive neighborhood. She's a French fashion designer and wanted a taste of home."

"Jesus, for that much money she could fly back to France for a meal." I laugh, still flabbergasted that anyone would pay that much for a meal cooked by me.

"I know, right!" I hear Cam make a cooing noise. "Oh darn, SJ's awake. Look, I'll email the details to you. She wants to have the dinner party as soon as possible, preferably this weekend if that's at all doable."

"Oh, that should be fine. We have no Gooey Gourmet bookings this weekend, and it gives me time to prepare the menu and buy the groceries." I've already got recipes swirling around in my head.

"Oh, on that note, she's also said she'll reimburse you for all your expenses, so just keep the receipts and present her with an invoice when you arrive."

"This seems too good to be true!"

"Believe it! Okay, I've gotta go. It looks like SJ's had a diaper explosion. Warren! I need a Code Brown clean up kit, STAT!" And with that Cam hangs up, and I'm left wondering how the hell I'm going to pull off this fancy dinner party with only a few days to prepare.

20

Thor

I tap my finger on the screen of my cell phone for what feels like the millionth time and see no notifications and no messages. Nothing from Lana since we got back from Florida. I've sent her two low-key casual messages, but she hasn't replied to either, and I'm starting to get a sinking feeling in my gut. Did I say too much after we had sex in her room? Did I freak her out by saying I wanted us to be more than a casual fuck? I know she's just out of a horrible relationship and perhaps fuck buddies is all she wants, but she's too polite to crush me.

Fuck! I need to speak to her, but I'm trapped here for the next few hours at least.

I flick my eyes back up to the game footage on the big projector screen in our media room and try to concentrate on what Coach Casey is saying about our penalty killing strategies for the start of the playoffs against the L.A. Pumas. We finished above them in the Western Conference, so we have home ice advantage for the first two games and Coach wants us to take full advantage. So that means daily skates, gym work, conditioning, strategy meetings, and working with our specific coaching teams.

After our talk, Coach came good on his promise to improve the goaltending team, and we now have a Canadian Olympic Gold Medal winning goaltender on the books. He's a machine and even though he retired from playing after 2014, he's fit and strong and makes me sweat my ass off after a session on the ice.

I absently tap my phone screen again, and I catch Bugs flicking his eyes over to me.

"Dude, cut that shit out," he hisses. "You're being as subtle as a sledgehammer, and you bet your ass Coach has noticed."

I'm about to reply, but Coach cuts me off.

"Yes, Mr. Parker, I have noticed that Mr. Bergman's attention isn't really in the room," Coach yells, causing several players to suck their breath in. "Hopefully drills with me in full gear before the afternoon skate will refocus him!"

I hear a few sniggers from behind me and realize I've been rumbled. "Yes, Coach," I reply in a slightly sulky voice while some of my teammates kick the back of my chair.

"Thank you. Now, let's continue looking at the penalty kill against L.A., so we at least have half a chance of taking game one of the series." Coach gives me one final shitty look and then turns his attention back to the game footage.

This is exactly the scenario I was hoping to avoid, and I'll have no time between now and afternoon skate to call Lana. After I've eaten a very quick lunch which I'm liable to throw up after Coach is done with me, we'll be skating until late afternoon.

With a huff, I fold my arms over my chest, put the whole situation out of my head, and give the footage my full attention.

"Dude, that was brutal to watch," Nate mumbles as I skate into my goal ready for the scrimmage game, my muscles screaming in protest.

I think Coach decided to make an example of me and kept my drills going for five more minutes so the rest of the team could watch as they came up the tunnel.

I squirt a fountain of water into my mouth and pray I don't hurl it all over my doorstep as my stomach roils.

"Nah, it's fine. No sweat."

Nate laughs and slaps my sweaty jersey. "Plenty of sweat, man."

I flip him off before I put my gloves back on, pull my grill down, and wait for the puck drop.

What follows is the most painful few hours of my hockey playing career, and when Coach finally blows his whistle and yells for us to hit the showers, I collapse onto the blue paint in front of my goal and pull my helmet off, letting it drop to the ice with a heavy clunk.

"Thor, a word." Coach's gravelly voice makes me look up, and I can see he's pissed.

"Yes, Coach." I haul myself to my feet and even though I tower over him in my skates and goalie gear, I still feel like I'm about to be scolded by my Mor for something.

"I don't know what's going on with you, but you

need to lock that shit down," he growls, stabbing his finger into my chest pads. "I will not have you lose focus and get hurt like you did last season. You had a lucky escape there, son."

I'm shocked by his words. I thought I was in for a standard ass whooping for being distracted, but Coach isn't like that. He cares about all of us and only wants us to play at the very top of our game. He's always said the same thing: "Leave your personal shit off the ice and leave your hockey shit on the ice."

It's great advice, so I nod to let him know I understand and decide that I need to see Lana and put a hold on our budding relationship until after the playoffs. Not just because of her brother, but because it's what I need to concentrate on my job. And from her lack of contact, I'd say she won't be too upset about it.

So imagine my surprise when I get to my cubby and turn my phone back on to see a message from Lana asking to meet at my apartment whenever I can.

Shit, I was hoping to have a little more time before I'd have to do this, but I guess ripping the Band-Aid off is sometimes the best option. So, I shoot off a text asking her to drop by any time after five, and I hurry into the shower.

A few hours later, there's a knock on my door and I anxiously pad over to open it. Lana is on my approved visitors list now, so she's allowed to come right up without an announcement. I've decided to dress casual in athletic shorts and a hoodie, my feet bare, so as not to give her the impression this is a date.

And I'm almost relieved when I open the door to see that Lana is dressed in yoga pants, sneakers and a Whalers hoodie, her hair up in a loopy bun. She's wearing no make-up and looks so fresh and young that my heart literally doubles its rate at the sight of her. She steps over the threshold with no words and the smell of vanilla and sugar fills my nostrils, causing them the flare.

With my self-control on a knife edge, I close the door and we stand there facing each other, neither of us wanting to speak first. I can see Lana's chest rising and falling under her hoodie, her cheeks flushed, and her pupils dilated.

Jesus, she looks so beautiful and tempting. How the fuck am I going to do this? Let her down just as we've got things started.

But before I can spiral completely out of control, a force stronger than both of our doubts pulls us together and my hands are in her hair and her lips are on mine. As my tongue seeks hers, she moans into my mouth and I pull the elastic out of her hair, letting the vanilla scented waves fall down her back. I quickly pick her up and carry her into the main room, sitting heavily on the couch so she's straddling me, my hard cock pressed against her hot center.

We continue to ravage each other's mouths while Lana grinds on my lap, my hands finding their way under her thick hoodie where I discover her bare breasts. The animalistic growl that escapes me makes Lana increase the pressure of her hips, and I cup her breasts in my big hands, rolling her hard little nipples between my thumb and forefinger.

When Lana reaches down to slip her fingers into the waistband of my shorts, it's like heaven and hell all at once. There's nothing I want more than to feel her lips around my fat cock, but we need to talk first. If we don't, I'll feel like a complete dirtbag.

So as painful as it is, I take my hands from Lana's warm breasts and hold her wrists to prevent her from pulling down my shorts. I pull my mouth away from hers.

"Babe, we need to talk," I gasp, feeling my dick twitch angrily at my poor timing.

Lana makes a frustrated little noise and slides off my lap, straightening her hoodie and tucking her legs underneath her. I subtly try to adjust my hard-on so it's not so prominent, but short of tucking him into my waistband, I just have to sit in a way that at least partly disguises my arousal.

"Okay, so talk," Lana huffs, her cheeks still pink from our make out session.

"Why haven't you replied to my messages?" I ask a little more aggressively than I mean and her eyes dart over to me, the crease between her eyebrows deepening.

Lana takes a deep breath and lets it out slowly as if she's getting her words straight in her head. "I guess I got a little freaked out. After we had sex and you said all that stuff about waiting until the off-season, Zac said it sounded like you wanted to keep us hidden and didn't want people to know about us." She bites her lower lip and looks away from me.

I try to regulate my expression so as not to show her just how pissed I am.

"Zac doesn't know shit," I grind out. "I told you my reasons for wanting to keep us on the DL. In fact, shit happened today that makes that even more important.

I completely zoned out worrying about why you weren't texting me back and Coach noticed."

"Oh no, did you get into trouble?" she gasps, putting her small hand on my forearm.

"You could say that." I laugh, enjoying the warmth of her palm more than I care to admit. "But my point is, I can't be that distracted when it comes to you and me. I want to enjoy every moment of being with you, not worrying why you haven't texted or returned my call."

"I understand." Lana removes her hand and slides a little farther away from me on the couch.

Shit, she thinks I want to end things.

"No, you don't understand." I close the distance again and cup her face in my hands. "I want to be with you. I really do. But I don't wanna sneak around. I want to date you out in the open, so everyone knows that I have the most incredible, talented, sexy girlfriend in the fucking world. It's just the timing sucks. You deserve my full attention, and I just can't give that to you during the playoffs. So, I propose we put this on hold until they're over."

Lana's blue eyes tear up and her lip trembles, but she continues to firmly hold my gaze, that beautiful determination ever present.

Taking a deep breath, she says, "I agree. Let's keep it in the Friend Zone until after the playoffs and then we can go to Matt together and tell him we're going to date, and he can like or shove it up his ass."

I laugh loudly and then bring my lips down to Lana's. "Please let me be there when you tell him that."

"Sure thing, big man." She puts her hands over mine and gently moves them from her face. "So, friend, now we can't fuck, what are we gonna do with the rest of the evening?"

The relief I feel that she's so cool about this washes over me, and I feel almost light-headed. "I guess you could give me another cooking lesson."

"Okay, we can do that. How about I show you how to roast a chicken? You can make so many dishes with the leftover chicken, like pasta and risotto," Lana replies enthusiastically, her eyes lighting up at the thought of cooking.

"Sounds perfect. Let's walk down to the market, and we can buy everything we'll need." I stand and offer her my hand, which she takes, rising from the couch. "And I promise not to fuck it up in anyway this time."

She laughs and pats my arm. "Don't make promises you can't keep."

This makes me roar with laughter, pulling her into my arms so I can rub my knuckles over her head before she squirms free and shoves me. "I already have one big hockey player who likes to give me noogies." She giggles. "I don't need another one."

21

Lana

I double and triple check the boxes of ingredients and pre-prepared elements as Zac helps me stack them into the back of Matt's Range Rover. I hang my chef's whites on the jacket hook and make sure my knife roll is secured in the locked box I like to keep it in when I travel around with it.

"I'm so sorry I can't be your sous chef tonight," Zac says again for the millionth time since I told him about this gig. He'd already made plans to go to Santa Barbara for some sun with his new boyfriend and their flight leaves this evening.

"It's fine, honey," I reply, patting his arm. "The woman assured me there'll be plenty of wait staff and her own personal chef will be there and is willing to help out if I need it. But with all the prep you've helped me with today, it's just a case of cooking the fresh elements and plating up for ten people. That's a walk in the park."

"And Thor's coming after his game?" Zac asks, side-eyeing me as he loads the last box.

"Yes, he's coming, but only to repay me for the

cooking lessons and to give the donors a little extra for their amazing donation. I told you. We're keeping it friendly until after the playoffs. No need to worry your pretty little head about me." I grip his face with my fingers so his full lips pop out and I plant a firm kiss on them. "Now go and pack for Santa Barbara and make sure this guy treats you well."

"Oh baby, Daddy's gonna treat me so good." Zac waggles his eyebrows and I make a fake gagging noise.

"Get outta here." I shoo him away, close the tailgate of the Rover, and walk around to the driver's door, having to hoist myself up into the high seat. *Doesn't anyone make an SUV for little people?*

As I drive out to the exclusive neighborhood, my excitement builds. I've designed a five course Parisian menu which has been such good fun to design and shop for. I found an adorable French food market and had a blast conversing in French with the elderly owner.

I made sure to design the menu so a lot of the elements can be prepped beforehand, transported to the house, and cooked there. I want to start with an apéritif, a Lavender French 75 cocktail that will refresh everyone's palette. As the guests enjoy their cocktail, I'll serve the Hors d'Oeuvres: fig and goat cheese tartlets with a watercress garnish, followed by duck in a bitter cherry sauce and summer vegetables. For the salad course, I'll serve pea and carrot salad and a fromage platter and chocolate mousse to finish. I feel a little self-conscious about handing over the bill for the food because I've spent more than I would hope to spend on a month's rent, but Cam assured me that they're happy to pay.

And as the GPS says that I've reached my destination, I can see why. The tall wrought-iron gates open, and I drive up to a huge mansion that makes a lot of hockey player's houses look like run-down shacks.

Shit, if I wasn't intimidated before, I sure am now. I carefully slide out of the seat and wonder if I should use the back door as technically I'm here to cook and not a guest. As I stand by the car feeling like an idiot, the front door opens, and a very glamorous woman beckons for me to approach.

"Darling, are you Lana?" she asks in a husky French accent, the smell of cigarettes and Chanel No.5 surrounding her.

"Yes, I'm Lana Landon, your chef for the evening. Is there somewhere I can unload the food without walking through your beautiful foyer?" As I stand on the doorstep, I've already spied the huge crystal chandelier and sweeping double staircase.

"Of course, darling. Raymond will move your car round to the kitchen door at the back and unload for you." She clicks her bejeweled fingers and a man I assume to be Raymond appears out of nowhere and holds his hand out for my keys, which I hand over before I'm pulled over the threshold by the woman.

"My name is Cherie, and I'm so excited to eat a good French meal." She kisses the tips of her fingers and guides me into the huge caterer's style kitchen. I thought Matt's kitchen was my dream, but this place is better than anything I've ever seen.

"Well, I'm excited to cook for you," I reply, accepting a glass of champagne from Cherie who then perches elegantly on a high stool. It's hard to judge her age because she has flawless skin and perfect makeup; however, I'd guess she's in her mid-fifties but looks much younger.

"I was intrigued by your menu when you sent it over; it's like you knew all my favorite things." She reaches over and lights a thin French cigarette, and I move slightly away as she blows a plume of smoke in my direction. "My son was also thrilled by the food. He'll be joining us later." Cherie stubs out her barely smoked cigarette and picks up the ashtray and her champagne.

"Thank you so much. I'm really looking forward to hearing what you and your guests think."

Cherie waves her hand at me absently. "It'll be beautiful, darling. Raymond will show you where anything is and he's available if you need another pair of hands in the kitchen."

At that moment, Raymond enters the kitchen through a door at the back and places several of my boxes on the counter.

"Thank you. I'll be ready to serve the apéritif at eight if that works for your guests," I state, walking over to the boxes to check which ones need moving to the fridge.

"Perfection, darling," Cherie replies. "And I'm sure my son will drop by and see you once he arrives."

With that, she leaves me alone with Raymond, who formally introduces himself as Cherie's personal chef and shows me round his fabulous kitchen. He's very kind and shows me how to work all the fancy gadgets and quickly finds the equipment that I need. Once I'm all set, I put on my chef's jacket and apron, pull my hair up into a tight bun, and wash my hands.

"Would Cherie mind if I put the Whalers game on in the background while I cook?" I ask Raymond as I begin to unpack the tartlets and set them out on baking sheets. "My brother plays for them, and it's the first game of the playoffs." I feel a bit cheeky for asking, but I really don't want to miss this game.

Raymond smirks and reaches for the remote, aiming it at the TV mounted high in a corner, the pregame show flashing up on the screen.

"I'm so glad you said that. I thought I'd have to sneak out to my car to check the score." He laughs. "Wow, so your brother is Matt Landon. Awesome."

"Well, if you think my brother is awesome, you'll love the extra surprise I've arranged for dessert," I reply, tapping the side of my nose, happy that at least one person here will be thrilled to see Alex when he shows up after the game.

"Oh, I'm intrigued." Raymond laughs but turns his attention back to the pregame show and I carry on prepping my tartlets.

The rest of the work is easy, and while the tarts cook, I mix the cocktail into tall cut crystal jugs, adding my homemade lavender syrup to flavor it. I manage to get the jugs into the fridge just as Matt takes the puck drop to start the game, so I join Raymond to watch the first ten minutes which is when the tarts will need to come out of the oven, and I can leave them to get to room temperature.

The Whalers come out strong and have several shots on goal before Ford finally finds the back of the net and Raymond and I leap up and hug each other, trying to keep our cheering to a minimum so as not to disturb the guests.

But as we settle back onto our stools, I wonder if any guests have actually arrived yet. I've not heard a doorbell ring or doors opening and closing. But then again, this is a huge mansion and we had to walk through several areas before making it to the kitchen at the back of the house. I push that thought away and look at the timer to see I have two more minutes until the tarts are ready, so I get the cooling racks out and begin to mix the dressing for the garnish.

Just as Alex performs a body bending save and deflects the Pumas' first real shot on goal, Cherie comes back into the kitchen and Raymond quickly shuts the TV off.

"Raymond, I'm out of cigarettes. Would you be a darling and go pick me up some more?" she says, sipping from her champagne flute.

"Of course, Madame," Raymond replies, grabbing his keys from the bowl on the counter.

"Merci," Cherie gushes, sweeping out of the room again.

As I remove the tarts from the oven, I hear Raymond mumbling to himself.

"Everything okay?" I ask, settling the tart cases on the cooling racks.

"Yeah, it's just my luck is all. The only place that stocks her cigarettes is a fifty-mile round trip. At least I can listen to the game in the car I suppose." Raymond looks at me a little sheepishly and adds, "If I miss your surprise, and it happens to be a Whalers player, could you get them to sign something for me?"

I laugh kindly. "I'll do one better. I'm sure I can score you some tickets and a signed jersey if you want."

Raymond pulls me into an awkward hug. "Thank you. I'll be as quick as I can. Good luck." And with that he disappears out the back door and I'm left alone in this huge kitchen. I just hope to god I can find anything I might need that Raymond hasn't already shown me.

Since Raymond left, I've had an uneasy feeling that something isn't quite right.

I can't put my finger on what it is, but this house is too big and too quiet to have ten or more people having a party. I hear no music, no voices, no one has been into the kitchen to get ice from the freezer, and I haven't seen any of the wait staff I was promised would be here to help.

As ridiculous as it sounds, Alex's warning about serial killers flickers through my brain more than once. So, I keep busy and reprimand myself for being a stupid scaredy cat, reminding myself that rich people can be weird, but that doesn't mean they're dangerous.

After quickly checking my phone to see that the Whalers are still leading by one goal to zero, I slide it into my purse and concentrate on plating up the Hors d'Oeuvres. As I move from plate to plate, adding a perfectly baked tart, a sprinkling of watercress and a drizzle of lemon verbena dressing, I'm completely lost in my task.

Once the plates look perfect, I pick up the first two

and turn around to place them on the island ready for the wait staff who are still yet to appear.

But as I turn, both plates drop from my grip and fall to the floor, smashing into thousands of pieces. My hands fly to my mouth, and I try to hold in the scream that so desperately wants to break free.

Before me stands the tall, lean figure of Etienne, dressed impeccably in his effortlessly stylish European designer clothes.

He can't be here. How is he here? What the hell is going on?

22

Lana

"**M**y darling Lana," Etienne says in the smooth voice which I once loved but now just sends a creepy shiver down my spine. "At last, I've found you."

I swallow the dry lump in my throat and dart my eyes around, looking for possible escape routes. At least in his apartment I know where to stand and where not to so that I could make a quick exit or get to the bathroom where I could lock myself in until he calmed down.

"What are you doing here?" I finally manage to say, trying to keep the quiver out of my voice. As subtly as I can, I pat my pants pocket searching for my phone, but then I remember I put it in my purse which is in the small mudroom by the back door.

Shit!

"Well, who do you think bid ten thousand dollars to secure an evening with you?" he replies with a smirk on his face. Money was never an issue for Etienne and dropping ten grand to see me is a minor inconvenience for him. His frivolous attitude to money was just another thing I grew to hate about him.

"But how? Why are you in America? How do you know Cherie?" I ask, so confused by the whole thing.

"Why darling, if you ever attended one of my parties in Paris, you would know that Etienne is my precious son," Cherie says as she enters the room and stands next to him. The sickening resemblance becomes blatantly clear now they're side by side, the aristocrat nose and cheekbones, the cold brown eyes and sandy hair. She places her hand on Etienne's shoulder and kisses his cheek, leaving a smear of red lipstick. "I saw how hurt he was by your deception in Paris, so when we realized you had run back to America, we put things in place so he could win you back."

Finally, I find my voice and my Landon spirit.

"Win me back?" I cry, moving so the kitchen island is between us. "I'm not his to win back. I don't suppose your precious son told you how he used to treat me?"

Cherie smiles and it's cold and reptilian. "Etienne told me that he had to issue corrections for your behavior which is a man's job. If you didn't make mistakes, he would never have to correct you."

Is she fucking serious? This woman is as crazy as her son, and I need to get out of this situation as soon as possible.

"Look, you've obviously brought me here under false pretenses, so I'll leave all the food for your guests, and I'm sure Raymond can plate it up when he gets back." I pull my apron off and stomp toward the back door. "I'm outta here."

I've barely made it three paces before Etienne is on me, his fingers gripping my biceps so hard I know from bitter experience that I'll have blue bruises there in the morning. But just his hands on me and the smell of his expensive French cologne fill me with panic, and I feel the walls closing in on me. My vision begins to blur, and I fight to catch my breath.

Breathe, goddamn it. Breathe!

But I can't take a deep breath and I feel my body become slack and pliable enough for Etienne to scoop me up into his arms and kiss my lips, which feel slimy and disgusting against my own.

"Ah, *mon petit amour,* we are together again," he whispers as he cradles me in his arms, my body frozen with fear.

"Shall we move to the salon so we can make arrangements for our return to Paris?" I hear Cherie say, sounding distant to my petrified ears. "I'm so tired of America."

"Of course, Mama," Etienne replies, and I feel him begin to move into another room. "We may have a problem getting her passport from that brute of a brother, though."

"There are ways around passports, my darling," Cherie replies. "I just want my baby to have everything he wants. And if that's her, then that's what you shall have."

Oh Jesus, are they really talking about taking me back to Paris against my will? Who even are these people?

As if the threat of being taken back to Paris is what I need to hear, I manage to control my panic enough to take a shaky breath, taking in enough oxygen so the walls move away, and my vision slowly clears.

I know from experience that Etienne is strong and quick, even when he's wasted. Unfortunately, he seems sober at the moment, so I don't even have that slight advantage. There's no point struggling while he's got his hands on me. I need to wait until he puts me down before I make my move. So, I continue to lay limp in his arms until he puts me down on a couch and moves away to talk to his mom.

They begin to converse in French, which is fine as I speak it fluently, but I'm not concentrating on what they're saying. I'm waiting for a moment when they're not looking over at me and I can make a dash for the kitchen and the back door. I know exactly where my purse is, which contains my phone and keys. Thankfully, Matt has the fancy kind of car with keyless entry and a push button start so there should be no fumbling around with the keys once I make it out there.

But at the moment I can see through my half-closed eyes that Etienne is watching me like a hawk, even as he talks to his mother about essentially kidnapping me. I know he's a dickwad; however, I never thought for a second that he'd stoop to this depth of crazy to have me. I can hear them talking about taking me to Matt's house before the game ends so they can collect my passport and some clothes, making it look like I've decided to return to Paris of my own accord. I would hope that none of my friends or family would believe that to be true, but I know how sneaky and manipulative Etienne can be.

As I continue to play possum and wait for my moment to make a run for it, I notice Etienne's hands are trembling. I know the signs that he's in need of a drink, so when he makes a move toward the bar which is at the far side of the room, I take my chance. Before

I can second guess myself, I let my flight instinct take over and haul up off the couch, desperately ignoring the way my head swims from panic. I don't even look back over my shoulder to see if they've noticed my move to escape. I just run through the living area toward the kitchen and the back door.

My ears are ringing with the blood pounding through my head, but it doesn't drown out the pained roar I hear as Etienne sees me running. All I can think about is getting out of this house with my purse. We're in the middle of nowhere and the only other property I noticed as I drove here was much farther down the street. I suppose if I had to, I could run there for help, but I'd rather get to my car and drive the fuck out of this nightmare.

As I reach the kitchen, I skid round the corner, my ballet flats sliding on the polished marble floor, and I almost wipe out in a heap. However, I must have inherited at least some of my brother's good coordination because I manage to stay upright and make it just four strides from the back door.

However, even as freedom is within touching distance, I feel a sharp pull on my ponytail, and I'm stopped so abruptly that my feet fly out in front of me, and I land on my butt on the marble floor. My breath whooshes out of me, and pain shoots up my back from the hard landing. Before I can catch my breath or make a move to continue my escape, Etienne sits astride my body, his hand still wrapped painfully around my ponytail.

"Not so fast, my love," he sneers, spittle splashing over my face. His expression is twisted and ugly. This is his true face, the one he keeps hidden from polite Parisian society and only lets me see. It's terrifying, and I feel myself shrinking back from it.

"Please, Etienne," I beg in a quiet, shaky voice. "Please just let me leave. I won't tell anyone what happened."

He laughs and shakes his head, his eyes flashing dangerously. "Of course, you won't tell anyone. I've learned my lesson from this, my love. When we return to Paris, there will be no need for you to work. I've decided to give up the restaurant and move out to the chateau permanently. We'll have all the space and privacy we need, and there will be no outside distractions like jobs and friends. We can be alone together, and it will be perfect."

Oh my god, he's actually out of his mind. He's essentially talking about keeping me prisoner.

I have to play this right. I know I can't overpower him or outrun him, so I need to be smarter than him. And one thing I know about Etienne, is when he's jonesing for a drink, he loses a lot of his focus.

So as difficult as it is for me to do, I relax my body under his and plaster a smile on my face. Even as I do this, his grip on my hair loosens, and he rises up on his knees so some of his weight eases off me.

"I'm sorry I tried to run," I whisper, placing my hand on his forearm, my skin crawling at the contact. "I know you're just trying to do what's best, and I'm being stubborn. Living at the chateau was always our dream and that sounds perfect."

Slowly, his eyes clear a little and his smile returns to normal. "Doesn't it, my love? We can make wine and cook, make love, and have children. What a perfect life we can have together."

The thought of all that actually makes bile rise in my throat, but I swallow it down and nod, which appeases him enough to completely let go of my hair and help me to my feet. My back hurts like a bastard, and adrenaline courses through my system, making me feel shaky and sick, but I walk as steadily as I can back into the living room. Cherie is sitting at the bar, smoking her stinky cigarettes, drinking a glass of brown liquor, and as we enter, she smirks. It's infuriating that this woman is standing by while her son abuses me, and in fact, she's enabling him. If I get out of this, she's going to be on the receiving end of one hell of a bitch slap.

As we get to the couch, Etienne roughly pushes me down, sitting next to me with his arm slung over my shoulder. It's not a gesture of affection as it once would have been; he's merely making sure I don't run again.

"Mama, please bring a large cognac," he says, twisting his fingers in the loose hairs at the nape of my neck, making my skin crawl. "It's been a trying time and I need to steady my nerves."

"Of course." Cherie fixes Etienne a drink, and I try to zone out his voice as he continues to wax lyrical about our future together. It's sickening and delusional, but I can tell by his tone that he completely believes it's a possibility. I almost feel sorry for him. Almost. Mostly I feel disgusted that he thinks he can hold me here against my will and force this life on me.

My hope is that I can stall things long enough for either Raymond to return from his errand, or for Etienne to get sloppy drunk enough that I can make another break for it. The important thing is to not let them take me out of this house until either of those things can happen. I'm not even thinking about the fact that Alex is due to come here because that won't happen for hours yet.

I have to get out of this myself. I've got no time to wait for him to come and save me. I saved myself once, I can sure as hell do it again.

Thor

I can't put my finger on it, but I've had an uneasy feeling in my gut, and I just can't shake it off.

I sit in my cubby during the second intermission, drinking the electrolytes my coach has just handed me, listening to Coach discuss our play for the last period. After our early goal, the Pumas kind of fell apart, and we scored twice more in the second period.

"So, as much as it pains me to do this, I'm gonna bench Thor for the last period and send Dexter into goal."

My head snaps up and I see everyone in the locker room looking at me. "Huh?" I ask dumbly.

"Thor, I'm sending Dexter out for the last period," Coach repeats and his words finally sink in. "You've played an amazing game, but these playoffs are a marathon, not a sprint, and I want to rest you whenever I have the chance. Dexter has come in leaps and bounds, and I want to make sure he gets plenty of ice time."

Even though his words sting, I completely understand why he's doing it. So, to show my pride isn't dented, I rise up off the bench and clump over to

Dexter to give him a fist bump and some insight into the Pumas game. Poor kid looks like he's about to shit himself, but once we've talked, he stands up and pulls his grill over his face.

"Thanks, man," he croaks.

"Just go out there and play like I know you can." I slap him on the back. "And don't fuck up my shutout!"

He laughs nervously as he follows the rest of the team down the tunnel for the last period.

"Want me out there, Coach?" I ask as he walks past me.

"No, you can start cooling down on the bike and then hit the shower." He looks back at me. "Great first game, Alex."

"Thanks, Coach." I try to keep the disappointment out of my voice, but I don't let it show on my face. This is all part of the game. Sometimes you have to give up your spot for the good of the team. Dexter is an amazing goalie, and my career is definitely in its twilight years. It's only sensible for Coach to give him more ice time, especially when we have a three goal lead.

So, I start taking off my heavy gear and change into athletic shorts and a hoodie so I can put some time in on the bike and cool down my muscles. I continue to take on electrolytes to replenish all the salts and fluids I lost during the game. I can shed up to ten pounds in one game, and that's just water weight, so I have to be careful not to get too dehydrated.

As I pedal, I watch the rest of the game on the TV in the exercise room. Damn, the team is pushing the Pumas to the very edge, and Dexter has made a couple of solid saves when they've managed to get through our defensive line. Good for him. I feel a swell of pride in my chest for the young goalie. He came up from the farm team this year, and he's definitely proving himself.

Once I'm done on the bike, I do some stretches on the mat, then strip down in my cubby so I can hit the shower before the last five minutes of the game. This is actually working out perfectly because it means I can get to Lana's dinner party sooner than I hoped. I check my cell and see a message from her just before the game started wishing me luck, so I quickly fire one back to her saying I'll be there a bit earlier than planned and then throw my phone in my cubby and hit the shower.

As I soap my chest and rinse shampoo through my hair, excitement swirls in my belly at the prospect of seeing Lana tonight. Since we both agreed to keep it friendly until the end of the playoffs, I've still felt the same thrill whenever I see her. But somewhere under the excitement is that same niggling feeling I can't quite shake. I've put it down to nerves about the game tonight, but seeing as we're set to win it by a comfortable margin, surely that can't be it.

I try to put the unease out of my mind as I dry off and watch the dying minutes of the game on the TV, watching my teammates running the clock down with a series of passes and plays, trying to get a final goal in the Pumas' empty net.

But as the buzzer sounds to signal the end of the game and the whole arena starts to thrum with the sound of the fans going crazy, I can't keep the smile from my face. This is the best feeling in the world, and I quickly dress in my suit so I can congratulate my brothers as they stomp into the locker room, loud and drunk on victory. I make a beeline for Dexter to offer my thanks for maintaining the shutout, and the kid looks like he's on top of the world. I want him to have the glory of this victory at the after party, so I go to Coach Casey's office and knock on the door.

"Come!" he barks, and I open the door.

"Coach, great play putting Dexter in goal. The kid had a hell of a game," I begin, making sure he knows there are no hard feelings about him pulling me from the game.

"He sure did." Coach looks up from his laptop and raises an eyebrow. "I'm sure you didn't come in here to blow smoke up my ass, Bergman. What can I do for you?"

"I was hoping to get to the dinner party that Lana Landon is cooking for, so I was wondering if I could head out now? Might be good for Dexter to meet the press tonight, give the kid some experience, and let him take the win."

Coach fixes me with his green eyes, and I can see the smirk trying to break out on his lips. "So, you wanna head off early so Dexter can get media experience, huh?" He narrows his eyes at me and now the grin is firmly in place. "Got nothing to do with the little sister of your teammate then?"

I start to splutter and protest against his accusation, but he just waves his hand at me and goes back to typing on his laptop. "Get outta here, Thor."

"Thanks, Coach!" I close his office door and try to forget about the fact that this guy seems to know everything. How the hell does he do that?

But at that moment, I don't really care. I push my way through the locker room and grab my duffel from my cubby, say a few quick goodbyes, and head out to my car, excitement rising in my gut at the thought of seeing Lana.

23

Lana

I've been watching Etienne get slowly drunk, and I can almost time it to the minute when he goes from controlled to sloppy. Cherie has been upstairs putting the finishing touches to her packing.

I know I'm on borrowed time.

I've listened carefully to their conversations, some in English, but most in French, and I know they're going to wait for Raymond to return with the car and then send him on his way before he can come back into the house and see what's going on. I figure that moment could be the one to make my move; it's obvious from the way they've been talking that Raymond has no idea what's going on. So, if I can scream or make some sort of commotion to get his attention, I could make an escape.

In the meantime, I have to sit here while Etienne pounds glass after glass of cognac and slobbers all over me. It's disgusting and I do my best not to shudder every time he strokes my arm or tries to kiss my cheek. Instead, I keep my panic under control and make sure I'm ready to move when my time comes, subtly stretching my legs to keep the blood flowing, so my feet don't go numb.

"We'll be so happy, my love," Etienne slurs into my ear, and I can't help the snorting dismissive noise I make.

Suddenly, he grabs my face and turns it toward him. "Oh, you don't think so?"

Shit, the last thing I want to do is poke the beast, so I think quickly, taking his face in my hands. The feel of his clammy skin under my fingers is repellent, but I hold in my disgust and look into his watery brown eyes.

"I'm sorry, baby," I coo. "I'm just nervous. That's all. We've waited so long for this. I don't want to mess it up again."

Ugh, it feels so wrong, saying these words to him and by the unfocused look he gives me, I don't think I'm being very convincing.

"You always were a lying little bitch!" he spits, shoving my face away. "You think I'm stupid? I can see you're just playing along. This is why I came here to collect you."

"Collect me?" I cry, finally losing the cool composure I've worked so hard to maintain through this whole experience. "I'm not your fucking property, Etienne."

"You are!" He grabs the tops of my arms again, pressing the already bruised skin, making me wince. "I tried to make you worthy of being with me, but you just prove again and again what an uncultured American slut you are." He shakes me so hard, my head snaps back and my teeth rattle in my jaw.

"Etienne! Stop! You're hurting me!" I beg, but the distant look has already cloaked his features and I watch in paralyzed horror as his hand draws back and the slap cracks against my cheekbone, whipping my head back again.

"You think I like correcting you?" he yells in my face, shaking me again. "Why won't you learn?"

That's it. I'm fucking done with this shit.

"Because what you're trying to teach me is bullshit!" I scream back, lunging at him, shoving him in the chest with all my might.

My sudden movement catches him unawares, and he topples off the couch onto the floor in a drunken heap. I'm almost too shocked to move, both of us staring at each other, unsure of what to do next. But that only lasts a second because as quickly as I can manage, I fly off the couch and make a run for the kitchen. However, Etienne is still too quick for me, and he grabs my ankle from his position on the floor, and I fall on my front onto the rug.

I frantically start kicking to release his grip, and when I feel my shoe connect with something that makes Etienne grunt in pain, I lurch to my feet and start running again. I weave around the furniture and make it back into the kitchen, my food congealing on the plates where it's been left untouched.

I dare not look back to see if he's following me, but when I reach the back door and grab the handle, I realize to my horror that it's been locked, probably by Cherie after my first attempt to escape.

"Too bad, my love. I have the keys," Etienne crows from behind me, jingling what I assume are the keys. "And the front door is also locked."

I whirl around, keeping my back to the door and see Etienne stuffing the keys in his pants pocket. He approaches me slowly, like I'm a wild animal that needs taming. And in that moment, I realize that's what I am to him. He needs to dominate and control me to make himself feel like a man and that's just pathetic.

As this thought lights up my brain, I can't help but release a hysterical giggle. Etienne isn't even a man, so why the hell should I be scared of him? I've seen the way a real man behaves: my dad, Matt, Zac, Alex. I have all these wonderful, strong, kind, thoughtful men in my life, and I allowed myself to be taken in by this pitiful asshole.

My laughter becomes louder and more maniacal the more I think about it, and the confused look on Etienne's face just spurs me on, blood from his injured nose dripping down his chin onto his expensive shirt. He looks ridiculous.

"What the fuck is so funny?" he growls, stopping his advance a few paces from me.

"I've just realized what a pathetic loser you really are," I gasp through my laughter. I know it's a risky move to provoke him by laughing in his face, but I really don't care anymore. He will not control me for one more minute. I'm prepared to fight him tooth and nail because there's no way in hell I'm going anywhere with him or his crazy mother.

It takes him a moment to register what I've said, and with a roar, he lunges at me, grabbing my arms and shoving me away from the door. My hip hits the edge of the kitchen island and I land heavily on the floor, quickly scrabbling to my feet as he stalks toward me. Before I can completely rise, Etienne grabs my hair and lands another head-rocking slap to my face, splitting my lip so blood floods my mouth. I grunt and fall back against the counter, using it to hold myself up.

And that's when I spot the heavy based saucepan I'd got ready to heat the cherry sauce. It's within arm's reach, so before Etienne can advance again, I shoot my arm out and grab the handle. With a swinging arch, I bring the heavy pan around and scream as it connects with the side of his head with a satisfying clunking noise, cherry sauce spraying everywhere. His head snaps to the side, and I see his eyes roll back in head as he falls to the floor like a tree, lying still.

Without hesitation, I fall to my knees and shove my hand in his pocket to retrieve the keys, pulling them free just as Cherie comes into the room.

"*Mon bébé!*" she cries, rushing over to an unconscious Etienne as he lays prone on the kitchen floor, blood seeping from the wound on the side of his head, mixing with the cherry sauce.

"I suggest you get your baby to a therapist, Madame," I spit out, quickly trying the keys in the lock until one fits and turns. "Once he wakes up, obviously."

With that, I rip the door open and rush into the mudroom where my purse is thankfully where I left it. The outer door is still open, and as I leave, I'm drenched with rain, soaking through my chef's jacket and chilling my skin. I frantically look around and see that my car is parked across the driveway, in front of the double garage.

Just twenty strides to freedom.

Holding my purse over my head to try and keep the rain out of my eyes, one of which is beginning to swell shut, I dash across the slick gravel, trying to keep my balance. I slam into the side of the Range Rover and grab the handle to open the door just as the driveway is flooded with headlights.

Oh shit!

Thor

I follow the GPS toward the house where Lana is cooking for the dinner party, and I can't help but peer at the expensive mansions through the rain. It's a nice neighborhood, one I haven't been to before in all my years living in Seattle. But as I pass large houses with lush gardens and elegant gates, I can't help but fantasize about living somewhere like this one day, perhaps with Lana. Making a home with her, having our children here, building a life we can be proud of.

Jesus, I never thought the fantasy of a house, wife, and children could give me a hard-on, but when it comes to Lana, everything about life with her makes me stiff as a board.

Chuckling to myself at how much I've changed since that little firecracker came into my life, I indicate and turn my car into the driveway of the house. The gates open automatically as I pull up to them and my tires crunch along the gravel driveway, my headlights flooding the area.

What the fuck?

I peer through the windshield as the wipers sweep the rain away and squint my eyes to check if what I think I'm seeing is actually there.

The tiny, rain-soaked figure runs wildly from the side of the house toward Matt's Range Rover, slamming into the side and frantically grabbing at the slippery door handle. Instinctively, I put my foot down on the gas and shoot across the drive, pulling up just short of crashing into the Rover. Panic clutching at my throat, I fling my door open and charge over to Lana who's still trying to get her door open. I reach out to turn her around, and she begins to scream, spinning around so her palm connects with my face with a wet crack.

"GET AWAY FROM ME!" she screams, her eyes blindly blinking the rain away.

The slap was hard, but it barely rocks my head. "Baby, it's me. Alex," I reply, my voice loud over the rain. "What the fuck is going on?"

It's then I see her bloody lip and swollen cheek, the look of absolute panic in her eyes.

My blood reaches boiling point in a matter of seconds at the thought of anyone putting their hands on my woman.

"Lana, what happened?" I gently hold her shoulders. Seeing her wince at my touch makes me even madder, but she finally lets her eyes focus on mine, and she visibly relaxes under my hands. "Baby, tell me."

She takes in a huge shuddery breath and says the word that chills me to the core.

"Etienne." Her shaky hand rises and points toward the house, her split lips trembling uncontrollably as she bursts into sobbing tears, falling into my arms.

"Motherfucker!" I growl, holding onto Lana as tightly as I dare, desperately trying to stop myself from rushing into that house and tearing him into small, unidentifiable pieces.

"Please, let's just go," she begs into my chest.

"But he's in there. Why the fuck is he in there?" I ask, completely confused as to what's going on.

"He arranged for the donation, to get me here," she sobs. "He and his crazy mom were gonna take me back to France."

What I'm hearing is completely unbelievable. *Who the fuck tries to kidnap their ex-girlfriend against her will?* This fucking asshole needs the whooping of a lifetime. I start to pull away from Lana, but she grabs the back of my soaked shirt and holds on for dear life.

"I hit him with a pan," she sniffles.

I can't help the choked laugh that bursts out of my mouth. I gently hold Lana away from me and look at her swollen, bruised face but also the determined set of her chin. There's my firecracker.

"You hit him?" I ask, a little taken back but not particularly surprised.

"Yes," Lana replies. "He's on the kitchen floor."

"Go get in my car and lock yourself in," I state through gritted teeth. I need to see this asshole for myself and then I fully intend to call the cops and get him arrested.

"But…" she protests.

"No buts. Go lock yourself in the car and call your brother." I press my keys into her hand and gently usher her away. "I need to have a word with this dickwad."

"No, please Alex." She clings to my arms. "Don't hurt him. You'll get into trouble."

I laugh loudly. "Baby, I think you've taken care of kicking his ass. I just wanna make sure he doesn't get away before the cops arrive. Now go to the car, please." I lean down and press a kiss to her forehead, and she finally runs over to my car. When I'm satisfied she's locked inside, I stalk toward the rear of the house and find the back door wide open, the sobs of a woman coming from inside.

I've got no idea what I'm going to find when I enter the house, and at first, I'm shocked to see the pristine kitchen covered in splatters of blood. I feel the panic begin to rise in my chest—perhaps Lana actually killed the guy. But on closer inspection, I see lumps of cherries in the red stains and realize it's some kind of sauce.

Thank fuck for that.

I see a middle-aged woman sitting on the marble floor, holding a man's head in her lap. Blood is seeping from a wound on the side of his head and his nose, but his eyes are opening and closing drunkenly so I know he's not dead. Shame.

"Oh thank god!" the woman screams in a heavy French accent. "We were attacked by the chef who came here to cook for us. She went insane when my son said he didn't like the food and hit him with a pan!"

I stare at her for a moment and then shake my head, pulling my cell phone from my pants pocket. I can't believe she's even trying to say this is all Lana's fault.

"Yes, call the police," the woman gasps. "She might still be on the property."

I nod to make her think I'm calling the cops on her behalf and dial 911, grabbing a towel from the counter, throwing it at the woman so she can hold it to the wound on Etienne's head. I don't know why I'm doing anything to help these two, but I want him to serve out every second of the jail time I'm going to push for, so I don't want him to bleed out on this kitchen floor.

When the call connects, I say "Hello, this is Alex Bergman. I'm at 901 Cedar Drive, and I need police and an ambulance. There's a man here with a head injury which he sustained while trying to kidnap my girlfriend."

As my words sink in, I see the woman's face change from pathetic helplessness to seething fury, her red lips peeling back to bare her teeth to me.

Keeping a close eye on the pair of them, I continue to give as much information as I can to the 911 dispatch handler, and she reassures me the police are on their way.

When I hang up, I take up a position leaning against the counter, my arms folded across my chest, making it clear to the pair of them that they shouldn't move and that I'm not in the mood to talk.

Thankfully neither of them tries to engage me in conversation, so I quickly call Lana on her cell phone to check she's okay and to tell her to show the cops where to go when they arrive.

"Did you call Matt?" I ask.

"Yes," she replies in a shaky voice. "He's really mad, but he's on his way."

"Okay baby. Put the heater on and get warm. There's a duffel in the back seat and there should be a clean hoodie in there," I instruct, not wanting her to get cold and go into shock. "Make sure the paramedics check you out first when they arrive. This shit stain can wait his turn." I glare over at Etienne, who is now sitting up, drinking brown liquor from a crystal brandy glass, held to his lips by his mother.

What a fucking pair of whack jobs!

24

Thor

Everything happens really quickly after what feels like hours of waiting. The wail of the sirens and blue flashing lights, police bursting through the front door with their guns raised. I put my hands up and identify myself, indicating that they'll find the kidnappers in the kitchen. Once I know the police are dealing with Etienne and his mom, I run out into the night to find Lana sitting in the back of the ambulance, one of the paramedics dealing with her cut lip. The other rushes past me into the house, and I almost tell her not to bother.

"Baby, are you okay?" I ask once I get to Lana. She looks tiny sitting on the steps of the ambulance, swamped in my hoodie.

"I'm fine," she replies, wincing as the medic dabs her cut lip.

"She has a few abrasions, a cut lip and a suspected fractured eye socket, along with lots of bruising," the medic tells me. "She's being a trooper, but I will insist on taking her to the hospital to get an X-ray on her cheek."

Lana growls in disagreement; however, she doesn't fight it. From the look of her, all the fight has finally drained away. She looks wrecked but definitely not defeated.

My little firecracker.

While she's being cleaned up by the medic, a cop comes out to take her statement and tell us that Etienne has held his hands up to the accusations. At least the asshole has the decency to do that.

I feel Lana tense next to me as Etienne and his mom are led to the police cruisers in handcuffs, so I gently pull her into my arms and stroke her damp hair. She curses softly under her breath, and I realize I'm holding her a little too tightly, so I loosen up my arms and she snuggles into me.

"We'd appreciate you coming down to the precinct tomorrow just to make sure we have all the information, Miss Landon," the cop says. "Here's my card if you think of anything else."

"Thank you," Lana replies, taking the card in her shaky hands.

The police begin to leave, and the medics start loading Lana into the back of the ambulance just as I hear the roar of Matt's Mustang.

"Lana!" he shouts, leaping out of his car, closely followed by Mila, both of them sprinting across the gravel. "What the hell is going on? Why are the police here?"

"I'm fine," Lana replies, looking tired and drained all of a sudden. I don't want her to go through what happened tonight with yet another person, but I know better than to get in between the siblings.

"You don't look fucking fine!" Matt yells. "What

happened to your face?" He quickly glares at me, and he'd better not be insinuating that it has anything to do with me.

"I told you all this on the phone," she says in a quiet voice. "Etienne and his mom are with the police. Everything is okay now. But I have to go to the hospital so could you yell at me there."

As if her words hit him right in the feels, Matt's face falls to pieces, and he pulls his sister into a fierce hug.

"I don't know what I'd do if I lost you, Squirt," he says into her hair, a tear slipping down his scruffy cheek.

When Matt finally releases her, he swipes at his cheek and allows Mila in for a hug, taking that moment to gesture for me to follow him round the side of the ambulance.

"What the fuck, man?" he growls. "Why are you here with my sister?"

"I was coming to help with her charity dinner," I reply, flustered by the question. "It's part of the deal— they get their dessert served by a Whalers player. Good job I came when I did."

"Yeah, okay," Matt says, looking at me suspiciously. "Thanks for calling the cops and making sure those scumbags didn't get away."

"No problem, man." I slap his arm and we return to the back of the ambulance where Lana is being strapped onto the gurney ready to be taken to hospital. She insists she'll be fine and that we can meet her there, so Mila drives the Rover and Matt and I take our respective cars, all of us following the ambulance in convoy.

Thankfully, the Emergency Room is quiet, and

Lana is seen almost immediately, being taken to X-ray to check her eye socket which is getting blacker every time I look at it. While she's gone, Matt, Mila, and I pace the waiting room, drinking bad coffee and not talking. It's awkward as fuck because I just want to let all my emotions flood out—the fear of losing her, the relief of having her my arms again, and the guilt about hiding our blossoming relationship from her brother.

After an hour of hell, Lana is pushed into the waiting room in a wheelchair by a nurse, who hands over her pain meds and instructions to ice her eye regularly. She confirms there is a hairline fracture, but it'll just have to heal on its own. While Mila goes to get the Range Rover and Matt follows the nurse so he can settle up the hospital paperwork, I squat down next to Lana and take her hand. I kiss her knuckles and rub her palm against my bearded face, feeling the tears finally sting my eyes and the back of my nose. Lana cups my face in her hand and leans forward to kiss my lips gently, tears falling down her face.

At this moment, no words are needed. We just have to feel it, our lips pressed together, our tears mingling, the magic of our connection fizzing between us.

That is until the spell is broken.

"What the hell is this shit?" Matt yells, causing us to spring apart, Lana covering her face with her hands, wincing when she touches her swollen eye. "You're kissing my sister after what she's been through tonight? Now is not the time to hit on her."

Lana does her best to roll her eyes. "He's not hitting on me."

"Then why was he sucking on your face?"

My head snaps between the siblings as they bicker back and forth.

"He wasn't sucking on my face," Lana growls back. "He was comforting me because we've been seeing each other, and he knows I need him."

With that, Matt's glare becomes firmly fixed on me. His blue eyes are dark and stormy. However, instead of killing me with his bare hands, he takes a deep breath and slowly releases it.

"I have no capacity to deal with that on top of everything else that's happened tonight, so I suggest you get the fuck out of here before I make Dexter our first string goalie."

I give Lana's hand one more squeeze and smile down at her. "I'll call you later, babe."

As I leave, I turn to Matt and say quietly "We really like each other, you know. This isn't my usual one-and-done. I think I'm in love with her."

And with that, I leave my firecracker in the care of her big brother, even though walking away from her is one of the hardest things I've ever had to do.

25

Lana

My brother is driving me crazy. I know he means well, but it feels like I've gone from one hostage situation to another. Ever since we got back from the hospital, he's hardly left my side. He put me to bed with my pain meds which thankfully knocked me right out. However, when I woke up this morning, he was asleep in the armchair in my room. I mean, that's creepy, right?

Thankfully, Mila came in to check on me. When she saw him there, she kicked his leg to wake him, told him to stop being a big jerk, and shooed him away.

"Thank you," I say as she puts the chamomile tea down on the nightstand.

"How are you, sweetie?" Mila asks, perching on the edge of my bed, gently stroking my hair away from my forehead. She's so kind and sweet, the complete opposite to my bullish brother.

"The meds are making me a bit groggy, but I guess I'm okay." I shift against the pillow and wince as my whole body protests. "Maybe a little sore as well."

"That's understandable." I notice Mila's eyes fill with

tears and she turns away. "You're so brave," she sniffs.

"Oh hey," I say, rubbing her arm. "I'm fine, really."

"I know. I just don't know how Matt would've coped if anything had happened to you."

"He's strong," I sigh. "And he has you."

Mila pulls me into a soft hug, and we sit and chat while I drink my tea. Eventually, Matt returns, fresh from the shower, looking suitably sheepish when Mila glares at him.

"I don't have practice until three so I can take you to the police precinct if you want," he says, putting his hand on Mila's shoulder, rubbing it lovingly.

Shit, this is going to be awkward. "Alex is going to take me," I say quietly. We texted briefly last night before I passed out, and he offered to go with me. "He has to confirm his own witness statement, so it makes sense."

"That's the only reason, is it?" Matt growls as Mila glares at him and nudges him with her shoulder.

"I think that's a great idea," she says. "It seems you two have some things you need to talk about."

"The fuck they do," my brother mutters, turning away and pacing the room. "What the hell's going on with you two? Have you been running around behind my back?"

"Matt!" Mila scolds, but he holds his hand up to silence her.

"No, Red. I think I deserve some answers. Especially if she's been fucking one of my teammates after I expressly told her not to."

That's it! I've had a gutful.

"You know what? I don't owe you anything," I yell.

"You're behaving just like Etienne—trying to control me and tell me who I can and can't love." I sweep back the comforter and climb out of bed gingerly, hissing air through my teeth as pain shoots up my back.

Matt looks devastated by my outburst, and even though it makes my heart hurt, he has to be told. There's being a protective big brother, and then there's what he's doing now. I will not go from one controlling relationship to another. As I storm past him into my bathroom, he mumbles "I'm sorry" before I slam the door.

After a tentative shower, I apply some concealer to my face to try and cover the ugly purple black bruise and quietly head downstairs. When I find Mila alone in the kitchen, I raise my eyebrow, and she confirms that Matt has gone to the gym to sulk.

"I'm sorry about what I said," I say quietly, fixing myself a coffee and bagel.

"Oh don't be. He needed to be told." Mila laughs. "I've been telling him for weeks to ease up on the overprotective shit, that you're a grown ass woman, but you know how he is."

"I know," I sigh. "And I love him for it, but sometimes he just needs to back the fuck off."

Mila chuckles. "Ain't that the truth." She eyes me warily and grins. "So, you and Thor?"

I feel a blush heat my cheeks at the mention of his name and the memory of what he whispered to Matt last night at the hospital. He thought I didn't hear him drop the L-bomb, but I did and even thinking about it now makes my stomach flip with excitement.

"That dreamy look you have on your face tells me everything I need to know." She laughs, wagging her finger at me. "He's a good man. You could do a lot worse than Alex Bergman."

I scoff and sip my coffee. "I think you'll find I already did worse, a hell of a lot worse."

Mila scrunches her nose up. "Sorry, honey."

"It's okay. Etienne is finally out of my life for good, and I'm ready to move on."

"With Alex?" Mila asks hopefully.

Just then, my phone pings, and a message from Alex lights up the screen, telling me he's waiting outside.

"Possibly," I reply, cryptically. "Anyway, he's here to take me to the precinct. See you later." I press a kiss to Mila's cheek as I grab my purse, heading outside where Alex is leaning against the side of his Lexus, muscular arms folded, smile on his face, looking absolutely delicious. My stomach flips and I feel giddy with anticipation. Every time I see Alex Bergman, he takes my breath away.

"Hey there, big man," I say as I approach. But instead of replying with words, Alex gently cups the uninjured side of my face in his big hand and kisses my lips with such tenderness my breath hitches in my chest.

"Hey, baby," he whispers, pulling away, his eyes clouding with concern as he looks at my smashed-up face. "How are you feeling? If you're not up for this, we can reschedule."

I shake my head with determination. "No, I want this done so I can forget about that crazy French bastard forever."

"That's my girl."

And before I can stop myself, I ask, "Am I? Your

girl, I mean?" I bite my lower lip and wince as the cut stings, averting my eyes from Alex's in case I've misunderstood the situation.

But he tenderly tilts my chin up so I can see the sincerity in his eyes.

"Yes, Lana Landon, you are my girl. That is, if you'll have me. I guess the cat's out of the bag with your brother, and I'm still breathing, so that's a good sign." He chuckles and presses another kiss to my lips, my heart soaring with excitement.

"Don't you worry about that big idiot." I laugh. "C'mon, let's get this over with."

"Anything you want, baby." Alex opens the door for me, and I kiss him again before sliding into the car.

A few hours later, I feel completely wrung out. Giving my statement was tougher than I thought, and I ended up crying angrily in front of the detective. She was so understanding, explaining that she deals with a lot of domestic abuse cases and that with my testimony and those of Alex and Raymond, Etienne and his mom should both serve some jail time; at the very least, they'll be deported.

As Alex drives me home, I feel both peaceful and slightly uneasy.

"You okay, baby?" he asks as we drive out of the city toward the Sound.

"Yeah, I'm fine. I guess I just can't believe it's over," I reply. "I mean I've been afraid for so long, it feels quite disconcerting to not have that in the background all the time."

Alex reaches across the center console and squeezes my thigh. "I'm here for you, whatever you need."

"Thank you." I put my small hand on top of his big one and that feeling of safety fills me with warmth. "I guess we need to figure out what to do about Matt. I told him off this morning, so he knows I don't want him butting into my life anymore, but you still have to play together. How's that gonna work?"

"Don't you worry about that," he reassures me. "I'll talk to him today. Maybe take him out for a beer after practice and straighten this all out. Perhaps I should go all old school and ask for his permission."

Alex smirks when I gasp in indignation at the suggestion and swat his chest with the back of my hand. "You're as bad as each other."

"I'm joking, babe. But if the only way he'll be okay with us dating is for me to get on my knees and beg, then I'll do it."

"Don't you dare, Alex Bergman!" I cry, laughing. "My brother has enough of a God Complex!"

Alex chuckles as we pull up to the house, putting his car in park and leaning over to kiss me. His lips feel warm and wet against mine, and despite the slight sting from the cut, I deepen it. My tongue glides against his as his hand slides into my hair, causing a thrill to shoot down my spine and land in my panties. God, I want him so badly.

As if sensing things are getting a little out of control, Alex pulls back, both of us panting slightly.

"I think we should stop before I move us into the back seat and do unspeakable things to you,"

Alex growls.

I huff out a breath and shift in my seat, the thought of what Alex just suggested not helping the situation in my panties.

"You're right, damn it," I pout, folding my arms. "We should really get everything sorted with Matt before we go any further."

"I promise I'll talk to him today." He leans over and kisses me one more time. "Now you go in and ice that cheek, take your meds, and have a nap. I'll text you later, and if you're feeling up to it, perhaps we can have a night in watching a movie."

"That sounds perfect."

And the thought of snuggling up on the couch with my boyfriend does sound absolutely perfect.

26

Thor

I haven't been this nervous walking into the Whalers locker room since my first day as a rookie. Unfortunately, after taking Lana to the precinct, I'm running late, and I can already hear the loud voices of my teammates echoing down the corridor.

Pushing into the locker room, I'm aware that the voices quiet down, and it's deathly silent by the time I throw my duffel into my cubby. Keeping my back to the room, I reach behind me and pull my sweater off and begin to unbuckle my pants. But before I can get much further, I notice Bugs standing next to me, already in his practice uniform.

"You okay, dude? We heard what happened. That's some fucked up shit."

I flick my eyes over to my captain and manage a tight smile. "Yep, all good thanks. Just took Lana to give her statement, and it looks like they're gonna throw the book at her ex and deport him."

"Good, good," Bugs replies, slapping me on the back. "I spoke to Matt as well."

"Ah shit," I groan, putting my hands on my hips and

turning to face Bugs. "He's pissed, isn't he?"

"Not gonna lie—he ain't happy," he replies, making a face. "He's already out on the ice hitting slap shots into the net."

"Fuck. Bet he wishes I was in the net without my cup on." I laugh nervously.

"Look, you two need to sort this shit out. Like now," Bugs says firmly. "We're all gonna stay in the locker room for ten minutes, so you can go out there and do whatever it is you have to do to fix it. I'm assuming you and Lana are an item, so be prepared to take a beat down." I shoot him a helpless look. "Just saying."

He holds up his hands and backs away so I can quickly change into my gear, double checking all my pads are securely in place because I know how it feels to take one of Matt's slappers to the chest.

As I clomp past my teammates, several of them mutter "good luck," and I feel like a condemned man heading for the gallows. But I know deep in my soul that Lana is my girl, and I'd take a lifetime of Matt firing shots at me as long as we can be together.

Lying in bed last night, I went over the moment I confessed my love for Lana to her brother again and again. It felt so right to say the words. There was no gut-wrenching fear like I thought there'd be, just a satisfying warm feeling that I never want to lose. I desperately wanted to say them to her today as we kissed in my car, but I want everything to be right before that moment and when that moment comes, she'll be in no doubt about my feelings for her.

That is if I survive the next ten minutes.

As the smell of the ice hits my nose, I hear the deep

grunts as Matt fires pucks into the empty net at the far end of the rink. I skate a few circuits around the other end of the ice before gliding along the boards to the far goal.

"Hey man," I say just as Matt pulls back and launches a puck with pinpoint precision into the top shelf. His dark blue eyes flick up to me, and he grunts in response, lining up the next puck. "No fun shooting into an empty net. Are you okay if I join you?"

"Fine by me," Matt grumbles, flicking the puck up onto the end of his stick, bouncing it menacingly, never taking his eyes off me as I take up my spot on the blue paint. My heart's hammering as if this was a Stanley Cup winning shootout, but I realize that this is actually more important. I respect Matt as a player, a teammate, and Lana's brother, and his approval means a lot. However, Lana and I want to be together, so what I won't be doing is asking for his permission.

"Ready?" Matt yells, dropping the puck to the ice and firing it at me. Luckily, he doesn't set it up quite right, so it sails harmlessly to my left.

What follows is a succession of screaming wristers and slap shots that hit me like machine gun fire. It's almost like he's not trying to score; he's just trying to hit me. When the next shot dings off my grill and knocks my head back, I decide he's had his shot, and I'm done with the shit.

"Time out!" I yell, skating away from my doorstep, pulling my helmet off and dropping my gloves and stick to the ice. "I hope you've worked out your frustration, man, because now it's time to talk."

Matt also takes off his helmet and drops his gloves,

his hair sweaty with exertion. I notice that the bench is slowly filling up with our teammates, and I hope this doesn't turn into a physical altercation.

"C'mon, then. Talk!" Matt barks, leaning on his stick, his mouth set in a hard line.

Shit, now the moment is here, I'm tongue tied. But then I close my eyes and picture sweet Lana: her smile, the dimple on her cheek and the ones at the top of her butt, her love for her friends and family, her bravery and resilience.

Fuck, I'm completely in love with her.

"You're what?" Matt asks and my eyes fly open. Shit, I guess I said that out loud.

"I'm in love with Lana. And I'm pretty sure she feels the same about me," I repeat. "We've tried to keep a lid on this thing, but hiding it and sneaking around is hurting us and everyone we love. So that's it. We're done. We're gonna be together."

Matt hasn't taken his eyes off me, and they remain stormy and dark. As he hasn't said anything, I continue.

"I respect you, man. You're my teammate and my brother, but I won't ask your permission to date your sister. She's her own woman, and if she wants me to be her man, then that's what she gets. I want to give her the world, but I'd rather do that with your blessing."

There, I've said my piece. The rink is eerily still, and it seems like no one is even breathing. I flick my eyes over to the bench and see our teammates leaning over the boards, waiting for the fireworks to begin. It has to be said that hockey players love a good throw down, and this one could be a doozie.

As I return my gaze to Matt, he begins to skate

toward me, his face fixed and stern. If he wants to punch me, I'll give him one free shot before I fight back. I don't want us to resort to violence, but if that's how he wants to play this, then so be it.

Matt comes to a stop in front of me, and I brace myself for the punch I'm expecting. However, instead of connecting with my face, Matt's hand shoots out, waiting for mine to join it in a handshake. My mouth drops open, and I'm stunned for a second. This is not what I was expecting. But I quickly regain my composure and fit my big hand in his, shaking it firmly.

"All I want is for Lana to be happy," he says, his voice thick with emotion. "Last night I got an insight into what really happened in Paris, and it makes me sick that she had to deal with all that on her own. But she did deal with it. And I'm so fucking proud of the woman she's become. She doesn't need a protector; she needs a partner, an equal. And if you're her choice, then I fully respect that." He nods at me, still not smiling, but then he's always been a grumpy bastard.

As we skate back toward the bench together, our teammates whistle and catcall, blowing kisses at us. Jesus, I love these guys, but I flip them off just the same.

"Okay, okay, that's enough of that shit," Coach Casey yells, stepping out onto the ice. "Let's get ready to take the second game of this series."

The whole team yells "YES COACH!" and begin to flood the ice, several of them slapping me on the back as they pass.

God, I love these fucking guys.

But the next person I'm declaring my love to is a pocket-sized firecracker with blue eyes that I hope to look into for the rest of my days.

Lana

As I approach Alex's front door, the butterflies that have been swirling in my stomach since he texted me take flight. And when he opens the door, his hair damp from the shower, wearing grey sweats and his favorite cotton T-shirt, they soar into the stratosphere. He fixes me with that sexy smile and reaches up to hold the top of the doorframe, causing his tee to rise up and show an enticing strip of his abs. His biceps bulge, and it takes every ounce of restraint not to climb him like a tree.

"Hey baby," he growls, cocking his eyebrow and flexing his muscles again.

I release a breathless sigh and look up into his eyes. "Hey, big man."

Alex reaches out and cups my face in his hands and presses a sweet kiss to my lips, ever careful of my injury.

"I've ordered the takeout and have that show ready on Netflix. So, all you have to do is take your shoes off, relax, and let me give you a foot rub," Alex says, stepping aside so I can enter his apartment.

"That sounds perfect," I reply as I let Alex take off my jacket while I toe off my sneakers. I follow him into his condo, and he hands me a glass of wine and shoos me over to the couch while he collects bowls of popcorn and pretzels.

"So, I assume as you still have all your limbs and you're breathing, things went okay with Matt at training?" I ask, sipping the fruity red wine.

"Let's just say we came to a gentleman's agreement,"

he replies, taking a gulp of his beer and putting it down on the coffee table.

He seems a little nervous and on edge, so I reach over and stroke to soft hair on his forearm.

"But everything's okay, right? I don't want there to be friction on the team because of me."

"It's all good, baby. Your brother is a good man, and once I told him how much I'm in love with you, there was nothing he could really say to that," he says softly, a sweet smile stretching his lips.

As his words sink in, I feel my heart swell so much I think it might burst clean out of my chest. "You love me?" I ask, tears filling my eyes.

Alex gently pulls me into his lap and presses his nose into my hair, kissing my forehead, my nose and finally my lips. "I love you so much, I didn't even think it was possible."

"I love you too, Alex." I fling my arms around his neck and plant kisses all over his sweet face, loving the tickle of his beard and the deep rumble of his laughter.

"Well, now that's sorted out, shall we watch some Netflix?" Alex laughs, giving my butt a light tap.

"Well, actually, I was hoping we could start with the Chill part of Netflix and Chill, if you're okay with that?" I ask, giving him my most alluring smile.

It seems to have the desired effect because Alex's ice chip eyes blaze with passion, and he scoops me up into his arms, carrying me into his bedroom. After he gently undresses me at an infuriatingly slow pace, he worships every inch of my body with his lips and tongue. He gently brushes them over the bruises I sustained, and I hear his soft sniffles as if the very sight of them hurt his heart.

When he's given me one toe curling orgasm with his mouth, he quickly rips off his clothes, rolls on a condom, and sinks into me. We both gasp and sigh as he makes love to me, really makes love to me for what feels like the first time. We writhe and rock together with no urgency because we know we have the rest of our lives to do this, his lips locked with mine, stealing my breath with every thrust.

As we fall apart, I clutch at his round ass, holding him inside me while we spasm and ride the waves of ecstasy. It's a perfect moment, and it feels like the first of many that we'll share. Together.

EPILOGUE

Lana

"**H**e's on his way, everyone!" I yell over the noise of rowdy hockey players. "Please move into the games room."

"And shut the fuck up, or you'll ruin the surprise!" Beth yells even louder, ushering the guests into the games room at the back of the house.

I've been planning Alex's surprise thirtieth birthday party for weeks now. Ever since the Whalers made it to the final of the Stanley Cup and lost out in game seven to the New York Bull Dogs, it's been my mission to cheer everyone up. Zac and I have decided to host a monthly supper club at our new apartment where our friends can come and be guinea pigs for new items on the Gooey Gourmet menu.

Well, when I say new apartment, it's really Beth's old apartment in Pioneer Square. You see when The Whalers made it to the cup final, Nate asked Beth to move in with him, right there on the ice after the last game. It was so romantic and really lifted everyone's spirits. Of course, she said yes, and they immediately set about getting a place together.

I was finally in a position to pay rent somewhere, so when I mentioned this at Champagne Tuesday, Beth immediately offered me her place. It's a perfect apartment, and I love sharing with Zac, even though it still shocks me to sometimes find his half naked hookups wandering around in my kitchen in the morning. It also makes it less awkward when Alex and I spend the night together, which, now the season is over, is every night.

So here we are, about to throw the legendary Alex Bergman a surprise birthday party. He's on his way to Matt and Mila's after picking up his family from the airport. There are so many of them, he had to hire a bus and a driver. I'm both nervous and excited to meet them. Even though I've been part of the family Skype calls for weeks now, it's still nerve-wracking to meet them in person.

"Okay, I see the bus pulling up," Matt calls from the front door. "Everyone shut up!"

I join Matt at the front door and try to keep the huge grin off my face. Alex has no idea we have this planned; he thinks he's bringing his family over to meet my brother and have dinner. Of course, his family are in on it. I called his *Mor* when I decided to do this, and she thought it was a wonderful idea. I can't wait to see the look on his face when he realizes we've all been plotting against him.

As the bus pulls up and the doors open, I see my handsome boyfriend disembark, and I still get the same thrill as ever, hardly able to believe he's all mine.

I can't wait to get my hands on him and give him a great big birthday kiss.

"Holy shit!" I hear Matt exclaim and I return my gaze to the bus.

And holy shit is right.

What follows is a procession of bigger and bigger men, each sporting a reddish blonde beard and shaggy hair with huge bulging muscles. Alex wasn't kidding when he said he was the runt of the litter.

"Hey Coach, if you're looking to sure up our defensive line, you may have a few candidates coming your way," Matt calls over his shoulder to Coach Casey, who just looks a little confused.

"Get ready, everyone," I whisper-shout. "Here they come."

As arranged, Alex's mom makes sure he's first through the door, and once he's inside, everyone leaps out of their hiding places and yells "Happy Birthday!"

Alex looks completely shocked and is still staring around wildly as I throw myself into his arms and kiss him passionately, momentarily forgetting we're in a room full of our families and his teammates.

"What the fuck, baby?" He laughs when I finally detach my lips from his.

"Happy birthday, big man. I wanted to do something for you just to show how special you are to me and how much better you make my life," I reply, hugging his muscular torso, pressing my cheek against his chest where his heart beats rapidly.

"All I need is you, but this is awesome. Thank you, firecracker." He presses a kiss to the top of my head as everyone approaches him to wish him happy birthday.

As I move away to give him some room, I'm quickly pulled into hugs by all his family, each hug tighter than the last, making me dizzy. His brothers, their wives, and children are so happy to be here, and finally I'm being hugged by his mom. She's also a tall, solid woman, and I feel tiny surrounded by these Scandinavian giants.

But as she holds me to her, I feel the love she has for Alex. "Thank you for loving my baby" is all she says, before wiping her eyes and moving away to speak to my brother.

This is the perfect way to celebrate the birth and first thirty years of the man I love, the man I hope to love for the next thirty years and beyond.

The End

Author Bio

Emily began reading romance novels in 2019 and became instantly hooked. She was inspired to write her own during the 2020 lockdown and first self-published on Wattpad. With the help of Instagram, she gained a loyal following and eventually secured a publishing contract with 4 Horsemen Publications. Emily is a recent but enthusiastic follower of the Dallas Stars and in particular the delicious Tyler Seguin. She loves an espresso martini, dirty-talking alpha heroes with tattoos, and a lazy Sunday breakfast.

Book Club Questions

1. What part of the book did you enjoy the most?

2. What part of the book do you think could have been improved?

3. Who were your favourite characters? Which characters would you like to see get their own book?

4. Which character gave you the strongest emotional response (either good or bad)?

5. If you were making a movie of this book, who would play the lead characters (they don't have to be actors)?

6. Share a favourite quote from the book. Why did this quote stand out?

7. What did you think of the book's length? Too long or too short? Are there any parts you wanted to be developed more?

8. What songs does this book make you think of?

9. If you had the chance to ask me anything about the book or being an author what would it be?

10. Which characters would you like to invite to a dinner party and why?

11. How realistic were the hockey scenes? Is there any way I can improve these?

12. Did you like the slow burn or do you prefer insta-love?

Discover more at
4HorsemenPublications.com

10% off using HORSEMEN10